MY RIDE WITH GUS

MY RIDE

WITH GUS

Charles Carillo

POCKET BOOKS
New York London Toronto Sydney Tokyo Singapore

This book is a work of fiction. Names, characters, places and incidents are products of the author's imagination or are used fictitiously. Any resemblance to actual events or locales or persons, living or dead, is entirely coincidental.

POCKET BOOKS, a division of Simon & Schuster Inc.
1230 Avenue of the Americas, New York, NY 10020

Library of Congress Cataloging-in-Publication Data

Carillo, Charles.
My ride with Gus / Charles Carillo.
p. cm.
ISBN: 0-671-53568-4
I. Title.
PS3553.A685M9 1996
813'.54—dc20 95-40509
CIP

First Pocket Books hardcover printing April 1996

10 9 8 7 6 5 4 3 2 1

POCKET and colophon are registered trademarks of Simon & Schuster Inc.

Printed in the U.S.A.

Hello, Joan and Rafael

and

Goodbye to six guys who brought us laughter:
Edward Sullivan
John Cotter
Frank Ambrosio
Bobby Russo
Paul Poppe
and Matthew Pearl.

MY RIDE WITH GUS

What I like about her, Jimmy Gambar told himself, is the way she gets me to do things I'd never do on my own.

White-water rafting. Motor bike rides on dirt roads. Camping. Just about every weekend since they'd met had involved one such adventure or another, and as they'd been dating for nearly two years, they were talking about nearly a hundred thrill-filled weekends.

Yes, Jimmy told himself; yes. He was seated alone at a table in the Windows on the World restaurant on New Year's Eve, awaiting the arrival of his girlfriend, Wendy Orgel. Far below, the lights of the Brooklyn Bridge twinkled like the strands of a magical necklace. It was a crystal-clear night, the perfect occasion to ask the woman you loved for her hand in marriage.

Especially now that it looked as if his partnership in the architectural firm of Reed & Walter was an absolute lock. Jimmy had the right future, and he had the right money. All he needed now was the right words.

"They're about to make me a partner," Jimmy planned to say. "And speaking of partners, how'd you like to become my partner forever?"

It sounded good in the shower, but now he wondered if maybe it was too corny. Maybe he didn't need words. All he needed, really, was what he carried in his pocket.

He pulled the small blue Tiffany box from his pants pocket and adjusted its red ribbon. Elegant. Stylish. Inside it was a diamond ring that had set him back thirty-eight hundred dollars. Jimmy had believed that the purchase of the ring would make him feel greater confidence in what he was about to do, but he was wrong.

Not that there was a problem. With the precise mind that made him as good an architect as he was, Jimmy had examined the relationship from foundation to roof, and found it solid. He liked Wendy, he approved of her, and yet he wondered. If he were truly in love, would he be weighing marriage as if she were an empty lot he was thinking about building upon? Wouldn't he be impelled to propose to her, unable to control himself?

No, he decided; that's ridiculous. For all thirty-eight years of his life he'd been doing things a certain way, and this was no time to change his game plan. Marriage was always a part of that plan, something he wanted to get done before he hit forty. He'd considered all the factors, looked over the data, and made a decision.

His decision entered the restaurant, threw him a wave and made her way to the table wearing, of all things, a tuxedo.

Jimmy was delighted. Only someone like Wendy could pull it off, and look even more beautiful than she would have in an evening gown. The getup showed off her long, lean legs and square shoulders, like those of a horseman. The whole outfit, down to the bow tie around her swanlike neck, was like a giant wink to the world.

What a night, and it hadn't even begun—drinks on top of the world, a proposal of marriage, dinner and dancing later at the Rainbow Room, and finally the all-time, nothing-held-back hump from Wendy, who, Jimmy suspected, was holding back a little something in the saddle for the man who would be her husband. Not that she wasn't a spirited, muscular screw. But if there was even more, he couldn't wait to taste it.

He rose to kiss her, feeling a slight pull in the muscles of his calves. The weekend before, at Wendy's urging and against his own good sense, Jimmy had jumped from a plane. Wendy had assured him it would be an exhilarating experience, unlike anything he'd ever known. And so, on a Saturday morning while the rest of the city slept late or made coffee or love, Jimmy Gambar had stood at the open doorway of a plane two thousand feet over a "target area" in New Jersey and stepped out into nothing. Wendy was right behind him, and though Jimmy's parachute had opened as planned, he'd failed to land correctly, bracing his legs a bit upon impact rather than rolling.

"You'll get it right next time," a helmeted and goggled Wendy said as she squatted over him, and though it shamed Jimmy to feel an urge to strike her at that moment, he quickly realized that this was merely Wendy's high-hearted, patch-it-up-and-keep-marching approach to life. He was learning from this woman, and would continue to learn. The time had come, and with the commitment his doubts, like the pains in his calves, would fade forever.

They kissed and hugged until Wendy gave Jimmy three small pats on the back, her signal that she wished to be released.

"Hi," Jimmy said

"Hi yourself."

"You look beautiful." He meant it. Nobody, but nobody, had eyes like this, twin balls of bright blue ice.

"And you," Wendy countered, "are the handsomest skydiver I've ever seen."

They laughed and kissed again before sitting down. A waiter took a bottle of champagne from a silver bucket and poured for both of them.

"This is beautiful," Wendy said. "Why does everybody make fun of Windows on the World? So what if it's a big tourist place?"

"I agree."

"I'm all confused. Which way is that?"

"That's New Jersey. Brooklyn's over there. See that giant clock by the Watchtower building, next to the bridge?"

"It's all wonderful, Jimmy."

She was right; it was. Jimmy reached for the box in his pocket with a shaky hand, but Wendy was faster. Like a man going for a cigar she opened her jacket, reached into the interior breast pocket, and passed Jimmy a flat, foot-long package, wrapped in shiny black paper.

"Open it," she said. "I can't *wait!* Open it, open it, *open it!*"

Jimmy considered insisting that she open hers first, but realized that this would be good foreplay to his gift. No way she could top him tonight. He tore away the paper to reveal an equally black and shiny box, and when he pulled off the lid he was looking at an outrageously pink silk tie.

"Do you *love* it?" Wendy gushed. "Put it on for the New Year!"

Jimmy couldn't move his hands. The tie he wore

was navy blue, to match his blazer and pants, all from Brooks Brothers. He despised loud clothing, and Wendy knew this as well as she knew the right and wrong ways to paddle a canoe through white water. Ever since they'd met, she'd been urging him to add a splash of color to his wardrobe, an urging that, Jimmy had to admit, had graduated to nagging. Once it was a pair of lime-green shorts, which Jimmy had refused to wear on holiday in St. Barts. Another time it was a yellow T-shirt, which Jimmy couldn't bring himself to wear through the Yuppie-clogged streets of East Hampton. He'd thought the issue was a dead one, but here it was rising from its grave in the form of the ugliest fucking tie Jimmy had ever seen.

He decided to try to kid his way out of it, mock-shielding himself from the thing as if it were glowing.

"Hey, Wen. We could get a sunburn from this tie."

"Very funny." She stroked his hand. "I know you don't usually wear stuff like this, honey, but I got so excited when I saw it that I went ahead and got it. It'll bring out your dark eyes. I've been picturing it around your neck all day long."

"Couldn't we switch outfits instead? I look good in a tux."

"Aw, please put it on, Jimmy. Be festive, for once."

For once. Unclench your teeth, he told himself; she doesn't mean it in a cruel way. She's all worked up over New Year's Eve.

"Could I wear it as a headband, maybe? Be a good thing to warn planes up this high."

A bomb. Two skinny cords appeared on either side of Wendy's neck, a reaction that took away its swan-like look and gave Jimmy a rare, horrifying glimpse of what she'd look like on her seventy-fifth birthday.

If she survived all the adventure weekends between now and then.

"I'm sorry," she forced herself to say. "I should have known better."

"Yes, you should have."

Her eyes glistened with tears. "Well for God's sake, Jimmy, don't rub it in. I feel silly enough as it is."

"Aw, look. I'm the one who's sorry. It's just that . . . you know."

"No," Wendy said, "I really *don't* know."

Jimmy sighed. "Me and bright colors. They just don't mix."

"What is that, your slogan?"

"Why are we fighting? Is there any point to us fighting tonight?"

Wendy wiped away her tears, forced a smile. "You're right. I'm sorry, okay? Let's just enjoy this beautiful evening."

They clinked glasses, sipped champagne, and ventured shy smiles at each other.

"Hey, stranger," Wendy giggled. "Boy, the things I'll never know about you."

"Me?" Jimmy spread his arms. "I'm an open book."

"All I really know about you is that you're a workaholic who despises bright colors."

"It's a start," Jimmy said. Casually, he tried to push the tie box across the table to Wendy, so he could get down to the business of his gift to her. But Wendy intercepted the box at mid-table.

"Tell you what," she said playfully, pushing it back toward his side. "Take the tie home. Put it way, way in the back of your closet. You never have to wear it, or even take it out of the box. I just want you to have it."

"What for?"

Wendy gave a girlish shrug of her shoulders. "I'll just like knowing it's there."

"No," Jimmy said flat out.

Wendy's face fell. This she could not believe. "No?"

"That's right. No. I don't want it." He shoved it back to her side of the table.

Wendy was dumbfounded. "God, Jimmy," she said in wonder, "you really are rigid."

"I'm rigid because my calves are still stiff from the fucking plane jump."

There: it was out, lanced like a boil, a remark he'd been swallowing back for a week. The cords in Wendy's neck became multistrand cables. The floor fell out from under Jimmy's feet, and there he was, hovering at 110 stories, this time without a parachute.

"That's really a shitty thing to say, James Gambar."

"Wendy, let's give each other a little break, here." He reached for the champagne bottle to top off both glasses, but it slipped from his sweat-wet hand back into the bucket. He wiped his hand dry on his pants and lifted the bottle, but Wendy put her hand over her glass.

"I try and I try and I *try* to bring you out of this enormous shell you've constructed for yourself, and you react by lashing out at me."

Jimmy tasted bile deep in his throat. He opened his mouth but said nothing.

"No, I mean it," Wendy continued. "What did you do with yourself before I came along? You worked, read your books, and went to the movies."

"A lot of people live that way, Wendy," Jimmy said in a hollow voice of rage that Wendy could not detect, any more than she could have heard a dog whistle.

She made a sad, chuckling sound. "A lot of people might be that way, but I wouldn't call it living."

"Okay, okay, you want me to live? Huh?" He ripped the tie from the box, coiled it like a snake and shoved it in his pocket. "Now I have the pink tie. Now I can live, right?"

Wendy had never seen him like this. "Have you flipped?"

"Oh, I've flipped, all right!" Jimmy boomed.

People were staring. The waiter rushed over. Jimmy got to his feet, and felt his knees shake as he pointed his finger at Wendy's face. The words were out before he could catch them.

"Go fuck yourself, Wendy."

She slumped in her chair as if she'd had the wind knocked out of her, while Jimmy ran to the elevator. Fortunately, it was right there, and one ear-popping ride later he stood more than a thousand feet below Wendy on the cold sidewalk outside the twin towers, wondering what in the hell to do next.

He did not wonder for long. He hailed a cab and wound up with one of the last of New York City's old breed of cabbies, a meaty-faced Irishman with a cocked cap over silvery hair and a pencil behind his ear. No Plexiglas divider separated driver from passenger. This was a man who believed in the goodness of his passengers.

"Where to, Mac?"

Jimmy could barely believe it. This guy really was from another time, or straight out of the movies. Jimmy looked at the identification plate. SULLIVAN, PATRICK. The cabbie chuckled. "Meter's running, pal."

It wasn't an upbraid. It was a working man letting a fellow working man know that hard-earned, after-tax dollars were being wasted by the electronic tick of a heartless machine.

"Hudson and Houston."

"Right-o."

Sullivan eased the cab into traffic as if he were carrying a load of eggs. Jimmy eased his grip on the door bar, a habit he'd gotten into from countless rides with scowling, turban-wearing cab drivers, who took off as if they'd just lit a fuse and Allah himself was on their tails.

"Mind a little music?"

"No."

Sullivan turned the radio on low. Sinatra sang "It Was a Very Good Year," and when he got to the part about the autumn of his life, Jimmy leaned forward to say, "I just broke up with my girlfriend."

"Did you, now?"

"We had a fight."

Sullivan clucked his tongue. "A fight on New Year's is a dreadful thing."

"I was going to ask her to marry me."

"Well, you'll have loads of chances to do that again."

"I will?" Jimmy's voice was as hopeful as a schoolboy's. Sullivan glanced back at him, blue eyes twinkling. "Of course! Know how many times I meant to propose to my wife before I finally hunted up the guts to do it?"

"How many?"

"Nineteen. And when I finally did it, I had me eyes shut. That was twenty-eight years ago next month." A grin split Sullivan's face. "Twenty-eight years and six children ago."

Jimmy sat back into the soft red leather seat. It was the first cab he'd ridden in ages that had good upholstery. No rips or tears anywhere, and no hunks of shiny silver electrician's tape to cover them.

"Love bounces back," Sullivan chirped. "You'll see!"

"Yeah," Jimmy said, "but I'll bet you never told your wife to go fuck herself."

Sullivan's grin vanished. His eyes narrowed to slits. Suddenly he looked like a longshoreman on a picket line. "You said that to the lady?"

Jimmy felt his face go crimson with blood. "Yes, I did. I was pretty upset, though. I mean, she drove me to it."

Sullivan hit the brakes as if a dog had just run in front of him. He wheeled to face Jimmy.

"Get out of my cab."

"What?!"

"You heard me. Don't make me get rough, now. Just keep your money and get out."

Jimmy literally couldn't move. He was mortified. Strangers' opinions mattered to Jimmy Gambar. A scowl on the face of a diner waitress or the rolling of a bank teller's eyes could ruin his whole day.

Jimmy swallowed. "Please," he said. "I've got nobody else to talk to."

"I said, *get out!*"

In a daze, Jimmy groped for the door and got out of the cab. He watched Sullivan drive off, vaguely hoping the man would turn around, come back, and apologize for what he'd said. With the faith of a child on Christmas Eve, Jimmy stood watching the cab until it was out of sight.

"I'm no good," Jimmy said out loud. The sound of his own voice startled him. Embarrassed that somebody might have heard him, Jimmy looked all around. He was all alone, and half a mile from home. But that was okay. In fact, it was a good thing. The walk to his SoHo apartment would be just the thing to help him figure out his next move.

Wendy! Did he go after her now, or wait until morning? Was she still at the World Trade Center, sobbing her eyes out, or had she gone home to await his call?

His abdominal muscles tightened at the thought of the confrontation. An open doorway beckoned Jimmy Gambar with sounds of music and laughter, and he drifted inside a club called Caliente.

There was a twenty-dollar cover charge. Jimmy went straight to the bar, slapped down another twenty-dollar bill and ordered a Jack Daniel's from a slender Puerto Rican bartender. He downed it in a gulp. He gestured for another one, and did the same thing.

"Slow down," the bartender cheerfully advised. "You got all night."

"I just broke up with my girl."

Jimmy couldn't believe he'd said it. He was not the sort of man who poured out his heart to bartenders. This one grinned sympathetically.

"New Year's Eve is a bad night for everyone," he said, pouring Jimmy a third shot. "This one's on me. But sip it, savor it. You look like you don't do this much."

Jimmy made a snorting sound. "Hell of a lot you know," he said, downing the third shot in a gulp. He pawed his hand into his pocket and dangled the tie before the bartender's eyes.

"Whaddaya think of this tie, hey?"

"It's a nice tie."

"Yeah?" Jimmy belched. "You think so? I don't think so. What makes this tie so great? Here, look at it. Touch it. Come on!"

The bartender reluctantly felt the material between

thumb and forefinger. "Silk tie, well made. S'matter, you don't like the color?"

"I think the color sucks. I think the *tie* sucks. My girlfriend gave it to me. Ex-girlfriend. Wanted me to put it on, and I refused. Whaddaya think about that?"

"I don't think anything about it."

"Come on, come on, whaddaya think?"

"I think if you really loved her, you woulda put it on."

Jimmy pointed at the bartender. "You," he slurred, "are a genius. This man is a genius!" He slapped the bar. "In thirty seconds, he has zeroed in on the root of my problem!"

"Hey, man, you're startin' to bother people."

"I'm sorry. A thousand pardons." He held the tie by one end and whirled it over his head. "See, the thing is, it isn't really a tie at all. It's a whip! Excuse me."

Jimmy bumped into four people while weaving his way to the dance floor, whirling the tie over his head. The bartender watched him go.

"What an asshole," he concluded.

Jimmy Gambar was not a man who often ignored his instincts, but when he did, he pulled the plug on the phone and hung a DO NOT DISTURB sign on the door to his better judgment.

He was flying on those three shots, enjoying the thump of a band that Wendy would have tolerated for all of fifteen seconds before fleeing from the percussion, the smoke, and the exuberance. For all her love of things physical, Wendy did not dance, and therefore Jimmy did not dance, and so what was he doing out there on the floor?

He playfully whipped the tie at the slender ankles

of a saucer-eyed Puerto Rican woman in a short leather skirt and a black leather jacket with many zippers, the uses of which Jimmy could not begin to imagine.

Like a toreador Jimmy stood, lashing the tie at the lady as if to keep her from goring him. Other dancers moved to give them a small circle of space for their routine, which ended with Jimmy, dizzier than he'd ever been, stumbling for the door to gulp cold air. The lady in leather, apparently unattached for the evening, followed him out, trailing Jimmy on the walk to his home the way a stray dog once did until Jimmy clapped his hands at the pooch outside his building.

"Take my arm, mon, I'm fuckin' freezin'."

I do not need this, Jimmy realized as he unlocked his door. New Year's Eve. Fucking amateur night. You fight with your girlfriend, you take a walk, things happen.

He did not start to panic until she was actually inside his home, pacing off the length of his loft like a real estate agent. She wore spike heels, and through his alcoholic haze Jimmy managed to feel a pang of worry for his newly varnished wide-plank wood floors.

"You own this?"

"It's a co-op, yeah."

"Nice fuckin' apartment."

She moved to a window for a better view of the twin towers, where, for all Jimmy knew, Wendy still sat, crying and sipping champagne.

"Dass a great view."

"I'm glad you like it."

"Whadda you, a lawyer?"

"Architect."

"You must make some pretty fuckin' good buildings."

She unzipped her jacket and tossed it on a chair. Responding to an internal beat, she began shimmying across the floor to Jimmy, hands extended high above the floppy sleeves of a blood-red silk shirt.

"Come on, man, let's dance."

"There's no music."

"Where's your stereo?"

"I, ah, only have classical music."

She stopped dancing and dropped her hands. "Are you fuckin' kiddin' me?"

"Classical music is nice. You should listen to it some time."

"Fuck classical. Where's the radio?"

"I don't have one."

"Man, dass fucked up. Where's my coat?"

Jimmy felt a wash of relief, until it was clear that all she wanted to do was remove a small glass vial from one of the many mysterious zippered pockets.

"And now you gonna tell me you got no glass dish, right?"

"As a matter of fact, I don't."

For the first time, her anger was showing. "Hey, asshole. Whatta you pickin' me up for? You don't like music, you don't like blow."

"I didn't exactly pick you up. I'd say you followed me."

She snorted. "Bet you don't like girls either, right? Juss like to whip 'em with your nice pink tie?"

"Maybe you'd better go."

"You finally got somethin' right."

She struggled into the jacket. Jimmy stood there, trying to figure out an apology and at the same time longing to get horizontal and pass out.

Just like that, she slapped his face, then slapped it again. Jimmy stood still for the punishment, dimly glad to get it, feeling that some debt was being paid for the way he'd wasted the woman's last few precious minutes of the year.

But she sensed that he was pleased, and pulled a switchblade from an unzippered pocket. Jimmy ducked the first slash past his ear, grabbed her wrist, and squeezed the blade loose.

"Motherfuckah!"

She launched her knee into his groin. In the explosion of pain that followed Jimmy shoved her away, and watched from his knees as she stumbled wildly across the long floor, coming to a stop when her throat banged into the curved metal neck of a five-foot wrought-iron antique lamp.

She staggered, put her hands to her neck, and summoned one final breath for an oath she could not quite deliver. Then she fell face-down on the floor, arms spread and ear to the wood, as if she were trying to eavesdrop on a conversation downstairs. The lamp, a birthday gift from Wendy, couldn't seem to make up its mind about toppling. It tottered momentarily on its heavy base before crashing to the floor.

Jimmy crept to her side and touched his fingers to her throat, which was cool and well on the way to cold. He shook her shoulder. He pinched her nostrils, held them for a ten-count. Nothing.

"Oh my dear sweet God in heaven."

He went to the bathroom and sat on the toilet lid, pushing his fists against his eyes. When he opened them he happened to be looking at a framed photo of himself and Wendy in matching sunglasses, on a beach in Montauk.

"You had to give me that goddam lamp?" he asked

the photograph. He got to his feet, wiped sweat from his face with a bath towel, and returned to the living room.

She was still there, of course, dead on the floor. Jimmy had actually allowed himself to hope that while he was in the bathroom, her body would somehow disappear.

He whirled around at the sound of a click, but it was only the digital clock on his desk changing from 10:36 to 10:37. A police car bound for the Battery roared down Greenwich Street, sirens wailing over some other tragedy. It was time to make the call.

Jimmy was surprised at how calm his hands were as he dialed the number, and got an operator's recording. *Dear God in heaven, it's been changed to an unlisted number.* But no—all the recording told him was that he had to dial the 718 area code first. There was no 718 area code the last time he'd phoned this number.

A boy answered politely. Jimmy cleared his throat.

"May I speak to Gus?"

"Junior or senior?"

"Senior."

"Hold on, please."

Jimmy heard the thump of the phone being dropped. Then came a shuffling noise, followed by the sound of a man clearing his throat, the way one would after being roused from sleep.

"Yeah?"

"Gus? It's Jimmy."

"Holy shit."

"Happy New Year."

"Not quite yet, it isn't."

They were silent. Jimmy could hear a TV set and

the sound of happy voices from Gus's side. Gus heard nothing from Jimmy's side.

"Could you come over?" Jimmy blurted.

"Now?"

"Please."

"All right."

Jimmy gave him the address. "Do you know how to get here?"

But Gus had already hung up.

CHAPTER 2

Jimmy was on his second cup of instant coffee when his doorbell sounded. He'd spent the time waiting for Gus slowly circling the body, as if it were a puzzling museum exhibit. He was careful not to touch it, as if there were a way in which he could make things even worse.

He jumped at the sound of the bell, splashing hot coffee on his wrist. He pushed the buzzer, opened his door, and walked out into the hall.

"Top floor," he called downstairs.

He heard the slow steps up the bare wooden stairs, and saw the salt-and-pepper top of Gus's thick, bristly head as he made his way, after what seemed like years, to the top landing. Gus was breathing hard but evenly as he approached Jimmy, preceded by his hard, bulging belly, snug against the zipper of a blue Windbreaker.

Jimmy extended his hand and Gus, after a momentary hesitation, accepted it for a brief shake.

"You don't check to see who it is before you buzz me in?"

"I knew it was you."

"It's New Year's Eve. It could've been any whacko in the city."

"You're right."

Gus nodded. "What's up?"

Jimmy jerked his head toward his home, and opened the apartment door wide. Gus walked to the body with the weary steps of a refrigerator repairman at the end of a long day, and squatted at the woman's side. On his feet, Jimmy noticed, were blue sneakers with Velcro tabs, over white athletic socks.

"Close the door."

Jimmy obeyed. Gus made a fist and touched his knuckles to the woman's neck.

"I just met her."

"That right?"

"I don't even know her name."

"Don't bother asking her now."

"I pushed her and her neck hit my lamp. She was trying to stab me. Look."

Jimmy went to get the switchblade, which had skidded to the other side of the floor.

"Don't touch it."

Jimmy obeyed. Gus rose to his feet, pushing hard on his knee to do it. He scratched his scalp, rubbed his face.

"Only I know, right?"

"Yeah."

"Was she with a group?"

"How do you mean?"

"When you picked her up."

"Not that I know about. I didn't exactly pick her up."

Gus walked slowly around the loft, studying the floors. Jimmy followed him, aware only of the thud in his own chest and the leathery smell of the cologne Gus wore. Gus returned to the body and studied it from all angles, like a golfer lining up a putt.

"All right," Gus abruptly said, "pick out your least favorite rug."

"Why?"

"We can't just carry her out of here. Come on, pick."

While Jimmy decided, Gus took a handkerchief from his pocket and used it to pick up the switchblade. He closed it and slipped it into one of her pockets as Jimmy watched in fascination.

"Will you pick, already?"

A minute later they rolled her up inside a worn blue Oriental rug from Jimmy's bedroom. It had cost Jimmy two thousand dollars at a shop on Lexington Avenue, but it was a good choice for this task because of its width. The top of her head and the heels of her shoes were well inside the ends.

"Now bring me some cord. You got cord?"

"The kind I use to tie up my newspapers?"

"Aaay, you're a good citizen. That'll do. Get it."

Gus tied both ends of the rug, and put a loop around the middle for good measure.

"Did she go to the bathroom?"

"No."

"She eat anything? Touch anything?"

"Don't think so."

"Anybody see you come in with her?"

"Don't think so."

"All right now, listen to me."

Gus stared into Jimmy's eyes like a hypnotist. He put his hands on Jimmy's shoulders and let his arms hang, the way a school guidance counselor might hold a troubled teenager.

"I'm parked right outside the door. I open the trunk, and in she goes."

"Okay."

Gus shook his finger in Jimmy's face. "We're carrying a rug downstairs, you understand? It's just a rug. You see any of your neighbors, you say hello, you wish 'em a Happy New Year, whatever."

"Okay."

"Unless you're not talking to them. Don't get friendly, all of a sudden. Be natural, is what I'm saying."

"Okay."

"It's getting cold. Maybe you want a warmer jacket than that."

As Jimmy hung up his blazer and took a brown leather jacket from his bedroom closet, he remembered that he'd left his trench coat at the World Trade Center. He wondered if he could pick it up in the morning, then wondered if something could be wrong with him for thinking of such a thing when he had a corpse on his living room floor.

"Jimmy, you comin', or what?"

"I'm ready, I'm ready."

"Say good-bye to this rug. You're not getting this rug back."

Gus made this sound like the worst part of the whole situation. He and Jimmy hoisted the thing onto their shoulders. The woman was as light as a cat, Jimmy felt, or else there was so much adrenaline pounding through his blood that he could have lifted an anvil.

"I'll lead the way," Gus commanded. "Nice and slow."

Jimmy fought the urge to rush. They successfully got the thing down one flight, and just as Gus's end of the rug passed the second-floor apartment, its door flew open. A thin, balding man in a snug black T-shirt stood in the doorway, a plastic bag full of empty bottles and cans in his hand. He was barefoot, and wore cutoff jeans as if it were the middle of July, the better to show off his out-of-season tan.

"Is that you, James?"

Jimmy forced a smile. "Hi, Dennis."

"Hello-hello, and Happy New Year! Moving a rug, are we?"

"Yeah."

"Not a very exciting way to spend the New Year." He cocked his head like a curious robin. "And where is the devine Miss Orgel tonight?"

"She had family obligations."

"Really." Dennis leaned back and stood like a flamingo, one foot flat against the wall behind his ass. "Guess we don't rate all that high on her food chain, do we?" he teased.

Jimmy forced a nervous giggle. "How are you? How are things?"

Dennis sighed. "Oh, puh-*lease.* Let's not even *begin.* Vance and I are no more. We had a *huge* blowup in Cancun."

"I'm sorry to hear that."

"Oh, it's nothing a fistful of barbiturates won't cure. . . . Did you get my memo?"

"No."

"I slid it under your door."

"Guess I missed it."

"I'm asking all the tenants to puh-*lease* rinse out their empties before they set them outside for Romundo. I have been noticing cockroaches *galore* in the hallways."

"No kidding."

"It's not a lot to ask, is it? It only takes a moment. I mean, these creatures could thrive for a *week* on the residue inside one tomato juice can."

Gus hefted his end of the rug, ever so slightly, the way an impatient donkey might shift his burden.

"It's not much to ask at all, Dennis. Be glad to do it."

"I knew you would. It wasn't you I was worried about. But *some* people in this building . . ." Dennis rolled his eyes, sighed, set the bag of empties outside his door, and went back inside without another word.

It seemed to take a year to negotiate the remaining flights, but at last they were out in the cold air. His left arm curled around the rug, Gus reached with his right into his jacket pocket for the keys to the trunk of his dark-green Oldsmobile. A helmeted cop on horseback came by, the animal's steel hooves loud on the cobblestones.

"Happy New Year!" Jimmy called to the cop, who nodded and kept going. Gus opened the trunk, which was absolutely empty, the spare tire and jack hidden in a compartment beneath a carpeted lid. They lowered it in together, and it fit with just the slightest bit of jackknifing. Gus closed the trunk, then unlocked the passenger door for Jimmy, whose knees shook as he sank into the green leather upholstery.

Gus got behind the wheel and put the key in the ignition without turning it.

"You always talk to cops?"

Jimmy swallowed. "He was looking right at me."

"You know that cop? He a regular around here?"

"I have no idea."

This seemed to please Gus, or at least it didn't get him mad. "Don't talk to any more cops," he finally said.

"I won't."

"Unless it's a cop who's your friend, and you always talk to him."

"I do *not* have any cop friends."

"Hey, what do you know. We got something in common."

Gus forced a slight smile as he started the car and revved the gas pedal.

"What was that fuckin' neighbor bustin' your chops for?"

"He's the president of the co-op board. He's all right."

"All right? That's your idea of all right? He stops you in the middle of the hall and gives lectures on cockroaches while you got a rug on your shoulder?"

"Gus. It's his job to look out for the building."

"He's havin' a rip-roaring New Year's Eve in there, washin' out his V-8 cans."

"His boyfriend just moved out on him. He's depressed."

"And so to ease his pain, he busts your chops?"

"Gus. What did you want me to do differently?"

"Nothing. Fact is, you were perfect. My only worry was that he'd offer to help us with the rug. Lucky for us he's a self-absorbed little prick. Did it even occur to him that another human being was holding up the other end of the rug? Did he even wonder who it was?"

"I don't know, Gus. We could go back upstairs and ask him."

"Nahh, I don't want to interrupt him. After all, it's

can-rinsing night. Gotta hand it to you Manhattan types. You sure lead sophisticated lives."

Gus chuckled. Jimmy stared at him, thoroughly unable to see what was so funny. Gus patted his knee.

"The worst is over now. That was our biggest worry, going from up there to down here. Didn't want to tell you that. Should be a breeze from here."

"But I talked to that cop."

"Ahh, don't worry about that." Gus pushed in the dashboard lighter and shook a Marlboro into his mouth. "Cops aren't used to friendly people, is all. Makes them suspicious." The lighter popped. Gus lit up, leaned his head back, and breathed smoke at the car ceiling. "But he figures it's New Year's, you're a little loaded, you decided to say hello. Aaay, why are we even talking about this? He forgot about it already. Let's go."

"Where?"

"Out of Manhattan, for starters."

Gus eased the car out of the parking spot and cruised slowly down the caverns of SoHo, toward the Brooklyn Bridge. Jimmy sat numbly, staring at the St. Christopher medal that jiggled from a chain on the rearview mirror.

"Want to give myself a lot of room, front and back," Gus murmured as they approached the ramp to the bridge. "All we need is for some asshole to rear-end us."

He reached over, patted Jimmy's knee. "How you doing? You doing all right?"

Jimmy nodded. He swallowed dryly. He had to say something, anything, and the words he chose surprised him as much as they did Gus.

"How's Mom?"

* * *

Not one thing about the way his big brother laughed had changed since they were kids. It was still three or four short, hard chuckles that stopped abruptly, the way schoolkids stop laughing when the nun appears in the doorway.

"She's alive," Gus said. "I just left them all watching the Times Square bullshit on television. That guy, what's his name, he never looks any older."

"Dick Clark."

"That's him. Fucker's got formaldehyde for blood."

"Do they know you came to see me?"

Gus shook his head. "I come and I go. They don't ask much."

"I pushed her and she hit the lamp, Gus, I swear to God. She'd just kicked me in the nuts. It was strictly a reflex—"

"Don't tell me what I don't want to know," Gus interrupted. "Did I ask any questions? Did I ask even *one question?* What good can come from my knowing?"

"But I want to tell you."

"All right, tell me. Might calm you down."

"She kneed me in the nuts. The push was like . . . an automatic reaction. Her neck hit the lamp. I mean, it was a million-to-one shot that she'd break a bone like that. What are you smiling about?"

"I love your odds. If you ran a casino you'd be broke in an hour."

"Million to one," Jimmy insisted. "The police would've understood."

"You didn't call the police."

"Maybe I should have."

"Too late now."

For the first time all night, Jimmy felt true fear, felt

that he'd slammed a door he could never open. Gus was right. As they passed the midpoint of the bridge Jimmy realized they had not just left Manhattan, they'd left America, and were journeying through time to sixteenth-century Sicily.

"This is a mistake," he murmured.

"No it isn't," Gus said. "And even if it was, you've got to live with it, little brother. What am I going to do? Dump you and the rug at some precinct in Brooklyn?"

Jimmy stared hard out the windshield, looking up at the huge digital clock he'd gazed down at with Wendy not two hours earlier.

"I could explain everything," Jimmy said.

Gus sighed, rolled his eyes. "Please, God, tell me that I'm not related to the man sitting next to me. Tell me the hospital switched babies."

"Gus—"

"You think like this, and you're a big success? *Madonna mi,* I should've gone into architecture."

"Watch it, Gus."

"What're you gonna do? Push me at a lamp?"

They were quiet until the car rolled off the bridge and was indisputably on Brooklyn turf.

"Anyway," Gus said, "you already did tell a cop."

"Huh?"

Gus jerked his head, as if to indicate someone sitting in the back of the car. "That cop on the horse."

"You said he forgot about it!"

Gus squinted, pursed his lips. "The more I think about it, the less I like it."

"He kept going!"

"So did we, and we're still thinking about it. Just hope he's not. He was young, you know? For all we know he's one of those ambitious sons of bitches. And anybody who likes horses has gotta be a hard-on. Ever see those fucks? They put a sugar cube in their lips, and let the horse bite it away. They *kiss* the fuckin' horse, is what they do. They'd rather kiss a horse than Sophia Loren." Gus made a face. "Or maybe it's the other way around. Could be he wants to get off the fuckin' horse and get himself a gold shield."

"But what could happen?"

Gus shrugged. "He checks in at the end of his shift. Desk sergeant asks him if anything happened, and he mentions that two guys were carrying a rug at midnight. Now two cops know about it. Who the fuck moves a rug at midnight?"

"My God, Gus, my God!"

Jimmy covered his face with his hands and sobbed.

"Good," he heard Gus say, "been waiting for that. Now it'll be out of the way."

Jimmy kept sobbing until the car passed the Brooklyn House of Detention and stopped at a red light at Atlantic Avenue. He wiped his eyes and looked around, the smear of his tears making the sights seem even more sinister than they were. He hated Brooklyn. To his eyes, everything about the borough was second-rate and crumbling, a place for losers, no matter how many stories *The New York Times* did about brownstone renovations and croissant shops in Park Slope and Brooklyn Heights. Even the streetlights seemed underpowered, as if Con Edison knew there was nothing much worth illuminating.

Three black youths in flashy clothes crossed the street in front of the car, eager to get to parties before midnight. One whacked-out teenager wearing a backwards Yankee cap stopped briefly to drum on the hood with his hands, to the howling approval of his drunken companions.

"Assholes," Jimmy muttered through tight teeth.

Gus shrugged. "Just kids."

"Yeah? What if he did that on the trunk, and the lid popped open?"

"I've got a nonspring lock."

"But what if you didn't?"

"He'd see a rolled-up rug."

"What if he and his buddies stole it?"

"Aaay, so let 'em steal it. Beautiful. They get the rug, and we haul ass out of there like two typical scared-shitless white guys. We're long gone by the time the cords break and the body rolls out. Think any of them would remember the license plate, or even the make of this car? Fuhgetaboutit. There's a scene, the cops show up. Bing-bing-bing, they book 'em, and it's all over."

Jimmy swallowed. "They didn't kill her."

"Oh, the cops are going to believe *that,* all right. You kiddin' me? No jury'd believe those kids were stealing a rug from a car trunk. A *black* jury wouldn't believe it. Bye-bye to the three of them for about fifteen years."

The light turned green. Gus turned left on Atlantic Avenue, chuckling softly.

"They'll never know how lucky they are, huh? They're going to get laid, instead of going to Dannemora. See how funny life is? See how slight the difference is between things happening, and not happening?"

"Yeah, I see."

"Guess you do."

Gus reached across and rubbed Jimmy's scalp with

his fingers, making it sting. As Jimmy pulled away and smoothed his thick hair back into place, Gus chuckled with pride.

"Aaay, you got the Gambuzza scalp. What a head of hair on you. Guess maybe you're my brother after all, Mr. Gambar."

They were out of downtown Brooklyn, now, riding deeper into the borough. Jimmy felt his soul sink at the sight of so many burned-out houses along Atlantic Avenue, with glassless windows that seemed to be gaping in silent cries of desperation. Empty lots were littered with scorched mattresses, battered stoves, automobile skeletons. It was as if a war the newspapers had not bothered to cover had been fought here, and who the hell had won?

"I want to stay off the highways," Gus explained, jolting Jimmy with the sudden sound of his voice. "Less chance of getting hit by a drunk."

Jimmy watched a black woman with outrageous red hair trot away from a man in a long leather coat. The man caught up to her, grabbed her arm, and whacked her across the face, losing his mirrored sunglasses from the force of his own blow.

"Nice, huh?" Gus murmured. "Guess they missed their appointment with the marriage counselor this week."

Jimmy swallowed. "I want to thank you for coming, Gus."

"Hey, there it is! Been waiting for a 'thank you' now for, what?" He squinted at the car clock. "Six miles and twenty-two minutes."

"I'm sorry."

"Fuhgetaboutit."

"Gus."

"I'm right here."

"What would've happened if we'd called the police?"

"Will you get that out of your head, already? You did what you did. Live with it."

"I am, but I can't help wondering."

Gus chuckled. "You are hot stuff, Jimmy. Who do you think you are, a fucking Kennedy? Think the rules don't apply to you?"

Jimmy said nothing.

"Stop me if I'm wrong, here. You've got this idea that if you'd gone to the cops, they'd figure you for an innocent. White-collar citizen like you. Big shot. Maybe they wouldn't even arrest you. Give you a fucking desk appearance ticket. Right?"

"I don't know."

"Yeah, well, *I* know. You've got a dead Puerto Rican on your floor, brother. That's strike one. Maybe she's even got a little nose candy with her."

"She did."

Gus narrowed his eyes. "She got it on her now?"

Jimmy shrugged. "I think so. She must. She took it out, then stuck it back in her pocket."

"It's not back there on your floor?"

"No way."

Gus nodded, and seemed relieved. "Anyway, that's strike two. A corpse, and drugs. Now you're under arrest. The newspapers all go for this one. On top of everything else, it's New Year's Day. Slow fuckin' news day, with every criminal in town sleeping it off somewhere. What the fuck have the reporters got to write about, besides the first baby of the year and the first murder?"

A horrified Jimmy looked at Gus as if he'd just been told that the biopsy had come back positive.

"And maybe the cops speed the clock up a little bit, just to make the first murder more than the usual male-black-in-a-ski-cap-and-a-hooded-sweatshirt bullshit," Gus continued in an almost professorial way. "So you got reporters squeezing this thing for all it's worth. One of 'em's bound to read your last name, and put two and two together."

"But I have a different last name!"

"You think reporters don't know when an Italian's chopped a few vowels off his name? Not in this freaking city. And that, little brother, is strike three. Next thing you know they're at my door, asking me to take a ride downtown. Before you know it, they're calling it a mob murder."

"That's ridiculous!"

"That," Gus said calmly, "is the system. 'Link.' That's the word they love to use, the friggin' reporters. 'Link SoHo death to Albertini Family.' See? It doesn't mean shit, so they can't be sued. All it means is that we're brothers, and we're both in fucking custody."

Gus rolled down his window, threw out his butt, and lit a fresh Marlboro.

"When did you figure all this out?"

"About four seconds after I saw the body."

"You're protecting yourself, is what you're doing."

"Aaay, nail me to the cross. Who else is gonna protect me? And remember, I came to your house before I knew."

"You're right. I'm sorry."

Gus sighed, leaking smoke from his mouth. "You see? People start out thanking you, and right away they look for a way to get out of it. Nobody wants to owe for nothin'. It's fucking *sad,* is what it is."

"Thank you, thank you, *thank you.* All right?"

Gus shook his head. "Sarcasm now. That's even worse. Let's just ride quietly for a while, what do you say?"

Jimmy obeyed for a few blocks. "What you're saying is, the police would have screwed me."

Gus nodded. "Completely."

"So I did the right thing?"

"You did the *only* thing. What with this fucking AIDS, every jail term is a death sentence. Good-looking guy like you walks into prison, they all see Marilyn Monroe. They'd get you the first night."

Jimmy shivered. "And you too," he said.

Gus shook his head. "Me, they wouldn't touch," he said, almost apologetically.

"Because of who you are?"

"Because of what I am."

Jimmy was too scared to be insulted. He let it go. "So you're saying I did the right thing."

Gus nodded. "You did the only thing. You listened to your bones, instead of your brains."

In the East New York section, Gus turned off Atlantic Avenue and rode slowly down a side street. Jimmy's heart hammered. He'd been lulled into an odd sense of security. As long as he was riding in his big brother's comfortable car, nothing bad could happen. Now that car would be stopping, and they'd be getting out of it. He licked his dry lips.

"Where are we going, Gus?"

"I have to see some people, just to say hello."

"Tonight?"

"I do this every New Year's Eve. If I don't stop by tonight, it'll look funny. Understand?"

Jimmy did not understand. He remembered how Gus had always made a point of spending holidays such as New Year's Eve with his wife, Carol, no matter what was going on. Well, things had apparently changed.

"But *I'm* with you," Jimmy said. "Won't that look funny?"

"No, no, no. People always patch up family problems during the holidays. You were sitting home alone, sad about your life, and you called your brother to wish him a Happy New Year. Makes sense, no?"

"Is that what we're going to tell them?"

"Tell? What's this *'tell'* business? What are you, in therapy? We're not telling them shit. We're going in for a little drink, is what we're doing. You've already been drinking, so don't have any more." Gus cocked his head. "You drunk?"

"I was. Not now."

"The fear burns the alcohol out of you."

"Gus, I'm nervous."

"Be nervous. That's good. These family reunions are never easy. Hey, we're here."

Gus stopped in front of a brick building that resembled a fortress and tapped his horn three times. It was obviously some kind of code, because a kid appeared out of nowhere to unlock the driveway gate.

The kid had slicked-back hair that made him resemble a vampire, especially when he was bathed in the shine of Gus's headlights. He closed and locked the gate after they were inside, then disappeared.

Gus pulled into a yard, his wheels crunching over dead brown weeds. Half a dozen cars were parked here side by side, but Gus drove to the other side of the yard to park his car by itself, under the bare branches of an ailanthus tree. He cut the engine.

"Here we are," he said, like a father soothing an impatient child after a long ride to a mountain cottage. "Come on, we're just in time to see the ball come down."

Jimmy followed Gus through a side door and down a rickety set of cellar steps, into a windowless room packed with stocky men, card tables, and cigar smoke. The ceiling was crisscrossed with pipes, and the walls were the color of tobacco juice. Noisy poker games were in progress, and a TV set over a bar blared with the revelry of Times Square. Jimmy thought dimly of the tuxedoed piano player at Windows on the World, his music a gentle thread through the whispered conversations of elegant people at eye level with the clouds. Now he'd journeyed to another planet, where loud people gathered below ground level and said "fuck" whenever possible.

The sight of Gus brought a roar from the crowd. Guys rose to greet him with hugs and kisses on both cheeks. The vampire kid appeared again and handed Gus a club soda with a wedge of lime in it. Gus slipped him a fiver, sipped his drink, and draped his arm across Jimmy's shoulders.

"Some of you might remember my brother Jimmy."

This was cause for another, far smaller roar of greeting. One elderly man kissed Jimmy on both cheeks, the prickly white stubble on his cheeks feeling sharp enough to draw blood. A countdown began on the TV set, and at midnight they were all hugging and kissing, the elderly man nailing Jimmy again. Gus shook Jimmy's hand, but did not attempt an embrace.

"Happy New Year, kid."

"You too, Gus."

"Sit down, relax. We'll be outta here in a minute. Just gotta take care of a few things."

Jimmy found a seat with the only two men in the room who'd ignored the midnight moment. They'd gone right on playing poker beneath a moose head that was missing one antler, scowling at the cards and each other. The one closer to Jimmy wore a hearing aid that resembled a ram's horn, curling out of and around his ear. He seemed to notice Jimmy for the first time and jerked his head toward the TV set.

"Fuckin' morons," he announced, as the cameras panned swarms of revelers. "Who in his right fuckin' mind would go to Times Square on New Year's Eve? Woujoo?"

"No."

"That's all you'd need. Standin' around in the middle of a million niggiz."

"They ain't all niggiz," his partner said, objecting not to the remark's racism but to its inaccuracy.

"Niggiz and spicks, all right?" the hearing aid said sourly. "Fuckin' Dick Clark's the only white guy there, and he's on top of the fuckin' building. Probably got there in a fuckin' helicopter."

Jesus, what the hell would Wendy say if she could hear these guys? Jimmy remembered the poor old white-haired Alabama native at a Puck Building fundraiser who'd gotten a five-minute, finger-in-the-face lecture from Wendy for referring to black people as "the colored." Five minutes after that lecture, Wendy was scolding a black busboy for dropping a gin and tonic and splashing her stockings.

"Hey." The ram's horn was talking to Jimmy as his stubby hands expertly shuffled the cards. "Want me to deal you in?"

"No, thank you."

"Just one hand?"

"I don't know how to play poker."

The men looked at each other in astonishment, then at Jimmy with a blend of pity and contempt.

"You're Gus's brother?" the Ram's horn asked. Fortunately for Jimmy they suddenly began squabbling about whose turn it was to deal, and forgot all about him. But suddenly a burly, chinless man in a snug, shiny suit was standing nose-to-nose with Jimmy, regarding him with a cocked eye.

"Holy Christ, you're Jimmy, aren't you?"

"Yes."

"I ain't seen you in terdy years. You remember me?"

"Angelo, right?"

"Yeah." He extended a hand, which swallowed Jimmy's in an iron grip. "Good to see you."

"You too."

Angelo released Jimmy's hand, which actually tingled at the sudden return of blood.

"Christ, but you was a lousy fuckin' athlete."

It had been so long since Jimmy had taken a dose of Brooklyn bluntness that he had to give himself a standing eight-count before even attempting a reply.

"Sports were not my thing," he finally replied.

"You're fuckin' tellin' me. You got chosen in last every fuckin' time. Remember?"

"Yes," Jimmy said. "Fortunately, I didn't pursue a career in professional athletics."

"Fuck is it you do, anyway?"

"I'm an architect."

"You build buildings?"

"I design them."

Angelo pursed his lips, as if it were occurring to

him for the first time that sketches and plans had to be made before bull-necked construction workers could start laying bricks.

"Me, I had a tryout with the Boston Red Sox. Woulda made it, but I fucked up my shoulder."

"Well, Angelo, that's the beauty of my field. Even if I fucked up my shoulder, I could still do my job." He clapped the astonished Angelo's shoulder. "Been nice reminiscing with you. Happy New Year."

"Hey, whoa, wait. Where's your brother?"

"He's around."

"I gotta talk to him tonight. He promised me we'd talk."

"Like I said, he's around."

Angelo smoothed his lapels. "Listen. What do you think of this silk suit?"

Jimmy's immediate impression was that the garment was way too snug, and that a lot of silkworms had died in vain. The thing somehow seemed as chintzy as a leisure suit, maybe because Angelo's body was inside it.

"It's nice," Jimmy lied.

Angelo nodded. "Know what it cost me? Take a guess."

"I have no idea."

"A guess. Come on, what's it gonna cost ya?"

"Eight hundred bucks."

Angelo beamed. "Not even in the ballpark. You ready for this? *Ninety bucks.*" He whacked Jimmy's elbow with an open palm. "Huh? Can you fuckin' be*lieve* it?"

"That's amazing."

"Wanna know why it's so cheap?"

"Not really, Angelo."

"Well, I'm sure your brother would like to know.

Where the fuck is he?" Angelo walked away from Jimmy without a word of farewell, scanning the crowd for Gus. The vampire kid appeared at Jimmy's shoulder.

"Your brother wants to know if you want anything."

"Where is he?"

"Do you want anything?"

"No, thank you."

"Your brother says you should have a coffee."

"I'll have a coffee. Can't you tell me where he went?"

"He'll be back."

The vampire brought Jimmy an espresso in a small cup and saucer that felt heavy as lead. Jimmy sipped the scalding liquid, bitter as the inside of a peach pit.

A wave of panic washed over him as it hit him that nobody, but nobody, in the world knew he was here except for Gus. Had he pissed his brother off in some way with his frantic behavior? Had he rendered himself too dangerous to live? Any one of the men in this room looked as if he could turn and shoot Jimmy dead without missing so much as one hand of poker. He suddenly noticed that the place had a dirt floor, and that he and the dead woman might very well spend eternity together in one hole, beneath the feet of gambling Italians.

His brain seemed to be fizzing, as if his blood had turned to seltzer. He began edging his way toward the cellar steps, just to see if he could get there. He was within ten feet of them when the vampire kid's hand gripped his elbow.

"Fuck you goin'?"

"I just want to get a little air."

"Don't go fuckin' wanderin' around. Your brother wants you here."

He shoved him toward the center of the room. Jimmy felt a scream welling up from his belly, creeping up toward his mouth as if the bones of his chest and throat were the rungs of a ladder, and just as it was about to reach his mouth Gus patted his back, squeezed his shoulders.

"Okay, kid, let's hit the road."

Jimmy gulped the night air like a diver who's just come up from the ocean floor. It was absolutely delicious, after all the cigar smoke in that low-ceilinged room.

"How the fuck could you leave me alone in there, Gus?" he snapped as they walked to the car.

Gus chuckled. "Alone? There were seventy-five guys with you."

"You know what I mean. Where the hell were you?"

"I told you, I had to talk to some people. Hey. Jimmy. Who came to who for help?"

"That goddam kid wouldn't let me out."

"Whoa, whoa. You tried to leave the social club without me?"

"I just wanted to get a little air out here in the yard."

Gus opened the passenger door for Jimmy. "Don't be pissed at him. I told him to look out for you, that's all. He goes overboard sometimes. Got a heart of gold, though."

The same vampire kid held the gate open for them as they drove from the yard.

"He might have a heart of gold, but he's a creepy-looking kid," Jimmy said.

"Think so?"

"Don't you?"

"He's our cousin, you know. His father was our father's cousin. Remember Fat Jack?"

"The guy with the funny eye?"

Gus let out a low whistle of admiration. "Good memory."

"And by the way, I had a nice chat with that fat fuck Angelo."

"Oh, shit." Gus slapped the steering wheel. "I was supposed to meet with him tonight. He thinks he's got a big idea."

"Something about silk suits?"

"I have no fucking idea."

"He went on and on to me about his silk suit."

"Whatever it is, it can hold." Gus grinned at Jimmy. "He tell you about his shoulder, too?"

"What do you think?"

"He works it into every conversation. 'Think it's gonna, rain, Angelo?' 'It might. The shoulder I hurt at my Red Sox tryout is achin' from the dampness.' 'How's your mother, Angelo?' 'She's fine, except I fucked up my shoulder during my Red Sox tryout.' "

"I remember him. He wasn't that good a player. He never would have made it to the big leagues."

"Aaay, he went to an open-call tryout, and they never called back. Gotta let him have his dreams, Jimmy. Keeps him from becoming a serial killer."

"He's a miserable bastard."

"Aaay, what the fuck are you so upset about?"

"I don't need to be reminded about how bad an athlete I was. I remember it well."

"For Christ's sakes, is that why you're pissed at

him? *Madonna,* what a short fuse you've got. You're so steamed at Angelo that you're forgetting about a slightly bigger problem we're tryin' to solve, here."

It was true. Jimmy gulped, and felt his stomach fall the way it used to on the Cyclone roller coaster at Coney Island, when the thing reached its peak and plunged down the rails.

"You're right, Gus."

"Of course I'm right. You've gotta do something about that temper of yours. Especially when you're dealin' with a guy like Angelo."

"Why? Is he . . . you know . . ."

Gus chuckled. "A killer? Nahh. He manages the produce section of a supermarket." Gus chuckled again. "Angelo, a killer. That is funny. How's he gonna do a job like that? He fucked up his shoulder at the Red Sox tryout."

"Oh, yeah. I keep forgetting."

Jimmy was glad to be back inside his brother's heavy green vehicle. Part of the reason was that Gus drove so carefully, making full stops at stop signs and pulling over to the right whenever other drivers wanted to pass. They rode for several miles without speaking, but at last Jimmy couldn't help himself.

"Where are we taking it?"

Gus smiled blandly. "How do you know it's still in there?"

"Is it?"

"What do you think?"

"I don't know."

"Figure it out," Gus urged. "Put yourself in my shoes. What would I do in a fix like this?"

Jimmy pushed at his eyeballs. "Well, it all depends on trusting people, on who you trust."

"Hmmm."

"Right?"

"Go on."

"This is big. I mean, it isn't usually like this."

"Usually? You think I do this often?"

"No! . . . *I* don't know. What the hell do *I* know?"

"You're getting flustered. That's bad. Calm yourself and keep thinking."

"Just tell me if it's back there, Gus!"

"Figure it out," Gus insisted. "This you must earn."

Jimmy sighed. He looked Gus in the eye and noticed how white the whites of the man's eyeballs were—no lines of red, no patches of tan, like the eyes of an Olympic athlete who got his eight hours of sack time every night.

"No," Jimmy finally blurted.

"No what?"

"No, there's nobody you could trust with something like this. It's still back there. Right?"

A tiny grin tickled Gus's lips, like the memory of an old girlfriend. "Not bad, brother," he said. "Not bad at all."

Jimmy's heart sank. "So I'm right."

"Yes. Can't you hear it? Every time I go over a bump, it thumps. Listen."

Gus might have been describing an automotive defect to a garage mechanic. He deliberately steered into a pothole, and sure enough, the bang of the wheels was followed by a bump in back, like a muffled hiccup.

"Feel it?"

"Stop the car."

Gus braked just in time to let Jimmy tumble out and vomit over a sewer grate. He felt as if all his internal organs were trying to evacuate, but in fact his belly was empty, except for an espresso and whiskey cocktail that felt like hot oil coming up. Strong hands squeezed his shoulders.

"Go on," Gus advised, "get it all out of you."

From a block away, to the eyes of Hector Martinez and Luis Melendez, the two hunched-over white guys could not have looked more like lambs ready for slaughter if they had had little white tails.

Martinez and Melendez were itchy. That very afternoon, the two seventeen-year-olds had been sprung from a juvenile detention center.

Martinez had spent two years there for beating and raping a sixty-eight-year-old woman. During his jail term, he was raped six times before turning jailhouse rapist himself. Martinez had done nothing to indicate a readiness for a return to society, but was pushed out by an avalanche of paperwork. Among other things, the woman he'd raped had no relatives, and she died a year after the crime. Nobody made noise when his parole hearings came up.

The only clean thing about Martinez was his skull, which he'd been shaving since his incarceration. His fierce, inky eyes were set back slightly on the sides of his face. He had a smooth, rolling walk that resembled swimming. He looked like a squid coming at you.

He was a choirboy compared to his companion, Melendez. Three years earlier Melendez, a small-boned boy with bulging eyes, had entered a bodega after midnight and demanded cash from a graying father of four named Pedro Arroyo. Arroyo looked down at the scrawny boy with the pistol in his hand and somehow couldn't help giggling. He believed that the gun was a toy. Without so much as a thought or a doubt, Melendez pointed at Arroyo's face and fired.

The gun jammed. Arroyo laughed out loud. It was the last time he ever laughed.

Melendez jumped over the counter and knocked Arroyo unconscious with the butt of the pistol. He found a large knife Arroyo used to slice open cardboard cartons. This he used to slice off the man's ears and the soft tip of his nose. Melendez was preparing to slice off Arroyo's upper lip when a cop entered the bodega to buy a pack of Luckies. The cop cuffed the boy, phoned for an ambulance, and vomited all over the counter. Then he had the presence of mind to put the nose and ears on ice, making it possible for surgeons to stitch them back onto Pedro Arroyo's head.

His spirit was another matter. He sold his bodega and moved with his family back to Puerto Rico, where his neighbors grew used to the sounds of his anguished screams in the middle of the night. Always, it was the same dream, about the boy's small hand on the knife's large handle. The screaming stopped with the man's suicide.

New York authorities had a hard time getting a reason from Melendez for the crime that chilled even the toughest of them. Bored by their questions, Melendez gave a simple explanation for what he'd done.

"The man be a pig. I made him *look* like one."

Melendez was one of the few inmates that Martinez never tried to rape. This was their first day of friendship outside of prison, and it was working out fine. So far that night they'd stolen a bottle of Jack Daniel's from a liquor store, drunk half of it, and robbed and beaten up a thirteen-year-old boy who'd been sent out by his mother to buy potato chips. They used the kid's money to buy quart bottles of Ballantine Triple-X, which they drank as they walked. Their victim had run home bleeding from his forehead, unaware of how lucky he'd been that the duo had chosen not to use their weapons on him. They were just warming up for the big night ahead.

Martinez had a six-inch monkey wrench, the kind a plumber would use to work on a small pipe fitting. Melendez had a 9-millimeter pistol. He'd hidden it under the floorboards of his old room, three years earlier. His family was long gone and their tenement building itself was abandoned, stripped of all plumbing and wiring. With a skeptical Martinez at his side, Melendez had climbed the pukey stairs of the tenement, kicked in his old door, and begun prying up the floorboards in the empty room. There it was, in fine shape, tucked inside a plastic bag. Melendez, who had not so much as grinned upon his release, was now beaming.

"You see?" he said to Martinez. *"Tole* you it'd fuckin' be here."

Martinez looked the gun over. "Can't believe nobody took it."

"They rip out the pipes, is all. Ain't nobody gonna bother with no floorboards. Come on, let's get the fuck out of here."

And now suddenly the main event was in front of them, in the form of Jimmy and Gus. Perfect. And white guys, to boot.

They didn't quicken their pace as they neared the brothers. They slowed down, as if to savor the approach to what their bones told them would be an all too easy attack.

"Fat one first," Melendez said.

"Yeah," Martinez agreed. "I'm gonna hit him in his fat fuckin' face."

"We gonna open his face."

"Yeah. Let the skinny one watch."

"He be pukin'."

"He gonna puke up his liver when he see what we do to his friend."

Melendez giggled. "This gonna be so much fuckin' fun." At last they broke into a run.

"Go on," Gus urged Jimmy. "Get it all out of you."

Jimmy heaved some more, and felt better. Gus passed him two sticks of Wrigley's Spearmint, but Jimmy's hands shook too much to unwrap them, so Gus did it for him.

"Oh, God, Gus, I feel like I'm going to die."

"No, you're not," Gus replied. "You may want to, but you won't."

Gus heard rapid footsteps behind his back. Martinez and Melendez had accelerated to pounce speed, their heels loud on the sidewalk. Gus turned and rose to face them, his hands balled into fists that he knew would be useless if these kids meant business. Martinez actually chuckled with glee as he pulled the wrench from his pocket, and was both startled and confused by the forbidding whack of Melendez's arm across his chest. On Melendez's face was a look Martinez had not seen in all their time behind bars. It was an expression of absolute awe.

Martinez pushed his arm away. "Fuck's wrong wichoo, man?"

Melendez pointed at Gus. He licked his suddenly dry lips and spoke in a reverential voice.

"That's 'Ghost' Gambuzza, man. Look at him."

"Bullshit."

"Look at him!"

Martinez said nothing, but he slowly slid the wrench back into his pocket. They stood and stared.

"Oh balls," Gus murmured. He squatted to speak

with his brother, but kept his eyes on the boys to maintain their trance. "Get up, Jimmy," he commanded. "And don't say my name, whatever you do."

Jimmy rose on shaky legs as Gus, still holding a thousand-volt hypnotist's gaze on the boys, guided him back into the car. Martinez and Melendez were not budging.

"Hey, Ghost, man," Melendez ventured, "what the fuck you doin' here, anyway?"

Gus behaved like a deaf man, got behind the wheel and calmly pulled away. The kids trotted after the car, but Gus didn't even look in his rearview mirror. Jimmy wanted to turn around for a look back, but Gus said, "Don't."

Jimmy obeyed. He looked in the rearview mirror and saw the kids stop running. They stood staring at the car, their hands away from their hips like Wild West gunslingers. Gus drove three blocks before calmly remarking, "That was bad."

"I'm sorry."

Gus shrugged. "Hey, you got sick. You couldn't help it. Now we just gotta hope that cop on the horse keeps his mouth shut."

"What's that got to do with this?"

"Nothing, as long as that girl isn't anybody." Gus lit a cigarette. "See, that's the missing piece. Who the fuck is she? For all you know she's some big-time entertainer, havin' a bad night. She disappears on New Year's. Now you got a mystery. All right, so the alarm goes out, and that hard-on cop tells his sergeant he saw something funny in the neighborhood that night. Two fucking guys putting a rug in a car. Maybe it's not much, but it's better than nothing. Good cop that he is, he jotted down my license plate."

"No way he did that! He never even took his hands off the reins!"

"All right, all right," Gus conceded. "But he remembers that it was a four-door green Oldsmobile. Boom, all the TV stations go with the story. 'Mystery green Oldsmobile.' "

Gus jerked his head back to indicate where they'd just been. "Our friends back there see the TV report, and they go bat shit." Gus pantomimed the dialing of a telephone, and startled Jimmy with a wildly exaggerated Hispanic accent.

"Hello? Lee-sin, mon, I seen that car, and Ghost Gam-boo-sa was dee pockin' driver!"

"Oh, for Christ's sakes!"

"Those kids," Gus said evenly. "All they do is watch TV. They dream about being on TV. They think they're not *alive* if they don't get themselves on TV. What the hell else have they got? They see a chance like this, they're gonna grab it. And let us not forget your friend Dennis in the hallway. He sees the TV report, and he stops washin' empties long enough to call the cops."

"Do you realize the series of long shots that have to happen for it to fall into place like that?"

Gus nodded. "Of course. But the only thing better for us than a bunch of long shots is no shots at all, which we no longer have."

"Oh God."

"You gonna be sick again? Want me to stop?"

"No . . ."

"Hey, relax. You were good. You didn't say my name. That was a very big deal, your not saying my name."

"Thank you."

Jimmy sat back and shut his eyes for a moment before suddenly sitting forward and turning to Gus. "You were on TV?"

Gus nodded, rolled his eyes. "That sleazoid show on Channel Five. They had like a five-second tape of me walkin' out of my house. Ran it six or seven times in slow motion, since it was all they had."

"What made them do that?"

"The article."

"What article?"

"Aaay, come on, Jimmy. Where do you live, in a cloud?" Gus sighed before flipping down the visor, which had a folded story from the *Daily News* clipped to it.

He passed it to Jimmy. "You never saw this article?"

Jimmy shrugged his shoulders in apology. "I only read the *Times.*"

Gus nodded his approval. "I like that paper. At least they wait until you're indicted."

"Okay if I turn on the interior light?"

"Go ahead. But read fast."

GHOST AND GODFATHER MAKE
BOO-TIFUL MUSIC TOGETHER
by JERRY CAPECI

They call him "the Ghost," and he's been haunting the hearts of diligent FBI investigators for more than two decades.

But like all ghosts, Augustus Gambuzza has proven himself to be as elusive as Casper himself—though not nearly as friendly.

"We know he's a key player," a law enforcement source told the Daily News. "But beyond that, we know very little. It's very frustrating."

Gambuzza, 45, has never had his voice recorded on a surveillance tape, and has never even been indicted or arrested.

But the stout, dark-haired resident of Brooklyn's Bay Ridge section might one day find himself in the shoes of his aging boss—reputed Mafia chief Federico Albertini, 67, who happens to be Gambuzza's next-door neighbor.

"Bank on it," said the law enforcement source. "The old man trusts 'the Ghost' more than he trusts his own children."

Neighborhood residents were predictably close-mouthed on the subject of Gambuzza, a father of two.

"He don't bother nobody," said a man who identified himself only as Rico. "He's a quiet man

PLEASE TURN TO PAGE 22

But there was no page 22.

"I lost it somewhere," Gus said casually, reaching up to shut off the interior light. "Blew out the window, I guess. Aaay, it's all bullshit, anyway."

"It is?"

"Absolutely."

"What happened when this story ran?"

Gus shrugged. "Nothing. I left town for a few days. By then, the TV cameras all went away."

"All but one."

"All right, all but one."

"What if the FBI is following you tonight?"

"Did I just say it was all bullshit, or what?"

"But what if they are?!"

Gus shook his head. "Jimmy, it's New Year's. That's double time. No way they'll put anyone on me at double time. There's a recession going on, or maybe you heard about it."

He took the article from Jimmy's hand and returned it to the visor. "Look at the bright side. The cop barely noticed us. The kids were drunk. They've forgotten about it already."

"Why don't *you* look on the bright side, Gus?"

"It's not in my nature. Never was. How's your stomach? Feeling better? We could eat something, if you like."

Jimmy was going to object to the idea of stopping again when Gus reached over and opened the glove compartment, liberating odors of garlic and tomato sauce that took Jimmy back to his boyhood. Gus removed a paper bag and asked Jimmy to remove the sandwiches. Tomato sauce soaked the rolls, which enclosed layers of eggplant parmigiana.

Jimmy's soul swelled. "My God, that smells good. I don't remember the last time I had Italian food."

Gus shook his head. "I can understand you rejecting certain parts of your heritage, but not the diet." Gus clucked his tongue. "Jimmy. Those restaurants in your neighborhood. I mean, please."

"You eat in SoHo?"

"Once or twice. Sun-dried this. Sun-dried that. I think the waiter was sun-dried, too. Skinny guy who kept poppin' up behind me with a pepper mill like a baseball bat."

"Not all the places are like that."

"Also, the waiter was a walking menu. He recited all the dishes like he was doing Hamlet. I don't care for that. I like a menu I can hold in my hands and read."

"You're right, Gus. The Brooklyn restaurants are

much better. I mean, what's the point of dining out at a place where there's no chance of gunplay?"

Jimmy passed an unwrapped sandwich to Gus, who gestured at the open glove compartment.

"I've got napkins in there, too. Reach me one, please."

To Jimmy's surprise they were cloth napkins, rolled and squeezed through silver rings. He pulled off the rings and passed one to his brother.

"You got candles in there, too?"

"Aaay, nail me to the cross, I like the little touches." Gus spread the napkin on his lap before taking a small bite of his sandwich. This was how Jimmy remembered him, growing up. No matter how hungry Gus was, he never wolfed his food, never gulped his drinks. Back in school, he was always the last kid out of the cafeteria.

"Eat up, Jimmy, you're thin. I bet you go to a gym, huh?"

"Once in a while," Jimmy lied. He actually went five times a week.

"Yeah? What do you do, that treadmill thing?"

"Sometimes."

"I should go to a gym. But what I need is an after-hours gym. Soon's they invent that, I'm the first to sign up." Gus swallowed his first mouthful. "Tell me about this girl."

"I told you, I only met her a few hours ago."

"Not that one. The one you've been dating. 'The devine Miss Orgel,' as your neighbor called her. She was serious business, huh?"

"How'd you know it was serious?"

Gus shrugged. "It fits. This is the kind of thing that happens when a relationship goes bad."

"Death?"

"No, no, no. Messes happen. When the pattern gets broken, things happen. This happens to be an extreme mess, that's all. So who's the girl?"

Jimmy wasn't answering.

"Look at this, he won't tell me."

"Why do you want to know?"

"We haven't had a conversation in twenty years. Tell you the truth, I'm running out of topics. Look, I already know her last name. Just give me her first name, for Christ's sake."

"Wendy."

"Jewish."

"Yes. Something wrong with that?"

Gus held up his hands defensively, his pinkies controlling the steering wheel.

"Did I say a word? I made an observation. If you'd said her name was Angela, I'd have guessed she was Italian."

"I've never dated an Italian girl."

"Big surprise. How long have you and Wendy been dating?"

"Almost two years."

"Steady?"

"Yes."

"What's she do?"

"Gus, why do you have to know?"

"I *don't* fucking have to know. I'm making conversation. If you'd rather ride quiet, that's fine with me."

"She's a lawyer."

"Criminal?"

"Real estate."

"Ooh, a barracuda. Excuse me, that was uncalled for. What'd you fight about?"

Jimmy sighed. "Believe it or not, it was over my taste in clothes."

"Get out of here."

"Swear to God."

"You look okay to me."

"She thinks I dress too conservatively. Too many dark colors. She wanted me to wear pastels."

"What kind of colors?"

"Pastels."

"Liberace colors?"

"Exactly."

"What'd you say?"

"Told her I didn't want to."

"You tell her what to wear?"

"Are you kidding me?"

"So where does she come off?"

"She said she was trying to improve the quality of my life."

"You're making this up! No, you're not. I forgot, she's a lawyer."

"Anyway," Jimmy sighed, "tonight she hands me a pink tie she wants me to wear."

"And you refused."

"Right. Christ, *look* at it!" Jimmy pulled it from his pants pocket and dangled it. Gus mock-shielded his eyes from the glare of it.

"I did that too!" Jimmy cried. "Tried to joke my way out of it!"

"Then what happened?"

Jimmy shrugged, stuffed the tie back into his pocket. "I walked out on her. Left her at the Windows on the fucking World, drinking champagne."

Gus exhaled, long and deeply. "Can't say I blame you. Sometimes women have funny ideas about how we ought to look."

"Goddam right they do."

"On the other hand—and this is just a suggestion,

for the future—you could've done what I did every time Carol wanted me to wear stuff I hated."

At the mention of her name Jimmy's blood jumped. He was only a boy when Gus married Carol, a gentle, blond-haired beauty who'd starred in Jimmy's very first sexual fantasies. Jimmy was wild about Carol, and always wondered if Gus could tell. What did she look like now? Maybe as a by-product of this wild night, he'd get to see Carol, twenty years after. Jimmy waited for his blood to calm before asking, "What did you do?"

Gus grinned. "When she wanted me to wear something I hated, I'd spill something on it."

"Jesus, Gus, that's pretty childish."

Gus shrugged elaborately. "What's the big fuckin' deal? You wear the friggin' tie for about fifteen seconds, then dip it in the gravy."

"You never would have done anything like that."

"You kiddin' me? Carol had this thing about gettin' me to wear light brown shirts. Some shit about the way it brought out my eyes. I spilled enough salad dressing on 'em, she got the message."

"That's just beautiful. Such communication."

"Once," Gus chuckled, "we went to a Chinese restaurant on our anniversary. She gives me a box, I take out the shirt. She gets one look at my face and shakes soy sauce on it. *She* shook the sauce on it."

"Now that's love," Jimmy said dryly.

"You bet your ass it is. Solved the problem without a single corpse, brother."

There was frost in Gus's voice; Jimmy remained silent for a minute. "Thing is," he gently continued, "I was going to propose to her tonight." He pulled out the Tiffany box from his other pocket and showed the wide-eyed Gus the ring.

"What'd it set you back?"

"Thirty-eight hundred."

"I don't guess I have to tell you most of that money goes for the blue box."

"Gus. She likes Tiffany stuff, okay?"

"Fine, fine. All I'm saying is you could've gone to Uncle Frankie on Canal Street."

"Oh, right. I'm going to give her a ring in a little Ziploc bag and ask her to marry me?"

"No, no, no. You buy a thirty-dollar silver pin at Tiffany's, and use the box for the ring. What's she going to do, ask for a receipt?"

"She might have," Jimmy said through tight teeth. "She just fucking might have."

It was only beginning to dawn on Jimmy just how unhappy he'd been with Wendy. Two fucking years of unhappiness! What the fuck had he been, unconscious all that time? The brothers were quiet for a while before Gus asked, "Did she live with you?"

Jimmy had to laugh. "No way."

"She got stuff at your place?"

"A toothbrush. Maybe one pair of panties. She's what you might call the independent type."

"You've seen the last of this girl, Jimmy."

Jimmy nodded. "You're probably right."

"No, no, no," Gus said. "I mean, *you have seen the last of this girl.*"

CHAPTER 5

Gus's voice was absolutely arctic. It was an order, Jimmy finally understood, and all he could do was stare at his brother, who forced a chilly smile.

"Let her pick up her stuff, give her a hug, and throw her out forever."

"Jesus Christ, Gus!"

"It's the only way."

"Why?"

The look of pity hurt even more than the words. "She's got you, Jimmy. You stay with this girl, and you go to fucking jail."

"Oh, right! Like I'm going to kill a woman every time we argue!"

"You'll tell her," Gus said soothingly. "You won't mean to. It'll be late at night, and you won't be able to sleep, and she'll ask you what's wrong. 'Remember New Year's Eve?' you'll say. 'Something happened that night.' You'll talk in the dark, Jimmy. People talk in the dark like it doesn't count. She won't even interrupt you while you give her the whole story. You'll be crying, and she'll hold you, and you'll probably hump like you never humped before." Gus nodded at his own scenario, eyes narrowed. "Then morning comes, and you're *both* fucked. You're going to have enough trouble holding this. You want her to hold it, too? Jews are very bad at that."

"I resent that, Gus."

Gus laughed. "Aaay, they make fun of us because we go to confession. At least it's free. They do the same thing for a hundred bucks an hour and call it therapy. You going to tell me she doesn't go to therapy?"

Jimmy licked his lips. "Three times a week."

"Ooh, fuhgetaboutit. She'd give you up by Thursday's session. 'Doctor, my boyfriend and I had great sex the other night, and I'm worried about it.' That's how it'd start. An hour later they show up at your office and take you out in bracelets. With her behind the cops, telling you she did it for your sake."

Jimmy felt numb. Everything Gus said made sense, and on top of that, his imitation of Wendy's loud, sometimes piercing voice was shockingly accurate. It was as if he'd been spying on him.

"You don't love her, anyway," Gus said. "Nobody who dates two years is in love. You've seen her in all seasons, twice. What are you waiting for? You're on a fuckin' hamster wheel."

"Yeah? How long did you know Carol before you knew you were in love?"

Gus hesitated before saying, "I loved her the first time I ever saw her. Before she ever even knew I was alive."

Again, Jimmy's blood jumped. He'd felt the exact same way the first time he saw Carol. Of course, Jimmy was twelve at the time. Any decent-looking woman who'd walked into the Gambuzza home would have had the same effect on him, or so Jimmy believed.

"Gus," Jimmy began carefully, "I think you're romanticizing it just a little."

"First time," Gus insisted. "Saw her walkin' to class in a plaid skirt and saddle shoes. 'Bout ten books in her arms. Blond hair in two braids to the middle of her back. Knew I was looking at my future wife before I ever spoke a word to her."

"Come on."

"Swear to God."

"That's not love, that's a Barry Manilow song."

"It worked for me," Gus said, softly but firmly. "Never looked at another woman."

Jimmy let it sink in. He knew Gus was giving it to him straight. What must it be like to feel that way about a person through so many years? No weighing of pros and cons, no nights of confusion about feelings, no fence-sitting. Look at her, love her, take her. My big brother, Alley-Oop. Jimmy felt it was ridiculous, but he also felt a pang of envy. And he was a little scared by the fact that he could not remember the first time he'd ever seen Wendy.

What was she wearing? What, if anything, did he say to himself when he saw her? He was drawing a blank—and worse than that, an apathetic blank. It didn't matter. She meant nothing to him. She'd *never* meant anything to him. Gus was right; she'd been a habit, nothing more. It was a painful truth Jimmy's stranger of a brother had forced him to see.

"I'll dump her," Jimmy finally said. "All right?"

"Don't just say it. You've got to be crueler than you've ever been. Let her cry, let her puke, let her threaten to kill herself. But don't take her back."

"Pull over at the next phone booth and I'll call her."

"No, no. Do it tomorrow, when we're in the clear."

"But I want to get it out of the way."

"Jimmy, it's all wrong that way. From a pay phone, you're going to dump her? She'll want to know where you are. You tell her Brooklyn, and she'll know something's up."

"I won't tell her."

"Oh, you'll tell her. They hear the word 'Brooklyn,' and they think two things—blacks and crime."

"Jesus, Gus!"

"Excuse me, three things—blacks, crimes, and dope. She'll picture a black girl standing next to you, with about ten pounds of cocaine in her purse." Gus chuckled. "Wouldn't be too far off, would it? Hey, come on, laugh a little, brother. It's just us. Nobody listening to make sure we're politically correct."

"I'll wait. I'll do it in person."

"Aaay, that's the spirit. And anyhow, what makes you think she'd be home on New Year's Eve? She's probably at the Rainbow Room. You had reservations, no?"

Jimmy was stunned. "How the hell did you know that?"

"Where the hell else is a white guy like you gonna go to make a big splash on New Year's Eve?"

Jimmy shook his head. "There's no way she went."

"Aaay, Jimmy, come on. This Wendy doesn't sound like the type who suffers in silence. She goes. She cries. Some guy comes along to ask her what's wrong. Ba-da-bing, ba-da-bing, and you're free. Bet you have a message on your machine. 'I met someone. It's over.' "

"You know, Gus, you have a real cruel streak."

"Nah. I have a real practical streak. People do as they do. You can't get mad, or disappointed."

"You never get mad?"

"Used to. But it never paid off."

"So you're not even a human being anymore, is what you're saying."

Gus shrugged. "I am what I became. Like everybody else. Didn't you become something else tonight? Something you'd never planned on becoming?"

"I'm not a killer."

"I didn't say you were. But you are also not your average friggin' architect anymore, livin' in a SoHo loft."

The loft, the loft; the only place in the world where Jimmy felt truly comfortable, and only when he was there by himself. Wendy was always complaining about drafts, stray splinters from the wide-plank floors, the lack of a doorman—it never ended. Jimmy covered his face with his hands and imagined himself home in his platform bed, reading a book. He could almost feel the cool sheets against his skin, the warmth of a bedside mug of coffee. It could all have been his, if he'd just gone straight home from the Trade Center. But no. He pulled his hands off his face and saw that they were riding near swampland. Cattails grew next to the road, and houses were scarce. Jimmy spoke like a child waking from a nap.

"Where the fuck are we going, Gus?"

"Tell you the truth, I don't know yet. I think better when I'm in motion. *Madonna,* we've gone sixteen miles, already. Lucky I gassed up before you called."

Jimmy felt dizzy. Big brother Gus, the Mafioso, had been filling his gas tank and making small talk with some gas jockey in Bay Ridge while he, the straight-arrow taxpayer, was pushing an Hispanic woman to her death.

Jimmy sat back and shut his eyes. The push, the

push: why had he pushed her so fucking hard? Or *had* he pushed her so fucking hard? He told himself it was a reflex, but would a plain reflex have sent her hurtling across the floor that way? He brought his hands to his chest and thrust them forward, saw the woman skittering across the floor and into the lamp.

An accident? Or a bull's-eye? The event was like a film on a loop, playing over and over in his head. Jimmy made the pushing motion with his hands again, this time slightly harder.

Giggling sounds. Jimmy opened his eyes to see Gus grinning and shaking his head.

"I don't believe this. You're duplicating the push."

"I was not! My arms are stiff, that's all."

"Jimmy, you can play it over and over in your head a million times, and all it amounts to is chasing your fuckin' tail."

"I wasn't playing it over in my head! My arms felt stiff. I was trying to loosen them up."

"Fine. Loosen them up. But what you gotta loosen up ain't your arms, brother. Trust me on that one."

"You think you know everything, don't you?"

"Me?" Gus yawned, wiped his wet eyes with the back of his hand. "I don't know a fuckin' thing. I'm just takin' care of our needs as they arise. Right now, need number one is coffee."

Up ahead, a silver-colored railroad car diner appeared from out of the fog, as if by order. Gus pulled up to it and parked by the steps leading to its front door. No other cars were in the lot.

"Large regular coffee for me, Jimmy. Get yourself whatever you want." He held a five-dollar bill out between his index and middle fingers, the way you'd offer money to the ballpark attendant who leads you to your seat.

Jimmy was offended. "I have money."

"Aaay, you're gettin' all upset? I just didn't want you to be diggin' through your pockets."

"I'm not upset. All I said was, I have money."

Gus stuffed the five in his shirt pocket and folded his hands in mock prayer. "Just please, please, *please* go and buy me a large regular coffee, Jimmy? I don't give a fuck if you pay with Adolf Hitler's money, long as the coffee's hot."

Jimmy got out of the car and climbed the steps to the place, which turned out to be a real railroad car, set on cement blocks where the wheels once were. But whatever touches might have been added to make the diner charming had faded long ago.

Inside, the linoleum was worn to the black, the red counter seat tops were torn and patched with silver electrical tape, and the Formica behind the griddle was splashed with ancient grease stains that time had baked into tattoos. A lone waitress was on duty, along with a balding fry cook who slept upright in his chair, a fist against his cheek.

The waitress sat hunched over at the counter, reading *People* magazine. She wore a powder-blue smock that zipped up the back and fit her bony body like a condom. She was only five-four or five, but her feet looked as wide as waffles inside white sneakers. At the sound of Jimmy's entrance she hoisted herself from a stool by pushing her hands against the counter, to spare her legs from effort. She was making the turn around to the service side of the counter when she asked the floor, "Help you?"

"A black coffee and a regular coffee, please."

"To go?"

"Yes."

She filled two blue paper cups with illustrations of

Greek statues on their sides. She covered the black coffee with a plastic lid and splashed milk from an open, unrefrigerated carton into the other. Jimmy thought about objecting to milk from a room-temperature container for his brother's coffee—good God, what if Gus got sick?!—but he let it go.All he wanted to do was leave. He put a ten-dollar bill down and waited for change, but the waitress did not move to take the money. She was staring at Jimmy's face.

"Could I have my change, please?"

She shook her head, smiling dimly. "It's on the house."

"Huh?"

"It's on the house, Jimmy."

His spine tingled. The waitress, a washed-out hag who looked to be crowding fifty, smiled broadly now, revealing uneven, tobacco-stained teeth. Her wiglike hair was her own, but it was dyed the color of taffy and looked more like rained-upon cotton candy than anything else. It was as if a beautician had blow-dried and teased it beyond repair, then abandoned it.

Here came her hand, red and raw, to touch Jimmy's cheek. "You don't recognize me?" Her eyes glistened with tears, and only then did Jimmy notice her eyes, blue as cobalt. Each iris was surrounded by a dark blue rim, like a ring around Saturn. Time could not change those eyes, the likes of which Jimmy had never seen since. They belonged, and still did, to Janet Ameruso, the girl he'd taken out on prom night.

"Hello, Janet," Jimmy said, his voice a blend of awe and sorrow. "Well. My God."

Janet bit her lower lip, wiped her eyes. "I'da been devastated if you hadn't recognized me."

"Of course I recognized you. How could I not?"

Janet chuckled. "Still the gentleman, huh, Jimmy?"

He could think of no reply. It was like seeing somebody after they've been mutilated in a train wreck, and trying to think of a nice thing to say. Jimmy gave her a make-over in his mind: shave her head and start over with untortured hair, steam out all the caked-in makeup, a few hundred hours at the gym to put some muscle on the bones . . . he gave it up. He realized that what needed repair was her spirit, obviously broken beyond repair.

"So," Jimmy finally managed to say. "How've you been?"

Janet laughed rustily. "Me? I'm workin' the swing shift at Brooklyn's worst diner. How've *you* been? You ever become an architect?"

"Uh-huh."

Janet nodded, her face soft with real happiness for Jimmy. "I knew you'd make it. If anybody was gonna get out of the neighborhood, it was you. Hey, that brother of yours is a big shot too, huh?"

She winked, hiked up her eyebrows, and touched the side of her nose in the universal sign for Mafioso. Jimmy wondered if Gus saw this through the front window. As if in response, a car horn sounded, tapped by the impatient Ghost.

"That's him now. I guess he wants his coffee."

"He's out there?" Janet's voice was thick with excitement. Jimmy was amazed to feel a stab of envy. "Geez, I'd love to meet him."

Jimmy shrugged. "Well. He's a little shy, you know. Let me bring him his coffee. I'll be right back."

On tingling legs Jimmy carried the coffee to the Ghost, who was not pleased by the delay.

"Hell's it take so long to get a cup of coffee?"

"I know the waitress. I went to the senior prom with her."

"Holy Christ, Jimmy, what a night you picked to play *This Is Your Life.*"

"Gus, what do you want from me? I have to talk to her a little bit. It'd look funny if we just ran off, wouldn't it?"

"Yes, it would look funny."

"Also, she wants to meet you."

"She knows I'm out here?"

"I guess I told her."

"You guess." Gus pushed at his eyeballs. "Tell you what. I'm gonna sit here and drink my coffee. I don't like to drink and drive, anyway. You go back inside, make nice, and then let's get the fuck out of here."

"You're not coming in to meet her?"

"I'd rather not do that. But I'll think about it. Let me feel the flow of the situation. Then maybe I'll come inside for a minute. Probably not. All right? Can you handle all that?"

"Gus, you act like I planned this."

"No." Gus removed the coffee lid, took a sip, and made a face. "If I learned one thing about you tonight, it's that you're not much of a planner, once you get away from your drafting board. *Madonna mi,* they brewed this coffee in the radiator of a De Soto. Go on, now, go and see your girlfriend. And before you go too far down Memory Lane, remember that I'm out here with the other one."

Jimmy returned to the diner, where Janet had moved to a booth. She'd combed her cotton candy hair and applied lipstick. Somehow she looked even worse, the way people look just before the coffin lid is closed. Jimmy sat across from her, where she'd transferred his coffee into a regular cup and saucer and set down a slice of cherry pie.

"By the way," she said, "Happy New Year."

"Happy New Year, Janet."

"You're looking good."

"You too."

"You lie. But you do it sweetly. Taste the pie, it's the only decent thing we sell."

Jimmy dug in and savored it. Janet was telling the truth. The pie was sweet and gooey, the cherries firm and juicy, the crust light and flaky. He was working on a mouthful of the stuff when Janet said flat out, "You never got married."

"How can you tell?"

"You look too good. Too thin. Still got a kid's face. Aaay, anybody lookin' in the window here'd think you were sittin' down to a piece of pie with your mother."

"That's not true, Janet."

"Jimmy, Jimmy, you're as nervous as ever. Just relax and let me look at you. Wouldja do that, please?"

Paper napkin in hand, she reached across and wiped a dab of cherry drool from the corner of his mouth. "You remember prom night? You'd better, or I'll kill ya."

"Of course I remember."

"You remember how you asked me out?"

"How? . . . No. That I don't remember."

"That's because you didn't. *I* asked *you."* Janet giggled. "To this day, I don't know if you really wanted to go with me."

"Sure I did. Of course I did."

Janet shook her head. "You were just as nervous as you are now, but God knows why. I was yours all the way that night. You coulda had me right there in the car." She lit a Kool, blew smoke toward the ceiling. "Just my luck to wind up with a gentleman."

Jimmy pushed his plate aside, startled to see that

he'd inhaled the pie. He stared at the fork lines of cherry goo on his plate. "I knew I was going away for good, Jan."

"I knew it, too. I didn't care. Hey. Look at me." Jimmy obeyed. Janet gazed at him, the Kool in a corner of her mouth. She removed it to ask, "Didja at least *want* to?"

"Yeah, Jan, I did. Honest to God, I did."

"Were you a virgin?"

Jimmy felt his face go crimson. "Yeah. In fact I was."

He feared that Janet would break out in peals of laughter, but all she did was nod, as if to confirm her own thoughts. "Ain'tcha gonna ask me if I was a virgin?"

"Jesus, Janet!"

"Hey, come on, it's twenty years later. What's the difference? Ain't you curious?"

"At this point, I don't see that it matters one way or the other."

"Christ Almighty, the way you talk! Are you an architect, or a lawyer?" Janet laughed out loud. "Tell you what. You take a guess, and I'll tell you if you're right or wrong."

Guessing games, in the middle of everything else. Jimmy sighed. He really didn't want to hurt her feelings. At the same time, he didn't want to seem like an idiot. "Well," he finally said, "I'd say you weren't."

"That's your answer?"

"That's my guess."

Tears flooded Janet's eyes. She stubbed her Kool out in an ashtray, bit her upper lip.

"Aw, Janet, I'm sorry . . ."

Jimmy reached out to touch her face, but she pulled back as if to avoid the flick of a whip. Then she folded her arms on the table and buried her face in the crook of an elbow, her back heaving with silent sobs.

"Jesus, Janet, you forced me to do this. I didn't want to guess, I really had no idea . . ."

She ignored him. Jimmy sat feeling stupid for thirty seconds that felt like a month. At last Janet lifted her face, beaming with suppressed laughter that burst suddenly from her like the roar of a lion.

"Aw, Jimmy, I'm terrible," she managed to say. "You don't remember that I was an actress, do you? I had the lead in *Come Back, Little Sheba* our senior year."

She reached across and pinched his cheek. "Did you think I was really upset? Be honest."

"Yeah, I thought you were upset."

"Don't be mad."

"I'm *not* mad."

"You are, but you'll get over it. It was just seein' you after all these years . . . I don't know, I just had to audition one more time. See that? I shoulda kept up with the acting. I was good, God damn it, I was *good.* I was gonna audition at the Strasberg Institute. Know why it never happened for me? 'Cause I didn't want to ride three trains each way to get there and back. Little thing like that, and I let my dream die. If I had it to do over again, I'd have *walked* each way. Over hot coals."

She took a paper napkin from the dispenser and wiped her eyes. "And by the way, your answer was correct. I'd been with three guys before prom night. I was hoping to make you number four."

She stroked his cheek. "The one gentleman I meet in my whole life, and he rides off on the white horse he came in on. Aaay, what're you gonna do? At least you chased your dream. Caught it, too, you son of a bitch."

Jimmy sipped his coffee, which was, as Gus had noted, terrible. He tried not to grimace as he asked, "Did you get married?"

"Oh, I got married, all right." She half-snorted, half-chuckled. "Yeah, I met my Vinnie two weeks after prom night. Gave birth to Frankie nine months after that." She winked at Jimmy. "So close to prom night that my mother thought *you* were a suspect. I let her think it." She laughed. "Stick around, meet my Frankie, he'll be here to pick me up any minute. Nice kid, my son. Does *not* take after the father."

It hit Jimmy in the solar plexus: had he gone all the way with Janet, he might now be the father of a twenty-year-old. A twenty-year-old! A human being old enough to father more human beings!

Jimmy rubbed his face hard with both hands, as if to erase the years.

"So what's going wrong in *your* life?" he heard Janet ask. He took his hands away from his face, hoping she wouldn't notice how they trembled.

"Why do you ask that?"

"Hey. Jimmy. Good luck don't bring nobody to *this* place."

Jimmy jumped as the diner door banged open. A wild-eyed young man with the kind of curls carved into the heads of Roman statues approached, twirling a set of car keys on his finger.

"Mah," he asked, his Adam's apple bobbing, "you ready, or what?"

"Come over here, Frankie, I want you to meet somebody."

Frankie bopped over to the booth, his open leather jacket flapping. He was all jangly nerves and impatience, a cup of coffee with hair. A thyroid condition, Jimmy said to himself, certain the kid had never been taken to a doctor for it. Frankie stuck a Marlboro into his heart-shaped mouth and lit up.

"Frankie, meet an old friend of mine, Jimmy Gambuzza. He took me to the high school prom."

Jimmy got to his feet and extended a hand. Frankie's grip was firm, and he held Jimmy's hand far too long, his face quizzical with an obvious thought: *Joo fuck my mother?*

"Frankie," Janet giggled, "let him go, already."

The boy obeyed. "Ya have a good time?" he asked Jimmy.

"I beg your pardon?"

"He means on prom night," Janet said.

"That's right," the kid demanded. "Ya have a good time, or what?"

Jimmy sensed that the wrong answer could cost him a few teeth. "We had a lovely time," he said at last.

Frankie's nostrils flared and his eyes narrowed. "I'll be in the car, Mah," he all but snarled as he stormed away. At the diner door he banged into the Ghost's shoulder and kept going without a word of apology.

Gus ignored the collision and walked almost meekly to the booth. "Excuse me, Jimmy," he said softly, "but I think we'd better be going."

Janet's mouth fell open in awe.

"Of course," Jimmy said. "Janet, meet my brother Gus."

Gus gave a courtly nod of his head as he shook hands with Janet. "Pleased to meet you, Janet. Happy New Year."

"Happy New Year to you, Mr. Gambuzza."

"Gus."

Janet held the Ghost's hand, as if to give a photographer a moment to immortalize the event. Then she suddenly dropped it, rose to her feet, and pointed out the window, her face ashen. The horrified brothers watched as Gus's long green car rolled back out of its parking space, then roared off with a squeal of rubber.

Janet let her head fall, revealing white-gray roots at the part line. "Ahh, that kid of mine. If there's anything he loves more than me, it's stealin' a car."

Stunned beyond belief, Jimmy watched his brother's car streak away as if it were a scene in a horror movie. Gus turned to Janet.

"Get your coat on, honey."

The three of them hurried outside to the battered Dodge Dart Frankie had driven to the diner. Gus took the wheel, with Janet beside him and Jimmy at the window.

"Oh shit," Janet moaned, "he took the keys!"

Biting his lower lip, Gus reached deep under the steering wheel with both hands. "Long time since I've done this," he murmured as his fingers found wires and twisted them together until the motor roared. They sped off in the direction that Frankie had gone.

"Okay, Janet, talk to me," Gus said calmly. "Where'd he go?"

Janet hesitated. "Not going to kill him, are you? He's just a kid with a little wildness in him."

A beatific glow came to Gus's face. "Kill him? Of course not. We just want to get the car back."

"He doesn't have a gun."

"I'm sure he doesn't, I'm sure he doesn't."

Janet pointed. "Go straight on this road. Usually he goes a mile or two and jumps out."

Gus seemed alarmed at last. "He just *leaves* it there?"

"Yeah. He ain't no thief. He's a joyrider." She turned to Jimmy. "He ain't no thief," she repeated.

But Jimmy appeared to be barely listening. He was staring all around at the interior of the car, as if it were a planetarium full of wonders. Gus wondered if he'd finally snapped.

"Hey, brother, you okay over there, or what?"

Jimmy nodded. "This is familiar," he said, thinking out loud.

Janet chuckled. "It ought to be. I picked you up on prom night in it."

"Oh my God."

Janet touched the windshield, making a mark in the fog from their breaths. "Yeah, these are the same windows we steamed up that night. Can you imagine?"

Gus said, "This car's twenty years old?"

"Hey, don't worry, the motor's fine," Janet assured him. "My Vinnie's one of those guys who spends every weekend with his head under the hood and his ass in the air, thank God. Runs like new. *I* should get the attention he gives this friggin' car."

Jimmy began quaking, as if the temperature had suddenly dropped fifty degrees. He was overloaded. He felt incapable of thought, language, or anything that required a sequence. Time no longer existed. It had *never* existed. Every philosopher, poet, or scientist who'd ever pondered the universe was way off the mark. Only Jimmy Gambar knew what the universe was; the interior of an ancient Dodge Dart. You wore a bad powder-blue tux and flesh-tone acne cream on your forehead as you swapped spits with a girl in a crinoline dress in the back seat, her tongue tasting of gin-spiked punch. You thought you'd left the car and the girl and gone on to carve a life for yourself, but suddenly you were back in the car, never having really left. The upholstery was tattered, the woman was old, and you? What the hell did *you* look like, anyway? Jimmy reached up to turn down the visor on the passenger's side, but the mirror that once was there was gone.

Gus chuckled. "Lookin' to see if your hair's all right?"

Jimmy was mortified. Janet suddenly started sobbing, and buried her face in Jimmy's shoulder, pretty much as she'd done so twenty years earlier.

"Please don't kill him," she begged. "Oh please God, he's all I've got, *please* don't kill him."

Jimmy stroked her stiff hair. "Aw, Janet, come on. All we want to do is get the car back."

"You will, you will." She turned to Gus, her eyes smeary with mascara. "But please don't hurt him."

"Not a hair on his head," Gus said calmly. He jerked his chin to indicate something up ahead. "But that cop over there might have other ideas."

Not a hundred yards ahead, the green Oldsmobile was parked at the side of the road behind a police car, its cherry-red roof light flashing. They were in time to see Frankie assume the position, his hands on the car's fender, his feet spread wide. Gus slowed the Dart to a crawl.

"Oh what a fucking mess," Jimmy all but wept. "Oh my God, are we cooked."

"Shut up," Gus snapped. "Your attitude does not help."

Janet looked at Jimmy in wonder. "Excuse me," she said. "There's not a scratch on that car. My son is an excellent driver. *He's* the one in trouble. This is no skin off your ass."

"Unless they decide to impound the car," Gus said. "Listen, let me do the talking. Janet, you be ready to play along with whatever I say, all right?'' Janet nodded, her faith in the Ghost absolute.

"What about me?'' Jimmy asked.

"Just don't interfere,'' Gus said. "Think you can handle that?''

Before Jimmy could respond to the insult, Gus had pulled the Dart up behind the Oldsmobile.

"All right, gang, let's go.''

Jimmy reached past Janet's face to grab Gus by the shoulder. "What the hell's your game plan, Gus?''

"Oh, something'll come to me. The cop's young. That could work in our favor. On the other hand, it could screw us to the wall.'' He shrugged Jimmy's hand off his shoulder and got out of the car.

Gus led the way to Frankie and the cop. He was indeed young, nearly as young as Frankie, who was now handcuffed and being led to the patrol car.

"Officer!'' Gus called. "A moment, please.''

The cop turned to face Gus, all arrogance and strut. He wore a winter cop coat, the kind that made all New York cops look oddly overweight. A brass name tag said PALMIERO. An Italian, Jimmy said to himself—that ought to work in our favor. Or does it? It was hard to tell. He was one of those cops who pulled the visor down low over his eyes and had to tilt his head back to regard the world chin first, like Mussolini. On his upper lip was a perfectly trimmed little caterpillar of a mustache.

"Who might you be?'' the cop demanded.

Gus forced a chuckle. "That's a little awkward to explain,'' he said. "May I first ask why you've arrested Frankie?''

"Speeding. Resisting arrest.''

"He resisted arrest?''

"Suspect failed to stop despite repeated warnings by siren."

Frankie, who'd been letting his head hang low, at last looked up, genuinely surprised to see his mother.

"Hey, Mah," he said warmly.

"Hello my baby," Janet said. "Are you all right?"

"Sure, Mah."

The cop tightened his grip on Frankie's elbow. "Also, suspect was not in possession of driver's license or vehicular registration."

"Well, I don't know about the license, but he wouldn't know where the registration was," Gus said. "You see, Officer, this is *my* car."

Palmiero's eyes widened. *"Your* car?"

Gus nodded. "I lent it to Frank earlier tonight. Thing of it is, I need it to get home myself."

Palmiero's eyes narrowed again. "You lent it, or he stole it?"

"I stole it," Frankie said, a goofy grin on his face. "Hey, Mah. I really am sorry."

Palmiero glowered at Gus. "What goes on here, sir?"

Gus forced a sheepish smile. "Could I just talk to you for a minute, Officer?" With a jerk of his chin, he made it clear that Frankie couldn't hear what he had to say. Palmiero put Frankie in the back seat of the cop car, the two of them bathed in the cherry light's swirling strobes. Palmiero swaggered back to Gus, who put his arm around Janet in the loose, possessive way a lover would.

"Officer," Gus said, "I'll put it plainly. I'm having a fling with the boy's mother. Actually, it's more than a fling. We're crazy about each other." Gus nuzzled his nose against Janet's. She played along perfectly, as if this was their special gesture. "The boy found out about it," Gus continued, "and he went a little crazy."

Palmiero nodded, his cop facade at last beginning to crumble. He turned to Janet.

"You're still married to the boy's father, I take it."

"Yes," Janet said, looking down at her feet in false shame.

The cop expelled a long breath. "Well, holy Christ. We've got us a mess here, haven't we?"

"Yes we have," Gus agreed. "So you can understand that we'd love to clean it up as easily as possible?"

The cop seemed to notice Jimmy for the first time. "Hell's this guy?" he asked.

"That's my brother."

"What's he got to do with your fling? Got a little three-way goin' here, have you?"

"No, no, no," Gus said. "Officer, I don't want to bore you with details. I'm just wondering if maybe this whole mess can't be straightened out some way so that innocent people don't get hurt."

Gus and the cop kept talking, while Jimmy reached for his wallet and took out all the cash he had, which amounted to a little over two hundred dollars.

"Whoa, whoa, *whoa,"* the cop said, pointing at Jimmy's hand. Gus saw what was happening, and shot a searing stare at Jimmy.

The cop's eyes were open wide beneath the visor. "Are you offering me a bribe, here?"

"Of course not," Jimmy stammered. "I was just . . . holding my money."

"Yeah? You gonna *buy* something?" Palmiero spread his arms toward the cattails, which rustled in the wind. "We're in the middle of nowhere, here."

Jimmy felt as if he might wet his pants. The cop thumped his shoulder with an iron forefinger.

"Think you can buy me off? Izzat what you think?"

Gus whispered to Janet, "Get hysterical."

Janet did not need to be told twice. She screamed as if she'd been stabbed. She ran to the cop car and pounded on the fenders, the hood, the windows. She hollered for the release of her boy, fell to her knees, and squeezed the knees of Palmiero, who stood before her, begging her to stop. It was, Jimmy realized, the performance of Janet's life.

"I'm gonna let him go!" Palmiero yelled at last. "Lady, get up, I'm gonna let him go!"

Janet stopped screaming. Palmiero got Frankie out of the car as if a bomb were ticking in it, unlocked the cuffs, and pushed him toward the other three.

"All of youse go home," he said. Just before getting in his car he pointed at Jimmy. "You," he said gravely, "are a very lucky man."

He roared away, the cherry light glowing as the car disappeared in the fog.

Janet, Gus, and Frankie lit up cigarettes. Nobody spoke for what seemed like years, until the silence was broken by Janet addressing Jimmy.

"That," she said flatly, "was pretty fuckin' stupid."

Jimmy tried to say something, but all that came out was a croaking sound. He looked in shame at the cash in his hand, then shoved it into his pocket.

"All right, all right," Gus said. "It's late, folks. Let's say our good nights."

Janet gave Frankie a shove toward Gus. He scratched his curly head as he mumbled, "Sorry I took your car."

"Forget it."

"What'd you do, hot-wire the Dart?"

"Uh-huh."

Frankie studied the Ghost, his eyes wide with admiration. "Cool," he said. He offered his hand, which

Gus accepted. Then Frankie shook hands with Jimmy, who turned to give Janet a farewell hug, but all she offered was a hard, dry handshake.

"Jimmy," she chuckled, "some day, you'll learn. I *hope."* The hug she saved for Gus.

"I owe you my life," she said fervently.

"You're a wonderful actress," Gus said.

Janet giggled. "Wasn't half bad, was I?"

"Oscar night," Gus assured her. "If we'd had a camera rollin', the prize'd be all yours."

"Thank you, Gus." She walked wearily to the driver's door of the Dodge. "Slide over," she told Frankie. "You think I'm lettin' you drive?" Then they were gone.

Jimmy and Gus walked to the Oldsmobile.

"That's some woman," Gus said. "You should never have let her go."

"I wasn't trying to pay off the cop. I just wanted to be ready for anything."

"Like a bribe."

"No!"

"Because that's what police officers think when they see people in trouble with money in their hands. They're funny that way, those men in blue."

"All right, I was stupid. I'm sorry. Okay?"

"Get in the fuckin' car, Jimmy."

They both got in. Jimmy sighed in relief. It was wonderful to be back in the Oldsmobile, away from the terrible things that happened when you left it. Gus clucked his tongue.

"That fuckin' kid put out a cigarette on my floor."

With finicky distaste, Gus made a tweezer of his thumb and forefinger to pick up the butt and throw it out the window. He rubbed his fingers on his pants. "All right, that's that. Nice little coffee break, huh?"

Gus started the car and rolled off into the Brooklyn night.

Jimmy sat quietly. He'd never felt worse. In the space of just a few hours he'd managed to convince the first and last women of his love life that he was a king-sized asshole. Not to mention the one in the trunk, who'd certainly have some choice things to say about Jimmy, if she were still breathing.

Gus patted Jimmy's knee. "Want to talk about what just happened?"

"I thought you were going to offer him money. I was just trying to hurry it along."

"What made you think I was going to bribe him?"

Jimmy shrugged. "The way you were talking. You were hinting around at it, Gus. Come on."

Gus shook his head like a disappointed professor. "Money," he began, "was the last way to go with that little hard-on. He was a by-the-book guy all the way, Jimmy. Did you see his perfect little mustache? Did you hear him talk? Were you *unconscious* out there, or what?"

"Well what the hell was your tactic, then?"

"To put him on unfamiliar ground, buddy boy. In his case, that means sex. Understand? It's New Year's Eve, and he's workin' the midnight-to-eight. This guy is no Romeo. If he does it at all, it's with his eyes shut tight. So I tell him a little tale about my fling with Janet. Cops love a good sex story. It fascinates him, but it also scares him. I'm talking a language he can't understand. All of a sudden, he ain't in command anymore. Suddenly he wants to be out of the situation even worse than *we* do."

Gus took a final drag from his cigarette and mashed it out. "So what do you do, in the middle of my beautiful work? You flash a wad of cash. You put him right back in a position of power." He jerked a thumb toward the rear window. "If Janet hadn't been there to bail us out, we'd both be in the fuckin' precinct right now, rollin' our fingers on the ink pad."

Gus couldn't help grinning. "I thank God that ninety percent of the men in this world are scared shitless of women. Did you see the look on that hard-on's face when Janet did her thing? I'm tellin' you, they went about it all wrong, tryin' to stop Hitler with bombs and tanks. All they really had to do was get any Polish soldier's mother to throw a tantrum at his feet. Whole fuckin' Nazi party would've backed off."

"So why didn't you just start off having Janet throw a tantrum?"

"Hey. Janet was my heavy artillery. You save your heavy artillery for last. Understand? Is any of this penetrating, or am I just blowin' hot air, here?"

Jimmy felt as if donkey ears might sprout from his head at any second. He wondered if his IQ had begun to drop the moment he'd crossed the Brooklyn Bridge, and continued to fall the deeper they drove into the borough. His hands shook. He squeezed them together, feeling flashes of shame over what Janet must be thinking of him.

Gus looked over, and noticed Jimmy's clasped hands. "Hey, what are you, praying?"

"No . . ."

"Sure looks like it."

Could he ask the question? Would Gus laugh in his face if he did? He didn't think he could bear any more humiliation on this night. On the other hand, he had to know.

"Gus," Jimmy ventured.

"I'm right here."

"Do you . . . believe in God?"

"Question is, does *he* believe in *me?*"

"Be serious."

"What do you want from me, answers? I've got no answers. I stopped worrying about answers years ago. All I can do is try to help you."

"What you were saying before, about confession. Do you go?"

"Yeah."

"You have a priest you trust?"

"With my life."

"You tell him everything?"

"I've told him things I didn't know I knew myself, until I knelt in the box."

Jimmy could not believe what he said next, even as he was saying it. He had not set foot inside a church since he was sixteen years old.

"Think I could see that priest?"

He braced himself for Gus's reaction—an explosion of laughter, sarcasm, whatever. But Gus just pursed his lips and nodded, as if Jimmy had suggested they stop somewhere for a plate of littleneck clams on the half shell, with a little lemon juice and red sauce.

"That," Gus said, "is not a bad idea at all." He made a wide, sweeping turn at the next corner. "See that? There's things we can agree on."

"I didn't mean tonight."

"There's *only* tonight."

"We're going to wake him up?"

He patted Jimmy's knee. "Sit back, relax. With every minute that passes, we come closer to a solution."

They were even closer to water, now. Jimmy could tell because a dampness penetrated his bones, followed moments later by a roll of fog that washed over the car like a blanket. Gus flicked on his high beams. It was as if a white sheet had been stretched out a foot in front of the headlights.

"Madonna mi, Jimmy, we're in a bowl of soup, here."

Between sheets of fog, Jimmy caught glimpses of houses like the one he'd grown up in, small dirty brick deals aglow with Christmas lights, fronted by carpet-sized lawns. It made him claustrophobic just to look at them. Even when he was a kid doing his homework in his room, Jimmy dreamed of high ceilings and skylights, of sunshine and long indoor shadows, of polished hardwood floors. And he'd made that dream come true, with his loft.

It was as if Gus had been reading his mind.

"What did you pay for that loft, if you don't mind my asking?"

"Three seventy-five."

"What's your monthly nut?"

"Comes to a little over three."

"Thousand."

"Right."

"Jesus Christ. And that's after-tax dollars."

"Did you like it?"

"Tell you the truth, I wasn't there long enough to form an opinion."

"It gets good light in the daytime."

Jimmy was going to say more about the loft, but he stopped himself. If he kept talking about it, he'd have to invite Gus over some time when he didn't have a corpse to get rid of. Just a guy and his brother, on a Sunday afternoon, having brunch in the buttery light from above. Maybe he'd bring Carol and the kids, too. Impossible. He wasn't even sure that he'd ever be seeing Gus again, after this night.

Gus jerked his head to indicate the people inside the houses they cruised past. "These people," he said, "go their whole lives without crossing the bridge to Manhattan. Never curious about it. They're happy as can be, right here. What do you think about that?"

"I guess I think it's pretty sad."

Jimmy looked out the window at the outdoor Christmas lights, all bleedy red and green through the fog. Here and there he saw short fig trees wrapped in tar paper, bent like aged priests.

"Lobster pots," Gus continued. "You believe some of them still go out in their boats and set pots under the bridge?" He jerked his head again, this time to indicate the Verrazano-Narrows Bridge. "Shellfish they eat, out of this water. Christ! Guess their bodies build up a tolerance to the poisons."

Gus spoke in amazement, but not with condescension. Jimmy couldn't help ask a question that had nagged him for years.

"Do you like it here, Gus?"

Gus shrugged. "It's home. Home is home."

"Yeah, but do you like it?"

"I don't think about it."

"How could you not think about it? You're a bright man, Gus."

"Maybe that's why I don't think about it. Ever think about *that?*"

"Ever been to Europe?"

"Jimmy, please. I've never even been on a plane."

Genuinely surprised, Jimmy said gently, "You've missed a lot."

"Oh, I don't know. Carol always wanted to go, but you know. It was hard to get away."

"You'd love Europe."

"Oh, yeah. But on the other hand, to paraphrase

Henry David Thoreau, I have traveled extensively in Brooklyn." He chuckled. "Surprised you, huh? Don't look at me like that. I have a library card."

"I didn't say anything."

"You didn't have to."

"Gus, God damn it, I know you can read."

"You went to Europe with Wendy, I'll bet."

Jimmy nodded. "For a month. Eight countries."

"How many of 'em did you fight in?"

"Seven."

"Where *didn't* you fight?"

"Greece. She got food poisoning, and she had to stay in the hotel room for three days. I left her in Athens and toured the islands."

"Shame it was only three days. Guess you didn't put enough poison in the food, huh?"

"Something like that."

"Europe. Jesus." Gus rubbed his chin. "Hey, maybe we'll go together some day, huh? We seem to be getting along all right. Would you say we were getting along, or what?"

What kind of a trap was this? Gus gets rid of a body for Jimmy, and in exchange Jimmy makes a little trip overseas to pick up a package with a postmark from, say, Turkey?

Jimmy hoped Gus couldn't see him flush. "Yeah, I'd say we were getting along," Jimmy allowed.

"Tell you what, then. When we get out of this, we'll go to Greece together, okay? Just you and me. Whaddaya think?"

"Are you serious?"

"Sure. Provided I can get a passport without going through a lot of bullshit."

"Why Greece? Why not Italy?"

"Italy, fuhgetaboutit. I try to get on an Alitalia flight,

they'll have every cop at the airport shinin' flashlights in my face. And anyway, Greece is the only country that doesn't have bad memories for you. What do you say? Deal, or no deal?"

Jimmy couldn't tell whether or not Gus was pulling his chain, but he knew it would not help his cause to refuse his brother. "Deal," he said.

Gus reached over to shake hands, and pulled over and parked a moment later. Jimmy looked out, half-expecting to see an all-night travel agency out there.

"Why are we stopping?"

"Because we're here."

Jimmy rolled down his window to look at a small stone church, set back behind a lawn. Already Gus was out of the car, heading for a set of steps leading to a side door. Over the door, a small yellow bulb burned inside a castle-shaped wrought iron fixture.

"It's kind of late, Gus."

"Long as the light's on, he's up. That's the signal for his parishioners."

"The trunk . . ."

"Ahh, nobody touches my car around here, except to polish it."

Jimmy couldn't believe it. "After what just happened to us, you're going to leave the car again?"

"Jimmy, Jimmy. You can't let that one bad experience color your view of all mankind. Have faith, my son. Come on, now, come on."

They climbed a short flight of steps, Gus leading the way and pressing a buzzer next to the doorknob. Jimmy gulped the salty air, anxious to get back to the comfort of the car. He was about to tell Gus that he wanted no more of the priest plan when a lock turned and the door opened.

A slender, oddly familiar bearded man in a priest's

collar and black shirt tucked into blue jeans stood before them.

"Hello, Gus," he began, but then he saw Jimmy and his mouth fell open. He threw himself at Jimmy and hugged him, burying his beard in Jimmy's shoulder. Gus spread his hands in mock puzzlement.

"S'matter?" he said. "Aren't you glad to see your kid brother?"

Father Joseph Gambuzza pulled back to examine his astonished brother at arm's length. He had the wide, wondrous eyes of a child, now filled with tears of joy. His beard was sparse, like the kind teenage boys grow during their first semesters away at college. Father Joseph had grown it to make himself look more mature, so that his older parishioners would take him seriously. Instead, it made him look boyish.

"My God, what a Happy New Year! Aw, Gus, *Gus!"*

"Joey, Joey. Did I tell you we'd see him again some day? Will you believe me from now on?"

"Always."

Joey released Jimmy and embraced Gus in the longest, tightest hug Jimmy had ever witnessed between two human beings.

"Come, come inside out of this dampness. What fog! You can hardly see the bridge."

They were in a room stacked high with boxes that Jimmy did not identify as shoe boxes until his kid brother asked, "What size you take?"

"Ten and a half."

"We've got that, I think," Joey murmured as he moved on feet clad in the same navy-blue, Velcro-tabbed sneakers that Gus wore. In seconds Joey located the right box, and presented it to Jimmy as if he'd been waiting all those years to do exactly this.

"Try 'em on. They're cut a little small, you might need the next size."

Jimmy sat and tried on the shoes, which pinched his feet. Joey fetched a box of elevens and, while Jimmy tried them on, the priest asked point-blank: "Why?"

Jimmy looked at Gus, then at Joey. "Why what?"

"Why come to see us, after all these years? Or is it just a miracle, and should I shut my mouth and enjoy it?"

Joey laughed as Jimmy's fingers, slick with sweat, sought to close the tabs. "It's a miracle, I guess."

"They fit all right?"

"Perfect."

"Once you break 'em in, it's like walking on a cloud." Joey squatted to feel the sides of Jimmy's feet. "Good, good." He turned to look at Gus. "I got this one lady, eighty-two years old, wearing these sneakers. First time in twenty years she's been able to walk up to the communion rail. You believe that? All her life she suffered in tight black shoes."

Gus nodded. "It's hard to break people's habits."

"Tell me about it. *Madonna,* how I begged her to try 'em on. Now she won't take 'em off."

"You got time to hear your brother's confession now?"

Joey turned to Jimmy, beaming broadly. "Be an honor."

"Gus," Jimmy said, "I want to talk to you first."

Gus shrugged. "Excuse us, Joey?"

"Of course."

Gus and Jimmy went out and stood on the little lawn, their breaths fogging the air between them.

"Are those sneakers comfortable, or what?"

"What the fuck are you up to, Gus?"

Gus spread his hands. "I did what you asked. Brought you to my priest."

"What kind of surprise is that to spring on me?"

"You want to talk surprises? Aaay, let's talk surprises. I walk into your house and find a corpse on the floor." He jabbed a steely finger into Jimmy's chest. *"That,"* he said, "is a surprise. This is a nothing, next to that. This is a friggin' *gift."*

A foghorn sounded. Gooseflesh bloomed on Jimmy's arms. "Is he a real priest?"

"You know, Jimmy, you have a way of insulting people without even trying."

"I'm sorry."

"Of *course* he's a real priest. What do you think, I built this church so he could play with it? His parishioners love him, by the way. Kids come to hear Father Joe like they're going to a Sunday morning rock concert. Attendance is way up. The collection plate, fuhgetaboutit, you can't even lift it after one of his sermons."

"Not to mention the money that comes in from the sneaker business."

Gus's nostrils flared. "You don't have to stay, Jimmy. Honest to God, you could go down the block right now and catch the subway. Hour and a half and you're back in your loft, safe and sound." He patted Jimmy's shoulder. "Go, go. I'll take care of your little problem, here."

Gus turned and walked heavily to the church steps. Jimmy hesitated, then jogged after him.

"I'm sorry, Gus, I had no right."

"So you want to go in and confess to him, or what?"

"He's my baby brother!"

"Don't think of him that way. If he hadn't recognized you, you still wouldn't know."

Gus put his arm across Jimmy's shoulder and guided him the rest of the way, as if Jimmy had just undergone surgery.

"Talk to him," Gus urged. "He's the only other person in this world you can trust right now, besides me. And I've got to tell you, I could use help carrying it. My friggin' shoulders are killing me."

"I'll talk to him. But maybe not about this."

"Aaay, I don't care if you discuss the Preamble to the Constitution. All I want is for you to relax." He forced a smile. "Believe me, he's got the biggest heart in the world. He's a good boy. One of us turned out right, anyway."

Gus decided to wait out in the car. Joey hugged Jimmy again, then urged him to sit in a red leather easy chair. Joey settled into a straight-backed wooden one. The priest leaned forward, elbows on his knees, grinning like a child about to be told his favorite bedtime story.

"I'm just trying to remember a time I was happier to see somebody, but for the life of me I can't, Jimmy."

Jimmy got up and went to the window. Gus sat behind the wheel of his idling car with the interior light on, reading a copy of the *Daily News* through half-glasses that gave him a professorial look. Gus licked a finger, turned a page. He might have been a chauffeur waiting for a rich man at a dinner party.

Jimmy looked back at Joey, still eager as a child. He was eleven years old the last time Jimmy had seen him, a sweet kid with all the good things the baby of a family can bring. Jimmy sat back in the chair and said, more to himself than to Joey, "You really are a priest."

"I sure am." Joey giggled as if it were a punch line. "Do you like it?"

"Hey, it's the best. And you're an architect."

"Yeah."

"Saw that picture of you in the *Times* last year, with the mayor at the dedication of that indoor garden. Must be wonderful to create something like that."

"You saw that picture?"

Father Joseph reddened. "Actually, I was at the ceremony."

Jimmy felt his mouth go dry. "You showed up?"

Father Joseph nodded. "I'd read about it. Thought I'd get a look at you in the flesh. Just a look."

Jimmy had to giggle. "You must have influence. I couldn't get tickets for any of my friends."

The priest tapped his collar. "This is my ticket, buddy. You'd be surprised at how many doors it opens." He chuckled. "Pretty good-looking lady with you, as I recall."

Now Jimmy blushed. "You should have come up to me, Joey."

"I did." He laughed as Jimmy blanched. "We shook hands. I said, 'I admire your work, Mr. Gambar.' And you said, 'Thank you, Father.' "

"Then what happened?"

"Then I came back here, to referee a CYO basketball game."

"Why didn't you identify yourself?"

"I was, ah, kinda hoping you'd recognize me. And

when you didn't, I figured, aaay, leave him alone. If he wants to see you, he'll find you."

"I wish you'd told me who you were, Joey."

"Really?"

"Of course."

Joey cocked his head, narrowed one eye. *"Really?"*

Jimmy had to look away. "No. I guess not. I'm sorry. . . . Joey, I don't know if I can do this."

Joey reached out to clasp Jimmy's arm. "We could go to my confession box, if you like. Might be easier. Come on, let's try it."

Joey led the way down a corridor to a side door that breathed incense when he opened it. They were inside a small, cold church, the sort of place you'd sooner expect to find in a mountain village. Near the altar a bank of red candles flickered, giving the place its only light.

"You keep those candles burning all night?"

"They're electric," Joey explained. "Watch, I got a switch with a dimmer." He went to the wall and twisted a knob. The red lights faded to embers, then roared like flames before Joey set the dial at a medium light. "See, it's easier than candles. Otherwise you spend your life replacing 'em, and scraping up wax."

"How do people pay to light a candle?"

"They don't. They all burn all the time, for everybody. Aaay, I hate that nickel-and-dime stuff. Free candlelight is the least you can expect from your church. There's a million ways to make it up. Here, over here."

Joey parted a black curtain. Jimmy entered the small, dark confessional and knelt down for the first time since he'd begun shaving. Joey sat on the other side of the screened partition, and cleared his throat to let Jimmy know he was ready.

"Uh. Bless me, Father, for I have sinned—"

"We don't have to go through that," Joey giggled. "I like to be relaxed about it."

"So what do we do?"

"We talk. Kind of neat in here, isn't it? Like when we were kids, and we'd make a tent out of chairs and a blanket. Remember you used to do that with me, when I was little?"

"I remember."

"Well, now I'm doing it for you," Joey said. "See? Life's a circle. What goes around, comes around."

"I guess so."

"Talk to me, brother."

Jimmy closed his eyes, opened them. No difference. What had Gus told him? *People talk in the dark.* And here he was, talking. "Something happened tonight. It was an accident."

"Were you hurt?"

"No. Well, yes, actually. A woman kicked me in the groin. Then she tried to stab me."

There was silence from Jimmy's side. "Wow," he finally said.

"That's not what I wanted to tell you about, though. See, I pushed her, and she banged her neck on something, and then she . . . stopped breathing."

"Hmmm."

Hmmm?! Maybe Joey hadn't heard. "I said, she stopped breathing."

"I heard, I heard. Gee, it's a shame."

"I mean, she didn't start breathing again."

"Jimmy, I got the picture. The woman is dead."

"Right." Jimmy swallowed, waiting for Joey to say something. "Hello?" Jimmy said, as if he'd been cut off from a telephone connection.

"I'm right here, still listening."

"So, that's about it. I called Gus, and he . . . came over."

"That's good."

"It is?"

"He helped you, didn't he?"

"Yes."

"He helps a lot of people."

"Little brother, let's not bullshit each other. This is Ghost Gambuzza we're talking about."

"That's right," Joey said softly. "And you don't know him."

"I don't, huh?"

"You left, Jimmy. Remember?"

At last, Jimmy was convinced that Joey was indeed a priest. That sneaky, deadly way of probing for the rawest of nerves . . . no way he could be a faker.

"I know I left," Jimmy said through tight teeth. "We're not here to talk about that."

"Yes, we are. We're here to talk about everything. Confession's a free-form thing. People kneel where you're kneeling now and tell me stuff they didn't know they were getting into when they crossed themselves. 'Ooh, Father, I ate meat on a Friday one night thirty years ago, when it was still a sin.' "

Joey's imitation of an Italian crone's voice was startling. "Then," he said in his natural voice, "they mention how they've refused to sleep with their husbands for those same thirty years, or ignored their dying mothers, or whatever. It's a fucked-up thing, I can tell you."

Jimmy literally gulped. "Do you talk to all of your parishioners like this?"

"You," Joey reminded him, "are not one of my parishioners. But, yes, in fact, I do. Depending on the circumstances. Everybody's different, you know.

That's something they forget to teach us at the seminary. Not everybody on this planet fits into society's pigeonholes. Very few do. The leaders would like us to think otherwise."

"Down with the Pope, is what you're saying."

"The Pope's a shill in a tall white hat, but that's irrelevant. He's got his own game to run. We were talking about you."

"We were talking about Gus, too. You apparently think he's a step from sainthood."

"Not true. All I'm saying is he's helping you, and he's not asking for a thing in return. Am I right?"

"No. He does want something from me. He wants me to take him to Greece."

Joey's laughter made Jimmy jump. "Oh, that beautiful man. Still thinks he can conquer his fear of flying. *Madonna,* you know how many times I've taken him to the airport, and taken him right back? One time they had to stop the plane on the runway."

"You telling me it's just a fear of flying thing he wants to overcome?"

"As far as I know."

"No suitcase full of cocaine to carry home? In my luggage?"

Joey whistled the way a mechanic does when inspecting a bad transmission. "My God, you *are* snakebitten. What happened to you all these years, Jimmy? Spend too many nights alone, eatin' Cup-A-Soup? Is something else bothering you that you don't want to talk about?"

"Something else? You mean besides the dead Puerto Rican? No. Nothing else, Father Gambuzza. But I'd be a liar if I didn't admit my big brother's wish to travel overseas with me made me jumpy."

"You sure there's nothing else eating you?"

"Just tell me why the fuck Gus is so hot to go to Europe with me."

"Ask him. He won't lie to you."

Jimmy clammed up. The priest sighed. "This isn't working, is it? You came to me for comfort, and you're even more wound up than before."

"I didn't come to you for comfort. I was brought here."

"And I'm so glad you were. God, Jimmy, I thought I'd never see you again."

Joey was weeping. Jimmy shifted on his knees, and noticed an odor he'd never before detected around a priest, most of whom smelled of cellars and haircuts. At last, he realized that his brother was wearing cologne.

"Joey, are you all right?"

He cleared his throat. "Forgive me. It's been quite a night."

"Yes, it has. I killed a woman tonight."

"No, no, no, *no.* A woman died tonight. You happened to be there."

"I'm thinking maybe I should go to the police."

There was ice in Joey's voice as he said, "What for?"

"Joey. Father Gambuzza. A woman is dead."

"But there was no crime. And no sin, for that matter. Your intention was not to harm anyone, but only to protect yourself."

"So what do I do now?"

"Live your life. Mourn her death. Be good to your family."

"I don't have one."

"I meant us," Joey said gently. "We've missed you, Jimmy. Mom's getting old. Gus's kids don't even know what you look like. And you didn't even call when Carol died."

Jimmy's chest tightened until he felt that he could barely breathe. It was as if all the air had been sucked from the confessional. He gripped the edges of the wooden slat his elbows had been resting upon, as if the confessional booth had turned into a barrel perched to go over Niagara Falls.

"Carol's *dead?!*"

"See that? You didn't even know. Going on three years, now. Ovarian cancer. She suffered, Jimmy."

Jimmy tried standing in the confession booth, but couldn't rise to his full height. He bumped his head on its ceiling, crashed back to his knees, and slammed his head into the screen, knocking it loose and into his brother's side of the box.

Joey caught the screen, set it aside, and cradled Jimmy's head in his hands through the opening.

"You all right, Jimmy?"

"Get me to a bathroom, Joey. Fast."

Joey led the way down an incense-scented hallway. At the end of it was a small bathroom, just a toilet bowl and a tiny sink. Joey snapped on an overhead light, and the little place became as bright as an operating room, its walls a high-gloss yellow. Jimmy saw his reflection in the toilet water before giving up the sandwich he'd eaten in the car.

A hand stroked his neck. "Easy, easy. Let it all come up."

Jimmy heaved again, then flushed the toilet. "I hadn't thrown up in years. This is my second time tonight."

"You're stressed out, seeing us after so many years."

"Well, there's that. Plus I killed a woman."

Father Joseph chuckled. "All right, have it your way. You killed a woman. You feel better now?"

Jimmy turned to look up at his brother. "Leave me alone in here a few minutes, would you, Joey?"

"Not gonna do anything stupid, are you?"

"No. I'm all out of stupid things to do tonight."

Father Gambuzza hesitated, then knelt beside Jimmy and stroked his back. Then his sides. Only when he came upon the bump of a box in his pocket did Jimmy realize he was being frisked.

"My God, do you think I'd kill myself?"

"You're confused," Joey said, even as he reached in to remove the Tiffany box from Jimmy's pocket. "I just want to protect you. You protected me when I was little."

"I have no weapons," Jimmy said. "Never in my life have I had a weapon. The most dangerous thing I've ever held in my hand was my T square."

Joey whistled at the Tiffany box, shook it. "What's in here?"

"Engagement ring."

"You getting married? Want me to do the ceremony?"

"No, no, no. Everything's off, Joey." Jimmy's eyes wandered to something on the wall that momentarily made him forget his worries. It was a clock with the somber face of the late Pope Paul VI on it. The hands now stood at ten minutes to two, giving the Pope the appearance of a jaunty mustache.

"I have a lot on my mind, Joey, but I must ask you what the fuck that clock is all about."

Joey scowled, and waved at the clock with a gesture of dismissal. "Ah, it was just a bad idea. Figured my parishioners would go for it in a big way, you know? Nice clock with Paulie's face on it. Thought it would be a big seller." He shook his head. "Major failure. I should have figured it. Nobody wants the Pope gazing at 'em all day. Where you gonna put it, the kitchen? Who could cook with those eyes peerin' down at you? The bedroom, fuhgetaboutit. Nobody'd ever get laid. Plus, this particular Pope was no barrel of laughs. I should at least have gone for the John the Twenty-third model. Fat bastard smiled now and then, at least. So now I got a garage full of Pope Paul the Sixth clocks. You want one?"

"No, thank you."

"You sure? Good for laughs. Makes a great gag gift. *That's* how I should've marketed it in the first place, as a novelty item. Take a couple, give 'em to your friends."

Jimmy felt a tear roll down his cheek. "I really have no friends to give them to, Father."

Jimmy dipped his face in shame, felt tears leak from his eyes. Joey's cologned hands cradled his cheeks.

"Hey, brother. What a lonely life you've had."

"Yes, Father."

"Isn't it funny, how confession works? We start out in my office, we move to the confessional, and we finally hit pay dirt in the toilet. Here." He handed Jimmy a roll of peppermint Life Savers. Jimmy crunched one, and felt the chemical sweetness overtake the sour taste in his mouth.

"Hey," Joey suddenly said. "Do you remember how you taught me how to subtract?"

"I did?"

Joey nodded. "You don't remember? Aw, man, I'll never forget it." He got off his haunches and sat next to Jimmy, his back against the toilet bowl, and gazed at the low, shiny ceiling as if it were a night sky full of stars.

"I just couldn't get the hang of it in school. Four minus two is two. What the hell did that mean? Sister Mary Florita couldn't get it into my head. Mah tried, but she couldn't teach me, either." Joey smiled. "Then one Sunday morning you and I were all alone in the kitchen. Nobody else was up. We're eatin' Cheerios. All of a sudden, you laid out a row of five Cheerios right on that checkered tablecloth. 'Hey, Joey,' you said. 'Here comes a hungry chicken.'

Joey made a pincers out of his thumb and forefinger. "You had the chicken pick up three Cheerios." Joey made the picking motion. " 'He ate three, Joey. How many are left?' 'Two,' I said. Man, you looked at me like I'd just ridden a rocket to the moon. We played Chicken and Cheerios all morning. You don't *remember* this?"

"I really don't. Wish I did."

"How can I remember it so clearly, and you can't remember it at all?"

"I can't say, Father. All I can say is, I've missed you."

"Me too you." Joey smiled. "To this day, whenever I'm balancing my checkbook, I got chickens and Cheerios in my head."

Joey kissed Jimmy's forehead. "You're sweating. You all right yet? Ready to come out?"

"In a few minutes. Just leave me alone for a little bit, okay Joey?"

"All right. Five minutes." Father Joseph pointed at the clock. "When the big hand is between Paulie's eyes, I'll be back."

He went out, closing the door behind him. Jimmy slumped back against the toilet, looked up at the clock, and cried big, gulpy tears for the late Carol

Gambuzza. The very first love of his life, whether Carol ever knew it or not.

Though he could not recall anything about the first time he'd laid eyes upon Wendy Orgel, Jimmy remembered the first time he saw Carol as if it had happened half an hour ago.

He was a seventh grader. It was a cold night, and he was in his bed, reading a book about pirates. It was long past midnight: Jimmy's lamp was the only one on in the Gambuzza house when he heard Gus's car pull into the driveway, the sounds of its trunk being opened, luggage being hoisted, and the soft voice of a girl speaking with Gus.

Moments later there was a tap at his door. Gus pushed it open and stood in the doorway. His hair was jet-black, combed straight back, and his huge muscles bulged the shoulders of his black leather jacket, which tapered to a narrow waist

"Hey, kid. Meet my wife." Gus pushed the door all the way open, and Carol stepped inside. Jimmy felt his heart flutter up his throat, like a bird trying to get out.

"This is my brother Jimmy," Gus whispered. "He's a vampire, my brother. Stays up half the night reading."

Jimmy made no move to get out of bed. He couldn't. He was literally paralyzed by the beauty of this blond eighteen-year-old in jeans and a denim jacket. She moved to his bed, sat on its edge, and extended her hand.

"Hi, Jimmy. I'm Carol."

Jimmy had never heard a gentler voice. If deer could speak, they would sound like this.

"H'lo," he managed to say. He extended a limp fish

of a hand, which Carol held for what seemed to Jimmy like years. Jimmy sat there, numb and dumb.

"Believe me, he knows a lot of words," Gus said. "Aaay, kid, I spent the whole ride home tellin' her you were the brightest kid in your class. You're makin' me look bad."

Jimmy still couldn't say anything. Fortunately his knees were up, allowing his erection to swell unobstructed under the blanket. For the first time in his life, he felt as if he might faint. Carol had enormous blue eyes and cheekbones like cliffs. Cornsilk hair hung to her shoulders. She tossed her head to get it away from her neck, sending an odor like the breath of a mint-covered mountain Jimmy's way. All at once, Jimmy understood how and why men fell in love. He noticed that Carol was still holding his hand. She winked at him.

"Your brother Gus is such a smart aleck," she said. The throb in Jimmy's groin intensified. Carol let go of his hand, smoothed the hair back from his forehead. "I'm happy to meet you, Jimmy. I know we're going to get along."

Jimmy licked his lips. "Are you gonna live here?"

Gus grinned. "See that, honey? Told you he could talk." Gus patted Jimmy's cheek. "Yeah, Jimmy. She's gonna live here. That okay with you?"

"Sure."

"All right, then. We'll see you at breakfast. Don't stay up too late. You'll be hangin' upside down like a bat, next thing you know."

They left the room, closing the door behind them. Jimmy felt as if his blood were boiling. Right down the hall, not fifty feet from where he lay, Gus and the most beautiful woman in the world were going to bed together.

He tossed the pirate book on the floor, flicked off his light. He listened hard for sounds from down the hall, but heard nothing. He took his erection in hand and came on the first stroke, before he even had a chance to summon up a vivid image of Carol. Jimmy had masturbated before, but he'd never cried out when he did it. The sound brought Gus running to his room.

"What's the matter, kid? Nightmare?"

"Yeah."

"Well, what the hell do you expect, readin' about pirates at midnight?"

"I'm okay, Gus. You can go." He turned to make a tent over the sticky puddle, hoping to contain its smell. Gus moved to the door, and hesitated there.

"You like my wife?"

"Uh-huh."

"Good. 'Cause she really likes you." Gus left. Already Jimmy's hard-on was growing back. This time, he bit the pillow to muffle his cry for Carol, Carol. . . .

A pounding on the door. This time it was his brother, Father Joseph Gambuzza.

"Jimmy! You comin' out now, or what?"

Jimmy opened his eyes, and saw that the minute hand of the clock stood between the Pope's eyes. He left the bathroom and walked slowly down the hall with Joey. "I can't believe Gus didn't tell me that Carol was dead."

"Pulling teeth is like picking flowers, compared to getting words from our brother. Don't bring it up to him, until you get your problem squared away."

"But I want to tell him I'm sorry!"

"He falls to pieces, Jimmy. Don't break his concentration until this mess is cleaned up, *capisce?"*

"All right . . . is he dating?"

"No chance. I try to set him up with every good-lookin' widow in the parish, but he always finds an excuse. Aaay, let's get the hell out of here, unless you got more to say."

"No. I'm all talked out."

"What do you say we wrap it up with an Act of Contrition, for old time's sake? Remember how it goes?"

"Think so."

"I'll start. 'Oh my God, I am heartily sorry . . .' "

The words came to Jimmy as if he were reading them from a book. The brothers did not so much pray together as they did a duet, the timing and cadences of which had more than a bit of Vegas to them.

"Olé!" Joey said at the end. "Bet you hadn't done that in twenty years!"

"Longer."

"And people think there's no such thing as a miracle. Hey, I've seen two tonight already, and the night's young."

Joey slid an arm across Jimmy's shoulders as they reached the rectory office.

"If I didn't sin, Father," Jimmy couldn't help asking, "why did I have to say an Act of Contrition?"

"That wasn't for what happened tonight," the priest kindly replied. "That was for the way you treated us. The way I figure it, your neglect was a sin of omission. But that's open to interpretation. One thing you learn as a priest—the only thing that's black and white is the wardrobe."

"You wear blue jeans."

"Aaay, it's New Year's. Got to live it up a little, you know what I mean?"

"Joey. Can we just sit for a minute? I'm a little dizzy."

"Sit, sit. Can I get you anything? A little sacramental wine? No?"

Jimmy eased himself into the red leather easy chair. "I'll be fine if I just sit for a minute."

"Sit as long as you want." Joey handed him a shoe box. "Here's your dress shoes. Not that you'll ever want to wear 'em again. Like walkin' on a cloud, am I wrong?"

Out in the car, Gus was just about finished reading the *Daily News*. It was a typical horseshit New Year's Eve paper, with foolish stories about hangover remedies, the best places around town to ring in the New Year and what's open/what's closed lists for New Year's Day.

Gus closed the paper, tossed it aside. He couldn't concentrate. He was second-guessing his decision to bring Jimmy to Joey. Gus rarely gave his decisions a second thought once they were made, but this was different. This was blood, and it was always hard to tell which way blood was going to flow.

On the other hand, he had faith in his kid brother. He couldn't remember a single situation in which Father Joey's presence hadn't improved things, so why should this be different? The kid had the touch, and if any night called for the touch, this was it. He sighed, dismissed the matter from his mind, picked up the paper again, and turned to the sports section.

A tapping sound at his ear. Slowly, Gus turned his head to see not a cop but Angelo outside his car, knocking on the glass with the bulky high school ring on his hammy hand. A goofy grin seemed to split his face in half. Gus rolled down the window.

"Shouldn't startle people like that, Angelo."

"You didn't act startled."

"Nobody *acts* startled. I *was* startled. I acted calm."

Angelo's heavy breath puffed into Gus's face. The guy always smelled as if he'd just eaten rare roast beef. "Could I talk to you, Gus?"

"For Christ's sakes, Angelo, have you been following me?"

"No!" Angelo was insulted. "I went home from the social club, and I figured you'd be here. Tell you the truth, Gus, I was a little pissed at you. We were supposed to talk about my thing tonight. Remember?"

"Anj. I had this family thing come up, all right? We haven't seen Jimmy in twenty years."

Angelo whistled. "Your mother, either?"

"She still hasn't seen him." Gus was mad at himself. He was giving away too much information to this stupid fuck, who listened with his mouth open.

"So what's he, inside with Joey now?"

"Yeah."

"What are they, catchin' up on the years?"

Gus rubbed his eyes. How was it possible to be as stupid as Angelo without actually dying from it? At the same time, he knew that a stupid man could sometimes get you into more trouble than a smart one. You always had some idea of what a smart man's next move was. Stupid enemies sometimes got the drop on you through the sheer thoughtless spontaneity of their actions. If Angelo was upset, who knew what the hell he might do with the little bit he thought he knew about the Gambuzza family reunion?

"All right," Gus sighed, "get in the car and tell me about your thing. But when my brothers come out, I have to go. No bullshit about that. You hear me, Angelo?"

Angelo spread his hands. "Whaddaya think, I'd interfere with your family?" He ran around the front of the car, got in, and extended a hand to Gus.

"For starters, Happy New Year. I mean it, Gus. You're a good man."

They shook. Angelo popped a Tic-Tac into his mouth, then offered the container to Gus.

"What, my breath's bad?"

"No, no, no, no. It's a nice taste, is all." Angelo closed the container with a fat thumb and pocketed it. He shifted to face Gus, cleared his throat.

"Thing is," he nervously began, "there's these Chinks right here in the neighborhood, Gus. We were so careful keepin' the niggers out that the Chinks slipped in under the radar! How about that, huh?" He spread his hands. "You wake up one morning and they're all over. Green grocers sellin' carrots at four in the morning. Restaurants with dead ducks hangin' in the window. What are you gonna do? Once they're in, they're in. Right?"

Gus maintained a level gaze at Angelo's eyes.

"Anyway, I got to know some of 'em," Angelo continued. "I mean, you know me. There ain't a prejudiced bone in my body. I got that way playin' baseball, before I fucked up my shoulder. If there's one place in the world you're gonna run into spicks and niggers, it's a baseball diamond, am I right?"

Gus nodded. "Yeah, you're a regular civil rights activist, Anj. What you really should have is a job at the United Nations."

"Fuck it, Gus, if you're gonna make fun—" Angelo flushed, lowered his eyes. "I apologize. Please. I'm sorry."

"Just get to the fucking point before the sun comes up."

"The point." Angelo nodded. "All right. So I get to

know some of these guys, and it turns out they've got an unbelievable operation goin' on, maybe half a mile from here. Look."

Angelo unbuttoned his trench coat to show Gus his suit. "They're makin' silk suits, Gus. Look, look at what I'm wearing. Feel, feel the lapel."

Gus reluctantly examined the lapel between thumb and forefinger.

"Ain't that like butter?"

Gus shrugged.

"Know what they charged me for this suit? Ninety bucks. Silk fuckin' suit for ninety bucks."

"How can they do that?"

"Bootleg silkworms."

"Bootleg silkworms?"

"That's what I said." Angelo looked left and right, as if to check for spies. "They got hold of these thoroughbred silkworms somehow, don't ask me how—"

"Whoa, whoa. First they were bootleg, now they're thoroughbred?"

"Hey, all right, my terminology might be a little off, but you know what I mean. These special worms come from China. They raise 'em like fuckin' racehorses, but my guys sneaked a few here in a jelly jar. And guess what? Turns out they grow like fuckin' weeds in America. They *thrive* here, Gus. Squirtin' out silk like there's no tomorrow." He couldn't resist playfully socking Gus on the shoulder. "Who knew, huh? Who the fuck knew?"

Gus rubbed his shoulder. "Don't ever touch me, Angelo."

"Hey, I'm sorry, I got a little excited, there. Thing is, these people are fuckin' geniuses, and they don't even know it. They think of everything. You gotta see where they work! Aaay, they even got a false wall in the place in case they're raided. Cut a secret passageway right into the wood paneling. A cop shows up, they disappear like roaches before he can even get down the stairs. I swear to God, they can't miss. They're perfect for us, Gus."

"Why's that?"

" 'Cause on top of everything else, they're scared of their fuckin' shadows. These ain't Chinatown Chinks, Gus. No gangs, no bullshit. They got nobody. They're looking for somebody. That's us." Angelo nodded, moved by his own fervor. "Come and see the operation. Takes twenty minutes of your time, tops."

"Now? They're working *now?*"

"You kidding? That's the beauty of the Chinks. Work is like rest to them. They go three days straight on a pot o' tea. And anyway, it ain't their fuckin' New Year. They celebrate in the middle of the fuckin' month, or some other fuckin' crazy time." Angelo chuckled. "Fucked up, huh? Like, excuse me, is there something wrong with January the first?"

Angelo was worked up. Gus knew he'd have to let him down gently. "Look, Anj, it sounds like you might have an idea, here," he began. "But what's the difference when I see these people? Like you say, they work every night. So what I'm telling you is, I'll meet them another time."

"No."

Gus tried not to show his anger. Very few people said no to the Ghost. He rarely put people in a position where the word was even an option.

Angelo wasn't kidding. His gaze was even and serious, though he appeared to be sweating around his collar.

"What do you mean, 'no,'?" Gus calmly said.

"I mean you *have* to see these people tonight. I set

it all up. Like I said, it's twenty minutes. Then you can deal with your family situation."

"You think you got some pair of balls there, don't you, Angelo?"

Angelo wiped sweat from his forehead. "I ain't tryin' to push you around, Gus. All I know is, I gotta get outta that fuckin' supermarket. And this is my first shot at somethin' good since I fucked up my shoulder."

They looked at each other, then turned toward the sound of the rectory door closing. Jimmy and Joey were on their way over. Gus and Angelo got out of the car. Jimmy blanched at the sight of Angelo, who stood like a duke, with his weight on his back foot.

"Hey, Angelo," Joey said. "Haven't seen you in church lately."

"Hey, what do you want? I suck at bingo."

"Open your coat," Gus said to Angelo. "Don't say a word, just open your coat and show Joey."

"Show me what?"

"Feel his suit. He says it's silk."

Joey felt the material exactly the way Gus had. Joey smiled sympathetically at Angelo.

"You're wearing polyester," he said gently.

Angelo pulled the lapel from Joey's hand. "Bullshit."

"Or if it's not polyester, it's a synthetic blend I don't know about."

"The fuck you say." Angelo turned to Gus. "You see that? One thing I gotta say about your brother, Gus. If he ain't heard of it, it don't exist." He turned to Jimmy. "You checked out my suit before. You know it's silk."

"No, I do not."

"Angelo," Joey said, "don't you think I'd be happier to tell you that the suit was silk?"

"It *is* silk. You're jealous 'cause you didn't discover it."

Joey pointed at Angelo's forehead. "The proof's right there. You're sweating like it was July. I mean, come on, Anj. Natural fibers breathe. You might as well be wearin' Saran Wrap."

Gus held up his hands. "Enough. This is not the fucking garment district. Angelo wants us to check out the operation this suit came from. He swears it'll take no time at all."

Jimmy's heart sank. "Gus," he pleaded.

Gus shot him a stare. "Jimmy, you ride with Angelo. Me and Joey'll follow."

Jimmy all but stammered, "Why can't I ride with you, Gus?"

"Just go with Angelo, all right? Keep him company."

There was no arguing the point. And so, with his heart flopping like a fish on a dock, Jimmy climbed into Angelo's battered Chevy and wondered what the fuck was coming next.

It couldn't be good. Angelo was the enemy, and Gus had paired him with the enemy. So it followed that Jimmy was considered an enemy—or was he? Jimmy hoped this might just be a Brooklyn male thing, the pairing up of men to keep anyone from riding alone. If that was the case, why couldn't Joey ride with Angelo? No, no. This was no random pairing.

The fog grew thicker. They were riding even closer to water. "Just kick that shit adda your way," Angelo boomed, referring to the garbage at Jimmy's feet—empty potato chip bags, dented Coke cans, and coffee cups with half-moon bites missing from their lids. The car also had a funny stink, as if a half-eaten hero sandwich might be moldering away under the seat.

Angelo's driving was as sloppy as the car. He was a one-hand-on-the-wheel guy with a habit of drifting to the middle of the road. Gus gave him plenty of room. Angelo chuckled as he checked the rearview mirror.

"Your brother don't exactly trust me, does he?"

"I wouldn't know."

Angelo lit up a Kool, flicked ashes on the floorboards. "Funny family you got there, Jimmy."

Jimmy didn't respond.

Angelo shrugged. "I mean, a middle o' the night meeting, after you stayed away . . . what, twenty years?"

"What's it to you?"

"Aaay, I'm not involved, I don't care. All I'm trying to do tonight is do Gus a favor."

"I'm sure he appreciates it."

Angelo chuckled. "You don't say much, do you, Jimmy? You disappear for twenty years, and you walk back like you left the room to take a leak."

"We're a quiet family."

"Aaay, come on, you can tell me. What made you come back?"

"None of your fucking business."

"All right, then, what made you leave?"

"Fuck you."

"Jimmy, Jimmy, don't be like that. You're in some kind of jam, ain't you?"

Jimmy looked in the rearview mirror for his brother's trusty headlights, wishing he could shut his eyes and will himself into the big green Oldsmobile. His hands trembled. He squeezed them in his lap, hoping Angelo wouldn't notice.

"I am *not* in a jam."

"Nah. Course not. Lots of big shot Manhattan guys ride around Brooklyn at two in the morning. Helps 'em unwind."

"You're in a jam, Angelo."

He laughed. "Yeah? How do you figure?"

"If you waste my brother's time with this little expedition, he's not going to forget it."

Angelo slammed on the brakes. "It's no waste of time, buddy. And don't you fuckin' forget it."

Jimmy thought the guy wanted to start duking it out, but in fact they'd reached their destination. As they got out of the car it occurred to Jimmy that if everything went sour and he got killed with Angelo, he'd hate to spend eternity in an unmarked grave beside such an asshole.

On numb legs Jimmy followed Angelo to Gus's car, parked twenty feet behind them. He was dimly aware that they were in a run-down area of row houses and flat-roofed factories. Gus and Joey both had their hands in their coat pockets. Angelo was doing the world's lamest imitation of a big shot acting cool, a sham betrayed by the quaking fingers that brought his cigarette to his lips.

"All right," Gus said. "Where are we going?"

Angelo jerked his head toward a cinder-block building. "Follow me."

Joey said, "I'll hang out here. I don't need to see a polyester palace."

Angelo scowled at Joey, turned, and walked toward the factory. Gus grabbed Jimmy's elbow. "Whatever the fuck happens, you stay with me," he whispered. "Now *move."*

The building had opaque wire-fibered windows, through which a dull gray light was visible. Angelo pounded on a graffiti-spattered metal door with his fist—slowly twice, rapidly three times, and again slowly twice. He turned to Gus and winked.

"That's the secret signal."

"I figured."

The door opened a crack. A roar of sewing machines filled the night air. An ancient Asian with a wrinkled walnut of a face peered up at Angelo through thick glasses.

"It's me," Angelo all but shouted. The man nodded, opened the door all the way and let the three of them inside. He was careful to shut the door and throw the slide bolt as soon as they were in.

A short set of wooden steps led down to one long room, the length and width of two bowling lanes. At least three dozen Oriental men and women sat hunched over sewing machines, feeding pieces of fabric under the throbbing needles. Each worked in a small circle of light from a shaded lamp.

Jimmy groped at his nose, itchy from the fibers that filled the air. Then he noticed that the stuff glazed the hair of everybody in the room. The women's heads looked like cotton candy. Everything stank of burning plastic, a distinct odor of artificial fabric that even a child could have identified. Only Angelo was dumb enough to believe the stuff was silk.

The walnut-faced man led the trio past tall piles of fabric to a man who sat like a lifeguard on top of a stepladder. He was skinny but tough looking, his eyes patrolling the work through a haze of smoke from the cigarette in his lips. Angelo called to him. His face was expressionless as he got off the ladder to greet Angelo. The two shook hands, and then the cigarette fell from his mouth when he saw Gus.

"Well, Chin," Angelo chuckled, "I guess you know

who this is. I *told* you I knew him personally! I *told* you I'd bring him here tonight! Didn't fuckin' be*lieve* me, did ya, ya Chinese bastard?"

Chin executed a full bow before Gus. "Mister Ghost," he said reverentially, facing the floor. "Welcome, sir."

"And this is his brother, Jimmy."

Chin shook Jimmy's hand but left out the bow. He turned to Gus like a kid at the ballpark meeting his favorite slugger. "So? How you like?"

"Very nice," Gus replied. "Working late tonight, huh?"

Chin nodded. "Always work. Always somebody here."

"He says they always work, and there's always somebody here," Angelo said.

"Yeah," Gus said. "I got that much."

Chin grabbed a suit off a rack and showed it to Gus. "You sell suit. Silk suit. Make much money."

"Mr. Chin," Gus said, "I need to speak with Angelo."

Chin nodded, replaced the suit on the rack and climbed back to his perch.

"So," Angelo said. "You want in on the chance of a lifetime, here?"

"It's not silk," Jimmy said.

Angelo sneered. "Another fuckin' expert. Gus, don't let your brothers fuck this up for you."

Gus patted Angelo's cheek. "Anj, you're not a bad guy, and I'd like to help you. But if these are silk suits, then I'm Bambi, wondering why in the world anybody would want to whack my mother."

Angelo's face fell. "Bootleg worms," he said weakly.

"No such thing, buddy. I had a talk with Joey on the way over here." Gus managed a sympathetic smile. "Did they ever *show* you these bootleg worms? Where do they keep 'em, in the fuckin' cellar?"

Sweat was trickling down Angelo's neck. "These people ain't jerk-offs, Gus," he said through tight teeth. "They built the biggest fuckin' wall in the world. You can see it from outer space, did you know that?"

"Yeah. And you can tell from outer space that these fuckin' suits are not made of silk."

The walnut-faced man let out a cry that sent all the workers scurrying from their machines. Chin leapt from the ladder and hit the floor running.

"Aw fuck," Angelo gulped. "Fuckin' *look!*"

He pointed to the opaque windows, through which the bleary red flashing of a police car's roof light was visible. Chin shrieked directions to his workers, who disappeared one by one inside the false paneled wall Angelo had described. Jimmy's knees literally gave out. He sank to the floor, kneeling like a man who's just witnessed a miracle.

Angelo reached for Gus, who pulled away. "Nothing doing," Gus said. "I'm walkin' out of here through the door."

Angelo couldn't believe it. "Gus, are you fuckin' crazy? That's Immigration! You wanna get mixed up in this? You?"

"If *I'm* in trouble, *you're* in trouble."

Angelo gulped, hesitated, then ran for the false wall.

Gus reached down and pulled Jimmy to his feet. "Gus," Jimmy begged, "we have to hide in the wall."

"Shut your fuckin' mouth and come with me." Gus's grip was like iron as he dragged Jimmy to the door. By the time he got his hand on the slide bolt, everyone had disappeared inside the false wall.

"Gus," Jimmy pleaded, "they'll search the trunk—"

"Do you trust me? Huh? *Do* you?"

"Yes," Jimmy lied.

"Then out we go. You first."

He unlocked the door and shoved Jimmy outside. The cold, fiber-free air cleared his head, and an instant later he saw his brother Joey across the street, waving them over to the Oldsmobile. On the car's roof, a cop's cherry-red light glowed in flashing circles. As Jimmy and Joey trotted to the car, Joey unplugged the wire leading from the light to a dashboard outlet and stashed it under the front seat. Joey got in the back seat as Gus and Jimmy piled in front. Gus started the car and got rolling without the faintest screech of tires.

They were a block away when he calmly asked, "Why'd you wait so long to turn it on?"

"Five minutes," Joey said. "You said five minutes." He tapped his wristwatch. "I timed it to the second."

Gus let out a long breath. "Felt like a fuckin' month."

"Worked though, huh?"

"They ran like mice. God knows how long they'll stay inside the wall, though."

"I let the air out of his right rear tire, just for good measure."

"Good thinking, Joey."

"May I ask one thing? May I ask *one fucking thing?"* Jimmy's voice was embarrassingly shrill.

"Go ahead," Gus said. "But talk softly."

"Why the hell did I have to ride with Angelo?"

"So you'd look surprised when I told you to leave with me through the door."

"You scared me half to death!"

"You'll get over it."

Jimmy's blood boiled. "Great fucking plan, huh?

You guys think that was such a great fucking plan? Well what if that had been a basement sweatshop, with no windows? Nobody would've seen the light!"

"We'd have used the siren," Gus explained. "Glad we didn't have to, though. People sleep through lights. Tough to sleep through a siren. That's all we would've needed, a fuckin' crowd in their pajamas."

He glanced in the rearview mirror. "Aaay, what am I lookin' for? He'll be in that wall for an hour. The Chinese won't let him budge. Then another half hour to change the flat. By the time he gets home, birds'll be singin'."

Gus stuck his tongue out, pulled at it with his fingers. "I got those fuckin' fibers in my mouth, now."

"They're all over your hair, too," Joey said.

"Hey, Joey, do me a favor and pick 'em off, would you?"

Joey leaned forward to pick fibers from the Ghost's hair. "I'll do you next," he said to Jimmy, who watched in awe as his kid brother groomed his big brother. Two descendants of the apes, picking each other clean on the great urban Serengeti known as Brooklyn.

Joey finished with Gus, then reached for Jimmy's head.

"Don't," Jimmy said. "I'll do it myself."

Joey chuckled. "Come on, Jimmy, let me do it. You can't see where they are."

"Just please don't touch my head, okay?"

Joey couldn't resist reaching for his hair. "Just this one strand—"

"Would you *leave* it!" Jimmy exploded. He turned to push Joey away, shoving at the left side of his chest. He felt the bulge of something hard and blocky under

Joey's jacket, something that Jimmy figured could be just one thing. A gun in a holster.

The priest sat back, hands on his lap. "Okay, Jimmy. Sorry I upset you."

"That's okay," Jimmy said, and in a funny way he meant it. He felt an odd sense of relief in knowing what his fate was, what it had to be.

Suddenly, it all made sense. They weren't going to kill Angelo. That was *never* part of the program. As big an annoyance as he was, Angelo remained a minor problem, and a well-connected one at that. What a pain in the ass it would be to make a neighborhood buffoon like him disappear cleanly.

No. No way. The thing to do was to get Angelo out of the way, so the Gambuzza brothers could focus on their far bigger problem. Jimmy had absolutely no neighborhood connections. Not one person he knew from his life back in Manhattan knew where he was tonight.

"All of a sudden you're quiet, Jimmy. You all right, or what?"

"Yeah, Gus, I'm fine."

"Listen, I'm sorry I couldn't let you in on the plan back there."

"That's all right."

Jimmy rubbed his hair with his hands, surprised to feel that his scalp was sweating. In that moment he figured that he had, at most, about an hour to live.

Chapter 7

Oh, they were so deliciously sneaky, you really had to hand it to them. Jimmy shows up after two decades of neglect, and of course these two men pitch right in to help their desperate, long-lost brother.

Who the fuck did they think they were kidding? What would Jimmy have done, if the situation were reversed? Suppose Gus had just rung his bell one night, out of the clear blue? Would Jimmy have buzzed him up? No way. No fucking way. He'd have given him the old Jehovah's Witness treatment, and left the bastard out in the cold.

And Father Gambuzza? Suppose Father Gambuzza had introduced himself that time, at the dedication of the indoor garden? Jimmy never would have believed he was a real clergyman. He probably would have called for security to escort the uninvited "priest" away. And now, together, these brothers of his were looking for a clever way to kill him.

The funny thing was, Jimmy couldn't blame them. He was a loose cannon. He'd shown tonight that he couldn't keep his mouth shut, couldn't stop babbling about The Thing in the Trunk. It was only a matter of days, maybe weeks, before the pressure got to him. He'd spill everything, and the ripple effect would be devastating. Gus would be finished, Father Joseph would be finished, their mother would wither away, Gus's kids would be lost. Way too big a price, any way you looked at it. The sensible thing—the *only* thing, Jimmy realized—was for them to kill him.

All because he'd refused to put a pink scrap of rag around his neck, to appease Wendy. One simple deed that he couldn't bring himself to do.

But no. Jimmy thought about it, and realized that the chain of people leading to his doom was much longer and more intricate than that. It began with Wendy, all right, but what about that cab driver? If that smug Irish fuck hadn't gotten so huffy about the way Jimmy had spoken to Wendy, things would certainly be different. If he hadn't tossed Jimmy out on the street far from his home, he'd never have gone anywhere near that damn Latin club.

And if you wanted to take it one step further, there was also the fucking bartender, who could have kept a better eye on Jimmy's alcohol intake, instead of pouring with such a free hand.

Wendy, the cabbie, the bartender . . . these were the people who'd led James Gambar to his downfall. Hell, they were accomplices! They'd practically *pushed* him into committing murder! If it ever went to trial, Jimmy thought, he'd have a lot to say about those people . . .

Trial? *What* fucking trial? For a moment, he'd forgotten that he was a dead man. A dead man! Jimmy couldn't help giggling over it, because any way he looked at it, he had very little to live for. But still, he couldn't help wondering how Gus and Joey would do it. And where would they dispose of *two* bodies?

A pair of hands on his shoulders; Joey squeezing from behind.

"Whoa, you're jumpy. You okay, buddy?"

"Fine."

"You've had some night. Hey, Gus, where are we going?"

Gus scratched his chin. "I thought we'd cross the bridge. We've been all over Brooklyn. That okay with you?"

"Hey, anything. I'm just glad to be cruising with my brothers."

Joey sounded so sincere, so completely without guile, that Jimmy's fear was momentarily replaced by awe. His kid brother must be a hell of a priest. No wonder they emptied their pockets when the collection plate came around. Who could possibly dislike him? He's about to help kill me, and *I* like him!

Jimmy tried to open the window for a gulp of air, but his button didn't work.

"I'll do it," Gus said, reaching for the four-button console to his left. Control, control; Gus even guided the destiny of Jimmy's window. "What do you want it open, just a crack?"

"All the way, please."

"Gonna puke again?"

"No."

The window slid down. Jimmy stuck his head out the way a dog would, tongue hanging loose, eyes squinting against the rush of air. When he pulled himself back inside his ears felt frozen, as if they'd crack like potato chips if touched.

It was a purifying experience. Resigned to his fate,

Jimmy wanted to come clean with his brothers, once and for always.

"Gus. Joey. I just want to say that I'm sorry."

"It was an accident," Joey said. "We've been over this, Jimmy."

"That's not what he means," Gus said. "Is it?"

"No, it isn't."

As the car rolled toward the ramps of the Verrazano-Narrows Bridge, an unusual sense of tranquillity filled Jimmy's being. It was all going to end in the corniest way possible, at the mountainous dumps on Staten Island. He was going to spend eternity as the commonest of Mafia cliches, in a grave of banana peels, foil wrappers, and Clorox bottles, beside a woman whose name he couldn't remember, if he ever knew it. The only cornier path to death would have been in a pair of cement shoes, blub-blubbing his way to the bottom of the East River.

Joey squeezed his shoulders again. "I was right, then. Something else *is* bothering you."

"Sort of."

"Say it, brother, before it's too late."

Before the ice pick in the back of the neck, the piano wire around the throat, the bullet in the brain, the whatever. Say it, *say it.*

"I'm just sorry I left you guys the way I did after Pop died. All this time that went by . . . I'm sorry, you guys."

He shut his eyes, awaiting a death blow that did not come.

"It was as hard on you as it was on us," said Father Gambuzza.

"Aaay, don't let it eat you," Gus added soothingly. "We can make up for lost time."

Jimmy's heart sank. It was the first time all night

that his big brother had lied to him, maybe the first time ever, and he didn't like it even a little bit. He had one more thing to say, and then it would be okay to die.

"It would all have been different," Jimmy said, "if not for that dog."

Gus couldn't help giggling. "You can't look at it that way. Believe me, you'll drive yourself crazy, looking at it that way."

"I know, I know, but I can't help it. It all boils down to that dog."

From the back seat, Father Joseph Gambuzza sighed deeply.

"That fucking dog," the priest said

The dog's name was Enzo, and none of the Gambuzzas could figure exactly what breed he was. He was like a Buick with a gargoyle's head, the mouth of which continuously dripped bouncy threads of saliva.

Enzo lived in a fenced-in yard next door. The fence was made of wooden slats nailed so close together that no light shined through the cracks. His whole life took place inside the fence. He shit mountains in the yard. He was never taken for walks, and never allowed inside the house where his master lived. That man's name was Federico Albertini, an Italian who looked and behaved like a mountain peasant who's come into money too late to change his wardrobe. Newspapermen filled many a slow day by running stories and photographs of Mr. Albertini as he went about his day in his worn gray jacket and crumply fedora—shopping in cheese stores, sipping espresso, or playing boccie on the dusty courts of Bay Ridge. Mr. Albertini had been arrested numerous times, but convicted of nothing. So what the newspapers could make perfectly clear without actually saying so was that Albertini was the most powerful Mafia chief on the Eastern Seaboard, and perhaps the country.

Bay Ridge was where he'd lived as a boy fresh from Italy, and Bay Ridge was where he wished to stay. He built a huge split-level house on what had been the neighborhood's biggest empty lot, next to the Gambuzza home. Thomas Gambuzza, father of Gus, Jimmy, and Joey, had played on that lot when he was a boy, and watched with wet eyes as the earth-claw machines tore at the hills and trees that had been his childhood. That a criminal would soon be his next-door neighbor was salt in the wound, with lemon juice for good measure.

Thomas was a bank clerk who struggled to pay bills. He and his family lived in the little brick house where his parents had lived, and though there was no mortgage to pay off, money was always tight. Thomas would examine the tax deductions on his paycheck, then look out the window at the house next door and imagine floor-to-ceiling stacks of cardboard boxes in the cellar, each brimming with twenty-dollar bills. Rarely did he feel proud of his honesty. Usually it made him feel like a fool, and he wished it was something he could have lanced and drained, like a boil. It was entirely possible that Thomas Gambuzza was the unhappiest honest man in New York City.

He was also an unlucky horse player, a hobby that ate up the little bit of walking-around money Thomas had. He was superstitious, believing with all his soul in the luck of the number seven. He would not play a horse unless the number seven was involved, and wagered wads of cash on some of the slowest thoroughbreds in history just because they wore the number seven, or competed in the seventh race, or at seven o'clock. So serious was his belief in the number that Jimmy was born seven years after Gus, and Joey arrived seven years after Jimmy. This, according to neighborhood legend, was no coincidence.

He was a drinker, and a nasty one. The boys' feelings toward their father were a cocktail of fear and puzzlement. His wife existed in what was nearly a state of catatonia, cleaning the house and serving meals with all the enthusiasm of a civil servant. Her husband's violence took a steady toll on inanimate objects—coffee cups, ashtrays, whatever was handy to smash. It was only a question of time before he took it out on his family.

"Big shot," Thomas would announce in the middle of a meal, gesturing toward the Albertini house. "What's the big deal about him, anyway? Huh?" And the family would wait for him to break something before resuming eating.

From a young age, Gus had taken it upon himself to become a surrogate parent to his younger brothers, especially when Thomas was in his cups.

"Take it easy, Dad," Gus said one particularly ugly night.

"Why?" Thomas demanded. "Why should I take it easy?"

"For your own sake."

"Yeah? What do you think, I'm afraid of the guy?"

"No," Gus replied. "Maybe just a little jealous."

It took a moment for the insult to sink in, and then Thomas whacked Gus across the face with a sound that echoed like a rifle shot.

The mother wept. The other boys were silent. At eighteen, Gus was a linebacker on his high school football team, so strong and fast that colleges across the country were after him. He could have killed

Thomas with one blow, but he took the slap as a statue might have, grinned the unfriendliest of grins, picked up his fork and resumed eating. Nobody seemed to notice that Jimmy chose this moment to run up to his room, where he sat on his bed and hugged his shaking knees.

The situation did not improve. Thomas's drinking worsened, to the point that he was putting his job in jeopardy. Just about every day he went to work with a hangover, and invariably the enormous Enzo would hear Thomas leave the house, make a running leap at the fence along the driveway and slam against it, paws and head above the jagged top in a barking frenzy that never failed to terrify him. Thomas was afraid of all dogs, even Chihuahuas. Enzo made him drop his car keys just about every morning. Once, when he'd carelessly gotten close enough to the fence to feel the dog's meaty breath on his neck, he'd wet his pants.

It all came to a head on a steamy Fourth of July, which happened to be Thomas Gambuzza's least favorite day of the year. It was on this holiday each year that Albertini treated the neighborhood kids to hot dogs, sodas, and a fireworks display on the street in front of his home. For hours, cherry bombs and fireworks sounded, and bottle rockets lit up the sky. The police did nothing to stop it. Street cops stood on the corner, eating hot dogs grilled by Albertini's people.

"What a patriot!" Thomas roared from inside his house. "Jesus Christ, what bullshit!" It was nearly five in the afternoon, and he'd been drinking steadily all day long. He stumbled around, looking for his car keys.

Gus, who was to attend Notre Dame University on a football scholarship in the fall, walked into the house. "Want me to drive, Pop?"

"I can drive," Thomas snarled. "Don't start with me, Mr. Football Scholarship." He poked a finger in his son's chest. "What are you saying, I'm too drunk to drive?"

"I'm saying you look tired, and I'd be glad to take you wherever you're going."

Thomas shook his head. "You even talk like one of 'em. They never answer your question. Always go off on some other thing. Keeps the juries confused. Whyncha just move in next door, the way you talk?"

"This is my family, Pop."

"Aah, look out, look out."

He pushed his way past Gus, went out to the driveway, fumbled his way into the car, and started the motor. Had he been a bit more observant, Thomas might have noticed that for once, Enzo was not barking, and the wooden gate next door was wide open. Perhaps he'd been distracted by the explosives going off all around him. Perhaps he was just too drunk to notice anything.

Just as he put his car into reverse, the unbelievably long frame of Enzo came loping down the driveway. Thomas was just bringing his foot down on the gas pedal when the dog's monstrous head and paws slammed through the open driver side window and onto his lap.

With a scream he put the gas pedal to the floor, and roared like a Roman candle down the driveway. Enzo flew free of the car, unharmed, but the rear bumper slammed into Mikey and Philip Albertini, the two youngest—and favorite—sons of Federico, who'd happened to be waving sparklers at the end of the Gambuzza driveway. Mikey, nine, was dead on the spot, but Philip, eight, lingered for seven hours at a local hospital before he was taken off life support.

It didn't happen immediately, and for a while it seemed as if it wouldn't happen at all. Truly heartbroken by what had happened, Thomas had gone next door and apologized to the Albertinis, weeping real tears and getting nothing back but cold, blank stares. They'd poured coffee and offered cookies to the visitor, gestures of hospitality accompanied by not the slightest hint of forgiveness. To the amazement of many, they let him leave the house alive.

A gas line was built under the street and piped into the Albertini front yard, where two flames burned in glass globes in memory of the boys. They burned night and day, through the funerals, the burials, and the start of a school year that Philip and Mikey would never know.

Snow encrusted the outsides of those flame goblets the day that Thomas Gambuzza disappeared. He'd left the house for work, and never made it to the bank. The police were called, but nobody had seen a thing. The cops said they figured he'd probably run away. What they didn't understand was that if there was one man in all of Brooklyn who wouldn't know where to hide, it was Thomas Gambuzza.

The disappearance was almost a relief to the surviving Gambuzzas. Thomas had been a ghost anyway, since the accident: now, perhaps, he would be at rest. Everyone else would have been at rest, too, if not for a remark made by Albertini to one of his associates, who had the bad judgment to repeat it to his wife, who saw to it that the whole neighborhood knew about it.

"The score," Albertini had allegedly said, "is now two to one."

He was referring to the death tolls in the Albertini and Gambuzza families. Everyone knew that the Don played to win. Satisfaction would not be his until two more coffins were filled.

News of his statement reached all the way to South Bend, Indiana, in a person-to-person call from Fiorentina Gambuzza to her son Gus, who walked straight from his dormitory phone booth to the bursar's office to announce that he was quitting college. He explained that he could not finish the semester, even though there were just two weeks to finals. He packed his few things, said good-bye to his roommates and his astonished coach, and embarked on the long, slow train trip that would bring him to Brooklyn.

On the way, Gus finished reading the last of his assignments, Martin Heidegger's *Discourse on Thinking.* It was for his freshman philosophy course, and though he knew he'd never be returning to Notre Dame, he was not the sort of person who left tasks uncompleted. Gus liked the book, liked the author's way of looking at things, and couldn't help wondering whether the man wouldn't have been even wiser had he only put in some time pounding the streets of Brooklyn.

He got home and didn't even unpack his bag first. He kissed his mother, shook hands with his brothers, and, though it was past ten P.M., walked straight to the Albertini home and rang the bell like an impatient bill collector. Jimmy, Joey, and Fiorentina watched from the window as the door opened and then closed behind Gus. The brothers went to bed but Fiorentina, weeping, sat watching the door until past midnight, when it finally opened and Gus emerged alive.

"Everything's going to be fine," he told his mother. Only then did Gus bring his stuff to his old room and unpack, while his mother warmed up a plate of leftover macaroni and sausages for him.

"Hey, Gus." Jimmy stood at the door of his room.

"What is it, buddy?"

"Are you back home again?"

"I sure am."

"What happened next door?"

"We just talked. Don't worry, everything's going to be okay."

Jimmy scratched his belly.

"Something you want to tell me, kid?"

"Nahh."

"You sure?"

"I'll tell you tomorrow."

"All right, go to sleep."

Jimmy went to bed. Gus sat with his mother in the kitchen and ate his meal while she watched him, hands folded where her plate would have been. It wasn't until after his second bowl of macaroni that Gus informed her that she was to become a grandmother, and that his bride, a cheerleader named Carol Redstone, would be arriving as soon as her exams were over.

The classic Italian-American response would have been to cry out in shame, or perhaps even faint to the floor, but Fiorentina had been through too much to let life's quirky biological processes overwhelm her.

No. Her drunk of a husband was gone forever, her favorite son was home for good, and a new life, the blood of her blood, would soon enter the world. How she'd feel about her daughter-in-law seemed irrelevant. She got up to hug Gus, dry-eyed as a lizard. If she'd shed a tear, it would have been one of joy.

CHAPTER 8

For the first time all night, Gus turned on the radio. It was tuned to a big band station, and the woodwinds and horns of Benny Goodman's band flooded the car from unseen speakers.

"That all right with you?" Gus asked Jimmy, meaning his choice of music.

Music to die by, Jimmy thought. He shook his head and murmured, "It's just not fair."

"Go ahead, change the station. Anything but rap."

"Not that. You. Your life. You could have played pro football."

"No, I wasn't that good. And even if I'd played, I'd be long retired now, with a whole other set of problems. Fucked-up knees. Maybe even in a wheelchair."

"You could have gotten a degree."

"Let's just say I've earned my equivalency through life experience."

"You don't even sound pissed off!" Jimmy all but shouted. "It all happened to you at once. Dropping out. Fatherhood. You were eighteen, Gus."

"Nineteen by then, but what's your point?"

"It was unfair."

"Hey, you discovered America. Life's a blow job from a vampire, Jimmy. You get the pain and the pleasure at the same time. Happy people ignore one and concentrate on the other."

"Is that right?"

"Absolutely. That's the only real difference between happy and unhappy people."

"I should be taking notes," Joey piped in. "This'd be some sermon."

"Oh, it'd be marvelous!" Jimmy said. "It'd be the first time in the history of the Catholic Church that the words 'blow job' appeared in a sermon!"

"Well, I'd edit it a little."

"Your problem, Jimmy," Gus said, "is you don't concentrate on your pleasures. You accentuate the bad."

"To tell you the truth, Gus, you caught me on a bad night."

"No, no. I've been riding around with you for hours, now, and you haven't told me one good thing about your life."

Jimmy felt the back of his neck burning. There was nothing to lose, now. It was up to him to write his own epitaph.

"You may or may not know it," he said evenly, "but I'm an excellent architect. I've been written up in magazines."

"I know all about that."

"I didn't let fate push me around. I *created* my fate. I won that scholarship to Miller Tech and made it all happen."

Gus and Joey burst out laughing. "Hell's so funny?" Jimmy demanded, and Gus's next words pierced

Jimmy as deeply as the bullet, the knife, the whatever it was he'd been anticipating.

"You, ah, didn't exactly *win* that scholarship."

Jimmy's tongue tasted salty. His scholarship to the Miller Institute of Technology in Massachusetts was his proudest achievement, the indisputable turning point of his life. It got him out of the family and out of Brooklyn. It led to his first job out of college, at an architectural firm in Boston, and to a second job in Seattle, which he'd applied for under his new name, James Gambar. He'd never dreamed the scholarship could have been fixed.

"What are you saying, Gus?"

"It means you had help you didn't know about."

Father Joseph's hands gripped Jimmy's shoulders again, squeezing away. "It's all right, it's all right."

Jimmy eeled out of his grasp. His lips quivered. "I had good grades. I had *damn* good grades."

"Of course you did! And a scholarship's an arbitrary thing, anyway. Bunch of alumni getting together with the faculty, sorting through the contenders. Who's to say who the best is? They've got to worry about picking a black, or a woman. Or maybe they've got to keep the alumni happy, give it to somebody's nephew, or all of a sudden the donations stop."

Gus turned to look at Jimmy up and down, forehead to feet. "What kind of shot did a guy like you have? White. Male. Unconnected. Kiss it good-bye." Gus forced a bland smile. "All I did was make it a fair contest. *You* won the race, though."

Jimmy was afraid to ask. His lips did it, without his brain's permission. "How'd you make it fair?"

Gus waved a hand. "The dean had some gambling debts. We made them disappear."

"That's all?"

"Christ, but you sound disappointed. What do you want me to tell you, that we threw a few faculty members off buildings?" He patted Jimmy's knee. "This is all irrelevant. We're not talking about a fix. We're not even talking about architecture. We are talking about *confidence,* man. That's the issue, here."

"Listen to him," Joey whispered.

"That atrium you designed in Baltimore," Gus continued. "You going to tell me you would have had the balls to build that thing without confidence?"

Jimmy swallowed. "You know about my atrium?"

Gus didn't bother answering. "If you think I was going to let some committee take away your confidence just because they didn't know you, you're out of your mind."

"So why tell me anything at all?"

"Because you brought it up, brother. And this is a night for the truth. We may never have another night like this."

I'm dead, Jimmy told himself. I am abso-fucking-lutely dead. He jerked his thumb toward the back seat. "And Joey, here. I suppose you did whatever you had to do to make him a priest."

"No," Gus calmly replied. "He did that all on his own."

Joey patted Jimmy's shoulder. "It's not nearly as competitive. Young kids aren't lining up to do what I do. Who the hell wants to be a priest? A man'd explode, trying to do it by their rules."

"At this point in my life," Gus said, "the priesthood looks good to me, under anybody's rules."

"You serious?" Joey said. "Because it's do-able."

"Get out of here!"

"Why not?"

"You and me, together? Running the same parish?"

"Tell me why not."

"For one thing, the press'd go wild."

"Fuck the press. What would they get out of it, one Sunday feature story?"

Gus had to laugh. "You know, maybe it's not as crazy as it sounds. Hey, Jimmy, what about you? Want to make it a trio?"

"Stop the car, Gus," Jimmy breathed.

"Aaay, we're in the middle of the friggin' bridge."

"Stop it!"

Gus made no move to slow down. Jimmy jammed his own foot down on the brake, making the car slam to a halt. A horn blared behind them, as a large red Chevy swerved at the last moment to avoid rear-ending them.

Gus banged his forehead on the steering wheel, and Joey was thrown to the floor in the back. Only Jimmy had braced himself for the sudden stop, and while his brothers gained their bearings he leapt from the car and started running toward Staten Island.

It was familiar turf, and it took him a moment to realize why. This was the bridge that twenty thousand runners crossed each year in the New York City Marathon, an event he'd entered with Wendy the year before. The only difference was that the race went in the opposite direction, from Staten Island toward Brooklyn.

The symbolism was so corny that Jimmy Gambar had to laugh. One minute you're running the same way as twenty thousand legitimate citizens on a bright, sunshiny day. Then, suddenly, you're an outlaw, all alone, in the dead of night, running the other way to keep from being killed by your brothers.

On foot, it was easier to notice the rise of the bridge's path toward a crest in the center. Jimmy could handle it, because he was in good shape. He looked over his shoulder and saw Gus and Joey running after him, losing ground with each step. No way in the world they could catch him.

Jimmy was giggling. He had a dim vision of himself actually escaping into the wilds of Staten Island, and beginning a new life there, eating berries and catching fish from the poisoned water. Then a sudden pang of guilt pierced his soul like a bolt of lightning. Even if he got away from his brothers, he knew that he'd never be able to live with himself. He'd lived a selfish, destructive life, and at that moment couldn't think of a single reason why he deserved to go on breathing.

He stopped running, walked to the edge of the bridge, and climbed onto a waist-high rail. The one thing he had left, the thing he'd had for nearly every moment of his adult life, was control. True, this entire night's events had been out of his control, but that was about to change. He'd show his brothers. James Gambar would orchestrate the terms of his own death, thank you very much.

Jimmy gripped an enormous cable, and looked down at the black water. There were worse ways to go. It would be fast. He crouched slightly, as if to prepare to jump, but his hands clung to the cable in their own reflex for life, separate from his brain's. He forced himself to release the cable and crouched again. Suddenly he was yanked backwards off the rail, as if he'd been lassoed.

He was in the grip of Gus, who had him around the waist.

"Do you know how fucking close that Chevy came to rear-ending us? Huh, asshole?"

The power of the man was extraordinary; Jimmy felt as if he were in the grasp of an earth-moving machine. Gus slid his other arm around Jimmy's neck. Joey arrived seconds later, gasping for breath.

"You really can run," he said to Gus. *"Madonna,* that was fast!"

Gus leaned against a girder, catching his breath. "I think I had one last run left in me, and that was it."

Jimmy could not turn his head a centimeter in any direction. He was giggling again.

"Somethin' funny, shithead?"

"You're wrong, Gus," Jimmy managed to say.

"About what, fuckhead?"

"With moves like those, you *would* have played pro ball."

Jimmy began laughing hysterically, and didn't stop until Gus tightened the grip around his neck and cut off his air. He felt himself losing consciousness, and sensed that the end of his life was about a minute away. It was not an unpleasant sensation. A tingle began in his feet and his palms, then gradually began traveling up his limbs and toward the vital organs. What a nice way to die, he thought, and he only wished Gus would loosen the hold on his windpipe long enough to thank him for doing it so gently.

When he came to, he was stretched out in the back seat of the car, which remained where Jimmy had stopped it.

"Hey, I'm alive," he whispered.

Joey was in the front passenger seat, and tapped Gus to let him know that Jimmy was awake. Gus spoke without looking back.

"You are really just about the most selfish person in the whole fucking world."

Jimmy said nothing, wondering if he might be

dreaming. Gus reached back with his right hand to point a finger in Jimmy's face.

"You want to fucking kill yourself, don't do it in front of me. I have a dramatic enough life without anybody's help."

"I'm sorry."

"A guy makes a pretty big splash falling that far, asshole. Did you think nobody would notice? Or did you want to stick me and Joey with this situation, after all we've fucking done for you?"

"Gus, Joey, I'm sorry."

"Yeah, you already said that."

"No, for a lot of other things, Gus."

Gus jerked his head toward Joey. "You got more stuff to confess, talk to him. That's not my department."

"It's all my fault." Jimmy winced. Each spoken word was like a tap on the eyeballs from a ball peen hammer, but he had to continue. "Gus, there's stuff I never told you."

"Yeah? Well I'm dying to hear it. How 'bout you, Joey?"

"Shhh. Try to be kind."

"Kind. Right."

"You remember that night you came home from college and saw me in the hallway? Remember you asked me if I had something to tell you, and I said I'd tell you tomorrow?"

"All I remember from that night was cutting a deal with old man Albertini."

"Well, I never did tell you that everything was my fault. Everything."

"Is that right?"

"The accident, and the two kids who got killed, and Pop getting killed. I'm to blame. It's me."

"You want to tell me why?"

Jimmy shut his eyes, licked his lips. "It's quite a story, even for your ears," he began.

The taunting Jimmy had taken earlier in the night from the bull-necked Angelo at Gus's social club had been cruel, but absolutely on the money. Little Jimmy Gambuzza had been a lousy athlete. In the schoolyard he was always the last kid chosen into a game.

This was not the easiest way for a boy to be in the Bay Ridge section of Brooklyn, especially when his brothers were jocks. Gus was a star athlete, and even toddling Joey could hit a baseball with the natural, unteachable moves of the true hitter. The sad truth was realized quite early by Jimmy—that the gene for athletics had leapfrogged from the oldest to the youngest brother, right over his head.

And so Jimmy occupied his time in other ways, spending afternoons at the local public library or making model planes and ships.

By the time he was ten, the models bored him. He wished to create something himself, beyond the boundaries of some foolish instruction sheet and a few scraps of plastic that came in a box.

He started collecting ice cream sticks. With these, and a bottle of Elmer's glue, he built a small cabin. That was just for starters. Next came a two-story house, with a thatched roof. The activity soothed his soul, and he suspected it made him feel the way Gus felt when he made a good tackle.

After a few more buildings, Jimmy felt he needed more of a challenge. He roamed the neighborhood, gathering ice cream sticks wherever he went. Soon he had nearly four hundred of them, hoarded for a project that had no name. It came to him one day after he picked four sticks out of the sand, and happened to look up toward Staten Island:

He would build a model of the Verrazano-Narrows Bridge.

The idea thrilled him so much he could barely sleep that night, and the next day he counted the hours until he could take a book about the bridge out of the library. Would he have enough sticks? How would he even begin? It didn't matter. He bolted his dinner that night, excused himself, and raced to his room to begin.

As close as Jimmy could figure it, the thing would be about six feet long. He opened the book to a picture of the bridge, took a deep breath, squeezed a drop of glue onto the end of one stick, and began.

Weeks passed. His mother never touched the strange pieces of glued-together sticks when she cleaned his room. Jimmy worked on the thing through May, and then June. It was not until the Fourth of July that he glued the final stick in place, and pronounced the bridge finished.

That's when he heard, between booms and bangs from the fireworks display next door, the sound of his father's footsteps heading his way.

Thomas Gambuzza was quite drunk, and in this condition he tended to slur his words. An hour earlier, at the lunch table, he'd told Jimmy to run to the corner and get him a pack of Chesterfields. Jimmy thought he'd been talking to himself.

The door swung open. Thomas, scowling against the smoke of the butt that burned in his mouth, squinted at Jimmy.

"Where the hell's my cigarettes?"

Jimmy's heart galloped. "Did you want me to get you some?"

"Did you want me to get you some?" Thomas's effeminate imitation of his son's voice was pitiless. "I tol' ya an hour ago. Hell ya been doing?"

"Nothing . . ."

The cigarette in his lips dipped straight down when he noticed the bridge, which was, as Jimmy had predicted, just about six feet long. Thomas held his hands together behind his back and leaned close to inspect it, like a respectful art patron examining a priceless painting.

"You did this?"

"Uh-huh."

"Why?"

Why? Jimmy had no idea of how to go about answering that question. He lacked the language and the understanding of his own motives for the project, which might have been summed up with words that could explain any genuine artistic endeavor: I just couldn't help it.

Instead, he said nothing. Thomas's brow knotted.

"I'm talking to you, boy. I'm standing here with my last cigarette, waiting for an answer."

"I don't know why I built it."

"Do you know why you didn't get me my cigarettes?"

"I didn't know you wanted any."

"So you didn't hear me tell you to get me a pack."

"No, sir."

"Do you hear me now?"

"Yes, sir."

"I spoke English before, too. Why didn't you hear me then?"

"I don't know, sir."

A volley of firecrackers exploded, seemingly right beneath Jimmy's window. Thomas hunched his shoulders, took a cigarette from his mouth, and pitched it into Jimmy's metal wastebasket.

"You got any paper in there, boy, you better get it out."

"It's empty."

"You know that for a fact, huh?"

"Yes, sir."

"You know everything, don't you?"

"No, sir." *Please come home, Gus,* Jimmy thought; *come home and come into my room. You'll know what to do.*

"You think you do," Thomas persisted. "That bridge, there. Now I know why I can never find you. You've been up here all this time, gluing sticks." He chuckled cruelly. "Just tell me why you did it, and I'll go away."

"I don't know why."

"I don't like that answer."

"I'm sorry, sir."

"Do you like what you made? Are you proud of it?"

Jimmy was prouder of the bridge model than he was of anything he'd ever done. But that's not what he wants to hear, he told himself.

"No, sir," Jimmy lied.

"Well then you won't mind this."

Thomas spread his hands wide to lift the model, then squeezed it like an accordian. It crunched and snapped horribly until his hands came together, and then he stomped on the few pieces that were still glued together until the floor was a mess of broken sticks and dried glue globs.

"Are you crying? Don't cry, now. You said you weren't proud of it. I didn't harm anything you cared about."

Jimmy stood there, trying to squeeze back tears, trying not to care, trying not to hate the man, who spanked his hands clean and mock-cheerfully announced, "I'm going out for cigarettes. That way I know I'll get 'em."

Jimmy gave him a few seconds, then tracked his father down the stairs.

"I'll get you for that," he whimpered.

While Thomas fumbled to put on his shoes and stomped around in search of the car keys, Jimmy sneaked out the back door, crossed the driveway, reached over the Albertini fence, and felt around for the slide-bolt latch. He unlocked the door, threw it open and clapped his hands.

"Come here, Enzo! Come here, boy!"

He turned and ran back into the house before he even saw the beast.

Jimmy was spent. The secret he'd bottled up for all those years was out, and as he lay there in the back seat he felt as if he'd been filleted. Boneless, soulless, he awaited his fate, but nobody was saying a word.

"So you see it was all my fault," he heard himself say. "Those two kids getting killed, and Pop." He thumped himself on the chest. "*My* fault. I'm sorry, you guys. I really am sorry. I made some fucking mess of the family."

Gus said, "Is this why you never came back after you left for college?"

Jimmy nodded, his head feeling heavy as a bowling ball. "I knew I'd have to tell you some day."

Joey reached back and squeezed Jimmy's knee. "You poor guy. Feel better now? A little better?"

"Yes I do, Father Gambuzza. And you were right, by the way. There *was* something more I wanted to confess. You're looking at a two-time killer. Tonight, and twenty-seven years ago. But fuck it, I'm ready to pay for everything now. Do whatever the fuck it is you've got to do."

Gus's eyebrows arched in what looked to be genuine puzzlement. "What'd you have in mind?"

Jimmy said, "Kill me."

A barge passed under the bridge, its foghorn making Jimmy and Joey jump.

Gus didn't seem to hear it. "Holy Jesus Christ hangin' up there on that friggin' pair o' two-by-fours. He thinks we want to kill him."

"Well *don't* you?" Jimmy all but bawled. "I'm dangerous. I'm a loose cannon. I've been nothing but trouble. Go ahead, do it. I fucking *deserve* it."

Gus jerked his head toward the back seat and said to Joey, "Get a load of this guy, beggin' for death. Like it ain't coming to all of us fast enough anyway."

"Shhh, Gus, he's upset."

Gus reached back and grabbed Jimmy's chin. "Get it through your head, Jimmy. We are *not* going to kill you. I can't believe I actually have to fucking *tell* you that."

He released the chin, and pushed Jimmy back against the seat. Jimmy wiped snot from his face. The revelation that he was going to live was not nearly as sweet as he might have expected it to be, blended as it was with embarrassment.

"God damn it, Gus, I did some terrible things," he said meekly. "I was just trying to come clean."

"I know, I know." Gus chuckled. "All these years that was the one piece that didn't fit. How did that goddam gate get open? Old man Albertini couldn't figure it. Finally told himself that Enzo worked the latch with his mouth."

"No way in the world a dog could've done that."

"Aaay, he thought that dog was Albert Einstein on four legs. You know how they get with their pets."

"Well, now you can tell him the truth."

Gus looked back at Jimmy and shrugged elaborately. "*What* truth?"

"That I killed his sons."

"Why would I tell him that? The debt's been paid off for years. Why pay it again?"

"The fact remains that I *did* kill those boys."

Gus shook his head. "You got such a funny way of looking at things," he said, almost sadly.

"Go easy on him, Gus," Joey urged.

"Easy? This *is* easy. Hey, Jimmy, why don't you confess to the Holocaust while you're at it? Dachau and Auschwitz. Those places were your idea, weren't they?"

"Fuck you, Gus."

"Ooh, I take it back. You *are* a tough guy. I'm scared to death, just being in this car with you."

"Gus," Joey said, "this isn't helping."

"Well maybe I'm tired of helping." He turned to grab Jimmy by the collar and pulled him up to a sitting position. Jimmy looked at Joey, who slipped him a quick wink to let him know to be patient, that it would all be okay, somehow.

"You listening?" Gus shook Jimmy like a rag doll. "Huh? You listening?"

"Yeah . . ."

"Because I'm gonna tell you something that's gonna free you forever, or maybe you're too far gone for that, so let's just say it'll give you something to think about."

He pulled Jimmy close, so that their noses were nearly touching.

"This was all Pop's fault," Gus said softly. "The guy was a king-sized dickhead. He was a careless, selfish, bullshit person from start to finish. All that talk about how honest he was? He was the biggest fucking thief you could ever know. He stole everything *but* money. When he broke that bridge, he stole your dignity. He stole our childhoods, being drunk all the time like that. Look at Mom. He stole her whole life, and all he could do was crow about the big gangster who lived next door. See what I'm getting at?"

Jimmy said nothing. A stink like a fart of a cabbage-eating giant penetrated the parked car. Jimmy knew they were near the mountainous, methane-breathing dumps of Staten Island.

Gus let go of Jimmy, who remained sitting, his bones having returned.

"These are hard things to hear, but I ain't telling you anything you didn't know. You, look what you did. Changing your name like that. Your *bones* knew he was an asshole. Who wants to walk around with an asshole's name?"

Jimmy looked at Joey, who sat listening with his eyes closed and his chin dipped, like a man saying his penance prayers.

Gus patted Jimmy's cheek. "So don't take the blame for what the old man did. *He* was a loose cannon. He was gonna get somebody killed, some way, some how. It was just your bad luck to be there when the odds caught up with him. Fact is, Joey and I should be thanking you for being the one."

"But Gus, I opened the gate."

"Big fuckin' deal. I saw he was drunk when he left the house. I should have taken the car keys, but I didn't. So maybe this whole fucking mess is *my* fault. Or *Mom's* fault, for not standing up to his bullshit. In the end, it comes to one thing—Pop was going to get somebody killed. It was his hard luck that it happened to be Albertini's kids."

Gus forced a smile. "Look, all you meant to do was

scare the shit out of him, right? Or maybe have Enzo take a chunk out of his ass?"

"Yeah . . ."

"That's fair, for what he did to you. The rest is on his head. Including what happened tonight, by the way. Think you would've grown up to be as uptight as you are if you'd had a father with anything on the fuckin' ball? Think you would've spent five fucking minutes, never mind *two years,* with a ball-breaker like Wendy if you had any kind of a father in your life? No way, brother. No freaking way. That's how I size it up, anyway." Gus held up a finger. "And remember. You can be the son of an asshole without bein' an asshole yourself. That's your salvation right there, buddy."

Jimmy said, "They killed Pop, didn't they?"

Gus smiled blandly. "Looks that way. Let's say they did. Nobody in this world can say he didn't have it coming."

"This is our father we're talking about."

"Yeah. That's right. He's gone, we're here, and there are other situations to worry about."

Joey opened his eyes, looked at Jimmy. "Listen to him, Jimmy, he's the smartest man I know."

"Well, the smartest man you know wants to get the fuck out of here before his car turns into a hunk of blue cheese. Staten Island on a damp night. Christ, but what was I thinking about? Let's go the hell back to Brooklyn."

Back to Brooklyn; in his whole life, had Jimmy ever heard such wonderful words? He sat back and spread his arms like wings across the back of the spacious seats.

"Are you guys saying you forgive me?"

Father Joey turned to smile at Jimmy.

"We're saying there's nothing to forgive, James."

Jimmy wept tears he was certain were as sugar-sweet as the nectar of apple blossoms.

"Aw, jeez," Gus said. "Now he's cryin.' "

"It's all right," Joey said. "Those are happy tears. I know 'em when I see 'em. Most of my widows at the parish cry that kind. Makes me wonder about this marriage business."

Jimmy took the deepest breath of his life. It was as if an anvil had been lifted from his chest, after twenty-seven years, and now parts of his lungs that had never known air were tasting it for the first time, swelling his body with new strength.

"Off we go," Gus said. He turned the ignition key, and there was nothing but a clicking sound. He took a breath and tried it again. This time, there wasn't even a clicking sound.

"Well, fellows," he said. "What we've got here is a dead fuckin' battery."

All three of them got out of the car to look under the hood. In this one way, they were equals—complete automotive incompetents. They pushed at fittings here and there, fiddled with wires, and spent a minute or so doing other useless things before Gus gave it another try. Nothing. For the first time all night, there was the look of defeat on the face of the Ghost.

"I fucked it up," Joey said. "Before, with the cherry light."

"Nah, I had the flasher on while we were parked," Gus said. "Must've drained the battery." He looked at his watch. "Quarter to three. We've been lucky so far that none of those hard-on bridge cops have shown up. Only a matter of time, though."

"What's the big deal if they do?" Jimmy asked.

"You're not supposed to stop on the bridge," Gus

replied, as kindly as he could. "They don't like it. All we need now is one of 'em sendin' for a tow truck. They take the car, and we're cooked." He managed to grin at Jimmy. "See that, brother? Your bad luck goes on and on."

"Bullshit," Jimmy said. He looked at his brothers, both of whom seemed windblown and exhausted. Jimmy, on the other hand, felt as if he'd been transfused with the blood of an Olympic god. He'd told them everything, *everything:* for the first time since he'd opened that gate to let Enzo out, Jimmy had absolutely nothing to hide.

Gus cocked his head at Jimmy. "You saying this ain't bad luck? Sure feels like it."

"You sound like *me* now, Gus. Before I was trying to figure out all the people I could blame for what happened to me tonight, from Wendy to the friggin' cab driver, and you know something? It's a pile of shit. I had them all conspiring to get me. Well, I was as fucking wrong as you can be."

Jimmy shook his head. "I was putting myself in the center of the whole fucking universe, like it all revolved around me. It doesn't. What happened tonight just fucking happened, and nobody in the universe can say why. No fuckin'-*body.*"

"That's right, James," Father Gambuzza said softly.

Jimmy patted the hood of the car. "If this had happened an hour ago, I'd've figured it for part of the grand conspiracy to screw me. It's not, Gus. It's a fucking dead battery. That's all it is. And all that matters now is to get it recharged so we can be on our way."

"A recharge," Gus echoed. "At three in the morning, in the middle of the bridge. Piece o' cake." He pointed a gentle finger at each of his brothers.

"Jimmy, Joey, you might as well walk back to Brooklyn. No sense in all of us being stuck here."

It didn't take a genius to figure out the Ghost's plan. He'd have to open the trunk, haul it out, and dump it over the side, hoping there'd be no witnesses. Then he'd have to sit in the car and wait to be towed. Suicide, any way you looked at it.

"No fucking way," Jimmy said. "Nobody move. *I'll* handle this."

Gus let out a bitter laugh. "What are you gonna do, architect? Design us a car that doesn't need a battery? We got a better shot of havin' Joey pray for the battery to get better."

"The fuck you think I've been doin'?!" asked Father Gambuzza. "Go on, Gus, try it one more time."

Gus tried it. Nothing. "So much for the power of prayer."

"Aaay, Gus," Joey protested. "It's not like a light switch, you know. Lemme keep praying, here."

"Don't waste your time, Joey," Jimmy said. He pulled out his wallet, and flapped it open to reveal a silver-colored badge. The year before he'd designed a police headquarters building in Memphis, and before he left town, the sheriff deputized him. Jimmy had kept the silly badge in his wallet just to amuse himself. Gus looked at it, and wrinkled his nose.

"Where'd you get that, from a fuckin' box o' frosted flakes?"

"Never mind where I got it. Just be glad I have it."

"The fuck you think you're doing?" Gus asked. Instead of answering, Jimmy walked to the bridge's interior lane, turned to face the scant traffic and stood there, arms spread high. An approaching blue Camaro beeped at him. Jimmy didn't budge. The car braked hard, its bumper not three feet from Jimmy's knees.

The driver got out. He was a chubby middle-aged man with a loose blue silk shirt, white slacks, and white shoes. He'd obviously had a couple of cocktails.

"What the big idea?" he demanded, his face growing redder by the moment.

Jimmy flapped open his wallet, and showed him his badge. "Special Agent Petrowski. Our battery went dead. We need a charge."

The man gaped at Jimmy, then turned for a look at Joey. Gus was nowhere in sight.

"A *priest?"* the man said. His normal color was returning as he muffled a belch.

Jimmy smiled at the man. "He sure looks like one, doesn't he? That's Special Agent Muldoon. Drug dealers are always shocked to find out who he is. We'd love to chat, but we really do need a charge. Pull around our car, here. We'll use your cables."

"Of course, officer, of course."

The guy hurried to do the job, moving with the assurance of one who spent many weekend hours tinkering with the motor. It took him less than five minutes. The tails of his silk shirt were smudged with grease. Jimmy shook hands with him.

"We won't forget this," he told the guy. "You've been a great help."

"I always do what I can," the man said seriously, wiping his hands with an oily rag. "We got a lotta scuzzos runnin' around this country."

"Damn right we do. Happy New Year."

"You too, Officer." The man drove off. Jimmy and Joey hugged, as Gus appeared from behind a girder.

"I never would have fucking believed it if I hadn't heard it."

"Acting was one of my electives in college."

"Lawrence Fuckin' Olivier, here. Get in the car and let's get the fuck outta here, Agent Petrowski."

They all got in. Gus eased the idling car into gear and continued crossing the majestic span.

"Aaay, you see that?" Joey asked. "And you made fun of me for prayin'. See how it helped?"

Gus chuckled. "No offense, Father Gambuzza, but that's bullshit. The battery did not come back to life."

Joey shook his head. "Wasn't prayin' for a resurrected battery. I prayed for a *solution.* See, this is where people make their mistakes. You don't pray for specific things. People who pray for this item or that item, fuhgetaboutit, they get zip. God does not like being treated like a stock boy. All you can do is ask him for help."

"God has a big ego, is what you're saying."

"Aaay, Gus. If he can't have one, who can?"

Gus shook his head in admiration. "You are a top-shelf bullshit artist, Father Gambuzza."

Joey lowered his eyes in mock modesty. "I thank you, Brother Gambuzza. And by the way, I really do think you'd make a great priest."

"How's that?"

"What you were ready to do for me and Jimmy. Stay behind with the car, while we walked away. Don't you see? The whole Catholic faith boils down to one sentence—'This is my body, which shall be given up for you.' I tell you, Gus, you're a natural."

Gus pooh-poohed the praise, and turned to Jimmy. "*You* amaze me, brother. I really didn't think you had it in you."

"I didn't, until tonight. Tonight I learned that you do what you fuckin' have to do, and then you fuckin' get on with your fuckin' life."

"Amen," said Father Gambuzza. "Another great sermon for me to use. Just gotta pull out the 'fucks.' "

Gus couldn't hide a grin. "Could I give you just a little advice, Jimmy?"

"You're my big brother. You don't have to ask."

"Next time you're in a spot like that, go easy on the details. That drug dealer business. That's an embellishment. You want to tell people just enough to get by. Don't showboat, is what I'm sayin'."

"I'll remember that the next time I'm in the middle of a fuckin' bridge with a fuckin' dead battery in the middle of the fuckin' night."

Gus laughed out loud. "Oh, baby! That guy sounded Irish. Did he look Irish?"

"As Paddy's pig," Joey said.

"Figures. The Irish love emergencies. They're prejudiced as hell against everybody but themselves, but in an emergency they dive right in and help out without thinkin' first. Month from now it'll occur to him that maybe you weren't a cop." Gus looked back at Jimmy. "Goddam lucky thing the guy you stopped was Irish."

"Lucky is my middle name."

A harsh, insistent ringing sound filled the car. Father Joseph Gambuzza pulled a cellular phone from a holster on his hip, the thing Jimmy had bumped against and mistaken for a gun. A gun! He'd actually believed that this wonderful, gentle young man had plans to kill him!

Gus looked back at Jimmy and rolled his eyes. "Did I tell you they call him night and day?"

"Yeah, yeah, I understand, buddy," Joey said soothingly into the phone. "Aw, hey. Don't get upset. I'm on my way." He clicked off the phone and slid it back into the holster. "Blind Billy's in trouble."

"Aw, Jesus, what is that guy's problem?"

"I'm sorry, Gus, I've got to go see him."

"We'll all go," Gus said. "Got nothin' better to do, at this point. Ride'll charge up the battery, too."

Jimmy's elation suddenly evaporated to dizzy horror. During those delicious moments of forgiveness he'd actually managed to forget about the immediate problem, which remained, as far as he could tell, far from solved.

"We're going to see a blind man?"

Joey pursed his lips and swayed his head from side to side, *mezzo-mezzo*. "He's not exactly blind," the priest began.

Blind Billy lived in a remote section of Brooklyn whose residents were so far from the loop of city life that many lacked Social Security numbers. They dug the poisoned beaches for clams and dropped lobster pots in the shadow of the Verrazano-Narrows Bridge. They raised chickens and geese in their backyards, and even goats. One guy actually had two cows in his garage, and kept his neighbors from complaining about mooing and manure by keeping them supplied with fresh milk and cheese. Another man on that same block had no electricity. He lit his home with oil lamps.

Between these two residents lived Billy DiGiacomo, a seventy-year-old widower who'd never slept anywhere but in the house he was born in. All his life, Billy had gotten by doing odd jobs for people in the neighborhood, not prospering but never starving. He'd clean out a cellar, clip a hedge, rake a lawn—anything requiring minimal skills and moderate muscle. Many in the neighborhood thought he was mentally retarded. This was untrue. It *was* true that he was illiterate, having failed to learn how to read during his brief formal education. Billy happened to have dyslexia, a condition that, even if explained to Billy's neighbors, would have amounted, in their minds, to the same thing: a fuckin' retard.

And so, like all children set apart from the general population, Billy had the lonely privilege of being allowed to do as he pleased. In his case, freedom took the form of working in clay. He started off making ash trays, worked his way through the animal kingdom, and finally settled upon saints. They filled the shelves of his home, which Father Joseph Gambuzza visited upon the death of Billy's wife, who happened to be the sister of one of his parishioners.

Father Joey was awed. He was convinced that he'd discovered Grandma Moses in clay. The saint figures had lopsided bodies and arms that didn't match, but there was an integrity to the work distilled straight from the purity of the man's soul. No, Billy told the priest when all the mourners had left: he'd never sold anything, never even tried to.

"I think you should," Father Gambuzza suggested. "I could help you."

Perhaps the success of the project was as much a testament to Joey's marketing genius as it was to Billy's rough talent. Touching as Billy's creations were, they could easily have gotten lost in the cluttered, cutthroat world of religious articles. Crude statues made by an old man were one thing. Such statues made by a blind old man were surefire.

And so Blind Billy was born, even though the man's eyesight, spared from a lifetime of reading, was perfect. The little booklet looped around the head of each saint had a head shot of the somber artist, in jet-black glasses, on its cover. The accompanying text identified him only as "Blind Billy," and was tantalyzingly devoid of details that would lead anyone to his whereabouts. All anyone could find out from the booklet was that Blind Billy had lost his eyesight in a kiln explosion, and that his finest work happened after that tragedy. God, the booklet made clear, had taken one of the man's gifts and replaced it with another.

Of course, Father Gambuzza realized that none of Billy's work could be marketed locally. He suspected it was the sort of thing that would work in the Southwest, where retired people moved to the desert on glittering promises made by glossy-paged brochures. They swapped cold climates and big houses for nonstop heat and cozy, antiseptic "units" in "complexes." But what they were really after, Father Gambuzza understood, was what they could never have—eternal life.

How sad to uproot oneself so late in life, only to be repotted in such bitter soil! These people looked hard for something to believe in, and so were liable to see the face of Christ just about anywhere—in rock formations, clouds, the wood-grain pattern of a kitchen cabinet door.

It so happened that one of Father Gambuzza's parishioners, a retired bookie named Rocco Amoroso, got sucked in by such a brochure and left Brooklyn for the promise of Phoenix, Arizona. Lonely and depressed, he wrote to the priest of the mistake he'd made. The letter dropped vague hints about the possibility of suicide.

Father Gambuzza didn't write back. He phoned the man five minutes after he had finished reading the letter.

"Rocco," he began, "I need your help."

Within six weeks, Blind Billy Inc. was on the books as a Phoenix-based corporation, and three dozen foot-high statues—wrapped in bubble plastic, sealed in boxes—were delivered to Rocco's unit.

The challenge of a fresh hustle evaporated Rocco's depression as he made the rounds of religious articles shops. The sun-baked population went wild for the kiln-baked work. Blind Billy statues were an instant hit, and soon stood on Formica shelves in units all over Phoenix. The buyers were happy, Rocco was happy, Father Gambuzza was happy.

Only Billy himself fell into an occasional funk over the deceit that was filling his pockets as they'd never been filled before. As with so many other people, it hit him hardest on New Year's. Father Gambuzza understood exactly how bad it could be, which is why Blind Billy was among the privileged few who had the number to the priest's cellular phone.

"Aaay, I don't know what I'm going to do with this guy," Joey sighed. "For the first time in his life he's got money, but he can't enjoy himself. On top of that, he's paranoid. Thinks an investigator's going to show up from Phoenix and arrest him."

"For what?"

"Fraud. Pretending to be blind. So all day he walks around in dark glasses, bumpin' into walls."

"You're kiddin' me!"

"You'll see when he answers the door. Gus, he wants to come clean. What can I do?"

"Easter," Jimmy said.

Gus and Joey turned around to look at him.

"Tell him to hang in there until Easter," Jimmy continued. "He wakes up Easter Sunday, and he can see. Let it be a miracle. Everybody loves a miracle, right?"

Joey nodded. "Goddam if that wouldn't work," he murmured. "Be fantastic for sales, too."

They were in Staten Island, now. Gus made the first turn he could to begin the trip back over the bridge.

"An Easter miracle," Gus chuckled. "Fucking fantastic. Funny how solutions come out of nowhere, isn't it? Still gives me gooseflesh, after all these years."

CHAPTER 10

Blind Billy opened the door on Joey's first knock. The priest had to laugh.

"Billy, Billy. What were you, standing behind it?"

"I'm jumpy, is all."

Scant white hair decorated the edges of the old man's scalp. He wore a ratty bathrobe, slippers, and round-lensed sunglasses on his bony face. He reached to remove the shades until he noticed Jimmy.

"It's okay, take 'em off," Joey said. "He's my other brother."

Blind Billy kept them on. "I never knew you had another brother."

"He's been away."

Blind Billy swallowed, stared at Jimmy. "You escaped?"

"I'm a fuckin' architect," Jimmy said.

"Hey, Billy," the priest said. "You gonna let us in, or what?"

"Come in, come in."

When they were all inside, Blind Billy pulled off

the shades to reveal sad, bright-blue eyes, like those of a child whose bike has just been stolen.

He extended his hand. "I'm Billy."

"I'm Jimmy."

They shook. Billy's hand was delicate, but the skin of his palm was as rough as a snake's.

"It's an honor to meet you."

"I wouldn't go that far, Billy."

Blind Billy led the way through rooms cluttered with red clay statues. There were angels, baby Jesuses, Marys, Josephs, and a variety of heavenly residents Jimmy couldn't begin to identify. They were all over the floors, the shelves, the tabletops. It was as if they were breeding.

"Jesus," Joey said, "you're backed up here, Billy. How come this stuff's still in the house?"

"The package man jacked the rates up again. Says the price of bubble wrap just doubled. My ass, it doubled. Wants the cash up front, the son of a bitch. Excuse my mouth, Father."

"I'll talk to him," Joey said.

"I'll talk to him," Gus said.

Joey smiled. "See that? We're here two minutes, and already one problem is solved." He led Billy to a couch, where they sat down together. A double plume of dust rose as their asses hit the cushions.

"What's eating you, Billy? Got the blues on New Year's?"

"Had a dream about my dead wife again."

"Same dream?"

Billy shook his head, wiped his eyes. "In this one she's an angel in heaven, and when I die I go straight to see her. I'm wearin' wings and everything, but she's cryin'. 'Catherine,' I say, 'what's wrong? We're together in heaven, everything's beautiful!' And she says, 'Yeah, but God says you gotta be blind for real.' "

Blind Billy snapped his fingers. "Like that, the lights go off. I'm a blind angel. I'm flyin' around, bumpin' into things."

"Then what happens?"

"I wake up sweatin' like I just run around the block a hundred times."

Joey sat back and exhaled, puffing out his cheeks. "Wow. Some dream." He might have been commenting on a long home run.

"Father, what can I do?" Billy whined.

"Well, for starters, you can turn down the heat. My God, what is it, ninety degrees in here?"

"I got some statues cookin' downstairs."

"Christ, you could grow orchids in here."

Blind Billy pulled at the lapels of his bathrobe in frustration. "Father, I'm afraid to go to sleep."

Joey patted his shoulder. "I've got an idea. Actually, it's my brother's idea." Joey looked at Jimmy and winked. Jimmy turned to look at Gus, and his soul sank. His big brother was gone.

"Gus?"

Jimmy prowled the dim hallway of the house, careful not to bump the statues lined along the baseboards. Light from an open door at the end of the hall beckoned. Jimmy made his way to the door, which led to a set of rickety cellar steps.

"You down there, Gus?"

The temperature seemed to rise five degrees with each step down, until he reached the dirt-floored cellar. A bright bare bulb burned from a hanging wire, directly above a long, rough-plank wooden table holding two dozen angel statues, each with a lopsided halo. Gus examined the enormous furnace as he lit a Marlboro.

"Ingenious," he said, more to himself than to Jimmy. "See this furnace? The top compartment's been added on. It's where he's got all his statues, cookin' away."

Jimmy studied the thing, and saw the fresh metal seam where the compartment had been added. It was a Rube Goldberg of a creation, with oddly shaped duct pipes leading to the main chimney. All of it, Jimmy was certain, was in wild violation of whatever laws governed the building of furnaces.

Gus squatted, opened the heavy metal door of the main furnace, and squinted in at the bed of red-glowing coals.

"Okay," he said, "let's get her."

It was a nonsequitur to Jimmy's ears; he had to think all the way back to how the night had begun. Her, the female Hispanic, the ballast in the trunk of the car, the cause for this unlikeliest of family reunions.

A tingling Jimmy followed Gus to a slanted cellar door, which pushed open onto Blind Billy's backyard. All over the scrubby grass were statues that seemed to be melting into red puddles, having endured endless rainstorms. Jimmy realized these were Blind Billy's discards, the statues that for one reason or another did not make the grade, and were set out here without a protective baking. And so they dissolved with each rain from the feet up, until Billy's little lawn resembled a boccie court scattered with angel heads instead of balls.

"Watch the heads," Gus warned. "Last thing you want to do now is twist an ankle, trippin' over a head."

Gus walked briskly to the street, like a Catholic school child during a fire drill. Jimmy could feel his heartbeat in his throat, and tried in vain to swallow it back. The unbelievably calm Ghost Gambuzza pulled his car keys from his pocket and slowly selected the right one (no rush, get it right the first time), looked all around, and opened the trunk.

"No blood," he murmured. "Lucky."

Jimmy's teeth chattered. "Why would there be?"

"Sometimes it drains out of them later. I was ready for a lake in here. We caught a break."

Gus indicated with a nod of his chin which end Jimmy should take. "I lead the way. Remember, it's a rug. We are carrying a rug."

"I had this lesson already."

Reaching for the rug, Jimmy wondered for the first time about this stranger's parents. Were they alive? Were they still together? And when their daughter was born, did they take turns getting up to feed her at night, work second jobs to make ends meet, tie her little shoes at the playground?

They got her up on their shoulders. Jimmy's eyes went misty, and he momentarily lost his footing. Gus made up for the slip, steadying the load from his end.

"I told you to watch out for the fucking heads."

"I'm all right. She feels lighter, doesn't she?"

A fierce, over-the-shoulder glare from Gus: What if somebody's fucking listening? Haven't you learned anything at all from me in all these hours we've spent together?

Gus moved slowly down the cellar steps, silent as the Ghost that he was. Only when they were back inside and had set the thing on the dirt floor and closed the slanted door did he speak again.

"You can go back upstairs now, if you want."

"No," Jimmy said, "I'll stay."

A tickle of a smile from Gus; Jimmy suspected that he'd just passed some secret test of loyalty.

The door to the steps leading to the house opened, and Father Joey stepped inside. There was an odd expression on his face, a blend of regret and resignation. He closed the door, leaned against it and sighed.

Gus jerked his chin in the direction of the ceiling. "Where the hell's Blind Billy?"

"He's in the bathroom," Joey said. "It's all right, his prostate's acting up. He'll be there for a while."

Father Joey approached the rug, and made the sign of the cross over it. "We didn't know your name, but we're sorry that you are gone. From the little we know, yours sounded like an angry life. May you find happiness now." The tears in his eyes looked real enough.

"Amen," Gus said. He squatted to lift the rug. Then they all froze at the distant sound of Blind Billy's voice calling out, "You guys down there?"

Gus looked at Joey. "Prostate, huh?"

Joey spread his hands. "He usually takes forever. What the hell can I say?"

Billy's slow footsteps sounded like approaching drumbeats as he made his way down the steps.

Jimmy's heart felt as if it might burst. "We're taking her back out, right Gus? We're taking her back to the car, aren't we?"

Gus shook his head. "Fuck no. Enough runnin' around, already." Gus pointed at the door Blind Billy was heading for.

"Jimmy, put your shoulder to that door. And if you don't want to spend the next twenty-five years of your life dodging horny black men who got nothing to do but lift weights all day, you will *not* let that old man in here."

Jimmy took his place at the door, hand on the knob, shoulder to the wood. He heard the footsteps stop, felt the knob turning, and then the old man was pushing the door from the other side.

"Guys? Guys, you in there?"

Jimmy thought he heard more approaching footsteps. It took him a moment to realize that it was the pulse of his own blood he was hearing, slamming against his eardrums.

Joey opened the furnace door wide, holding his head back to keep his eyebrows from being singed. Even from five feet back, his face glowed red in the incredible heat of the fire, like a chunk of the sun being held hostage. Then he took a pink-beaded rosary from his pocket, crossed himself, knelt before the closed side of the furnace, bowed his head and began to pray.

The door boomed against Jimmy's shoulder. Jimmy was jolted, but held it closed. Blind Billy muttered puzzled curses on the other side.

Gus seemed to move in slow motion. He squatted and lifted the rug in the middle, holding it like a sagging log meant to be used as a battering ram.

Walking backwards, he paced off the steps to the open door like a shot-putter measuring his approach steps, took a deep breath, trotted toward the door and shoved the thing in with a motion that landed it smack in the middle of the coals. Flames curled around the rug until its ancient colors began to burn blue-green.

Jimmy held the door closed, though Blind Billy tattooed its other side with blows of his fist. Streaming with sweat, Gus walked to Jimmy and held out his hand. Jimmy moved to shake it, but Gus slapped it away.

"What did we, just meet?" he whispered. "Give me the tie."

"Huh?"

"The fuckin' pink tie."

"Why?"

" 'Police seek a man last seen whipping a pink tie around on the dance floor.' "

Jimmy dug the tie out of his pocket and handed it to Gus, who hurled it into the furnace as if it were a snake that meant to bite him. He shut the furnace door and wiped his face with a handkerchief, to the sound of a nearly hysterical Billy bashing at the door.

"Wait till there's a lull," Gus whispered. "Then rush the fuck away from the door."

Jimmy waited. Sure enough, the old man grew tired of banging on the other side. He stopped to take deep breaths. Jimmy jumped away from the door and Joey got to his feet.

The priest brushed dirt from his knees. "He's gonna come flyin' in here," Joey predicted.

"Don't be lookin' at the door," Gus instructed. "Everybody come to this table. Act like you're checking out these statues."

And so when Blind Billy came rushing in thirty seconds later, the Gambuzza brothers stood casually gathered around the statue table, like browsers at a flea market.

Tears of frustration streaked Blind Billy's face. "Youse didn't hear me knockin'?" he snarled. "For Christ's sakes, what are youse all *doin'* down here?"

Father Joey said, "Knocking? Why didn't you just come in?"

"The fuckin' *door* was jammed!" Blind Billy

screamed, flecks of spit flying from his mouth. "I mean, Jesus *Christ!* Didn't youse hear me?"

Father Joey rushed to Billy's side, and slid a supportive arm across his shoulders. "Hey, Billy, you feel all right? You look pale."

"I been out there bangin', and bangin' . . ." He sputtered, pulled at the wisps of hair on his head. "Youse all abandoned me up there!"

"Billy," Joey said, "I just wanted to show them what you've been workin' on. Stuff looks great."

Billy eyed them suspiciously. "Youse really didn't hear me?"

"Well," Joey said, "the furnace is kinda loud. Listen, forget about that, let me take you upstairs. You could use a drink."

"I musta banged on that door for ten minutes!"

"Billy, Billy. How are you ever going to get over your problems if you dwell on them like this?" Joey and Blind Billy went up together.

Gus slumped on the bench by the statue table and let his arms hang like lead bars between his knees, truly relaxed at last.

"We'll let it burn a little," he told Jimmy, "then we'll pull the damper and shake a little more coal over it." He grinned. "Nothin' to worry about now, brother. That's the hottest fire in all of Brooklyn."

Jimmy's eyes brimmed with tears. He moved to the bench and sat beside Gus.

"You'll get over it, believe me," Gus assured him. He stared into Jimmy's eyes and managed a weary smile. "Look at you. You should see what I see, Jimmy. You know, I didn't like the pretentious uptight asshole I picked up in SoHo tonight. But I gotta tell you, I like the guy I'm sittin' next to in this fuckin' crazy cellar. These few hours together, you really did grow up."

"Think so?"

"I *know* so. Hey, one of us changed. I know it wasn't me."

Gus put his hand behind Jimmy's neck, pulled his head close and kissed him on the forehead. Jimmy couldn't look him in the eye.

" 'S'matta now, buddy?"

"Gus. I'm so sorry about Carol."

Gus's eyes flared in surprise before going wet with tears. "Joey told you, huh?"

"Yeah."

"You really didn't know she died, huh?"

"How could I know? I would have come, I swear to God I would have come, Gus. You know how I felt about her."

Gus bit his upper lip, wiped his eyes.

"Don't be mad at me, Gus. I'm just so, so sorry."

Gus nodded. "She was special," he choked. They embraced, long and hard, as the furnace popped and sizzled.

Jimmy followed Gus back upstairs and down the hall to Blind Billy's living room, where the smiling sculptor grabbed Jimmy by the cheeks and delivered identical bristly kisses to each one.

"You're a genius!" Blind Billy all but sobbed, and it took Jimmy a moment to realize he was talking about his Miracle at Easter idea.

Oh, but they couldn't leave just yet: Blind Billy found a bottle of Cold Duck at the back of his refrigerator, dug out four dusty jelly jars, and poured a toast to the Gambuzza brothers. They clinked and drank. Blind Billy wiped his sweaty forehead with his sleeve.

"Cheez, you know, it is hot in here. Damn if I didn't overload that furnace." He draped an arm across the shoulders of Jimmy, who felt as if his stomach were munching on his liver.

"But better too much coal than too little," he continued. "If it ain't hot enough, the statues chip and get chalky." He lightly squeezed Jimmy's neck in the vise of his elbow. "Come on, drink up. Gus, Father Joe, what's with this brother of yours? You sure he's a Gambuzza?"

"Absolutely," Gus replied. "But hey, there's always blood tests." He looked at his watch. "Billy, we gotta be goin.' "

"One thing," Billy pleaded. "Father Joe, would you bless my house for the New Year?"

"Aaay," said the priest, "I thought you'd never ask."

The three men bowed their heads as Father Joseph Gambuzza mumbled in Latin and made the sign of the cross toward each of Blind Billy's walls. They were the only people awake in the neighborhood at that hour, and the only creatures, with the exception of one. Two doors down, in the heated garage of a retired plumber named Alonzo Calderain, a black leopard named Camille restlessly paced the confines of her cage, roused for the first time since her illegal arrival from the jungles of Africa by the smell of roasting human flesh. The creature had grown fat and lazy in captivity. For the first time in years, she took a swat at her cage door. It popped open, no testament to the animal's prowess. Calderain, grown fat and lazy in retirement, had neglected to lock it after the evening feed.

* * *

Blind Billy put on his sunglasses and insisted upon walking the Gambuzzas to the car. It was Joey who first noticed the leopard, loping along in the middle of the foggy street.

"What the hell is that?"

Blind Billy pushed his sunglasses up on his forehead. "Oh, my God, lemme run and call Alonzo!"

He fled to the house. The leopard's ears perked up at the sound of Blind Billy's footsteps. She began walking toward the brothers in a loose-shouldered stroll, her big belly hanging low.

Gus stood with his hands in his pockets. "Nobody move," he said. "Just stand abso-fuckin'-lutely still."

"Let's get in the car," Joey said.

"Don't move," Gus insisted.

The leopard was slowly getting closer. Jimmy couldn't take it. The wooden leg from a broken kitchen chair was sticking out from Blind Billy's curbside garbage can. Jimmy grabbed it.

"I'll handle this," he said.

"Get the fuck back here, Jimmy," Gus said, barely moving his lips to speak, but Jimmy went into the street on shaky legs, holding the stick out like a sword. His heart hammered, his throat palpitated, but he was going to protect his beloved brothers if it was the last thing he did.

The leopard stopped walking. Jimmy continued to approach it, and when the stick was a foot from the animal's nose, a funny thing happened. She sat down, yawned, and pawed idly at the stick the way a playful kitten might have.

Jimmy didn't know what to do. He suddenly felt that his courage was dissolving into foolishness, a belief that was confirmed when he pulled the stick back and the animal swatted at it, knocking it from Jimmy's hand.

"Camille!"

A fat, scowling man came trotting over from his house, his terry cloth robe flapping over striped pajamas. In his hand was a leash. He slipped its collar over the animal's head, stroked her head, and kissed the top of it. Then he looked angrily up at Jimmy, who now had Gus and Joey at his sides.

"What are you teasin' her for with that stick? Huh?"

Jimmy had no answer. He spread his hands to begin making some kind of an explanation, and only then noticed that the back of his right hand was bleeding from a long, slender gash.

He looked at it in wonder. "I got scratched by a leopard," Jimmy said.

Blind Billy came running out. "Is everybody okay?"

Alonzo pointed at Jimmy. "This guy here was teasin' my Camille."

"I wasn't teasing her!"

"Yeah? What was all that funny business with the stick?"

"I was just protecting us!"

Alonzo squinted one eye at Jimmy. "The truth, now. Did she run to you, or didjoo go to her?"

Jimmy looked at Gus, then Joey. He swallowed. "Well. I guess I went to her."

"All right, then."

Blind Billy said, "What'd you tease her for?"

"*Tease* her! Jesus Christ, Billy, what was I supposed to do? You ran to the house, scared shitless!"

Blind Billy shook his head. "No, no. I was afraid, Gah-fah-bid, she was gonna run away. She did that, she wouldn't stand a chance, poor thing. Coulda wound up dead, or in a zoo."

Gus and Jimmy couldn't help giggling. Alonzo sighed.

"All right, all right, you had no way of knowin.' No hard feelings, all right? Come inside, I got somethin' for your hand." He wrinkled his nose, turned to Billy.

"You cookin' somethin'?"

"I ain't lit my oven since my wife died."

"I smell meat. You guys smell meat?"

"I don't smell a thing," Gus said.

"Well, come on and let's fix your hand."

Alonzo brought Camille back to her cage, and was careful to lock it. He got a bottle of hydrogen peroxide and cleaned Jimmy's wound before bandaging it with gauze and tape.

"Is that enough to kill the germs?" Jimmy asked. Alonzo seemed insulted by the question.

"Course it is. Look at her cage. Three times a week I change the straw. Whaddaya think, I treat her like an animal?"

Jimmy went to the car, where Gus and Joey were waiting. Joey was in the back seat this time, and insisted that Jimmy sit in front.

Jimmy didn't argue with him. He got in, closed the door, and slapped the dashboard with his hand.

"Would you believe I apologized to that guy for disturbing his leopard?"

Gus reached across, grabbed Jimmy's head in both hands, and kissed his temple before starting the car.

"What's that for?"

"For having brass balls. *Madonna,* that was a beautiful thing you did. How were you supposed to know she was domesticated? Huh? You were only thinkin' about us. Is this a beautiful family, or what?"

* * *

It was nearly four A.M. by the time they dropped Joey off at the rectory. He had time for a brief nap before he had to get up and say the six o'clock Mass.

"Pain in my ass," Joey said. "Nothin' but widows. They make faces if I yawn. Aaay, but what am I complainin' about?" He turned to Jimmy. "We're not gonna be strangers, are we?"

"Of course not. Thanks for everything."

"Hey. You kiddin'?"

The three of them hugged and kissed before Joey trotted off. As Gus was pulling away from the curb, he patted Jimmy's back.

"Now for the hard part," he said, and Jimmy felt like a man who'd just spent twelve hours in the dentist's chair, only to be told that the pain was about to begin. What the fuck else could happen? Did they have to return to Blind Billy's to bank the ashes and sift through them for earrings, fillings, and gold teeth?

"*What* fuckin' hard part?"

"Mom's waiting to see you."

Jimmy's heart sank, touched bottom, and made its way back to the surface. "You said you didn't tell her."

"Hey, I lied. So kill me."

"I've done enough killing for one night."

Gus held up an admonishing finger. "Don't even friggin' kid about that. Just sit back. Relax. Our problems are solved. Take a little nap, if you want. I'll wake you when we get there."

Jimmy slumped back in the seat and shut his eyes. He took long, even breaths and tried to fall asleep, but he could sooner have flapped his arms and flown to Australia. This was the one trip he'd vowed to himself that he would never, ever take again. Gus knew how he felt.

"Gettin' rid of the thing was easy compared to this, huh?"

Jimmy nodded, his eyes shut. "Piece of cake."

"You'll handle it. You're a fuckin' leopard tamer, man. This is just a trip back home."

"So how come I'm sweating?"

"Aaay, you think too much. There's no ghosts, no monsters. Just a little old lady and her grandsons."

Jimmy swallowed. "Mah's a little old lady now?"

Gus rolled his eyes. "Whaddaya think, we dipped her in amber when you left? Twenty years, Jim-a-nootz. Twenty friggin' years. You even remember what your old room looks like?"

"I remember," Jimmy said. But what he meant was that he could not forget it. Especially the last time he walked out of it.

It was early September, but the warmth of summer did not linger that year. The radiators in the Gambuzza home were on, and the one in Jimmy's room whistled steadily when night fell. That was all right. Jimmy could endure the noise for one more night.

He stood in his room, looking at the two zippered suitcases containing all his worldly goods. On his otherwise bare desk top were his wallet, which held $358 in cash, a train ticket to Boston, and his brand-new draft card. Whenever he needed assurance that he was indeed a man, Jimmy looked at his draft card. When he needed assurance about his mission, he looked at the train ticket. ONE WAY, it said. Damn right. Only Jimmy knew that he'd never again be coming home.

He went to the window for one last look at the Albertini yard. Enzo slept on the lawn, his enormous head atop his clublike front paws. He was old, now. If you opened the gate, he probably wouldn't even bother stepping out of the yard. Enzo yawned enormously, baring yellow fangs. Sticky threads of saliva bridged his upper and lower jaws.

A hand on Jimmy's shoulder. He whirled to face Gus, handsome in brown slacks and a brown leather jacket.

"Gonna be late for your own party, kid." He grinned a big-brother grin. "My brother the architect. Never thought I'd hear myself say it."

He held out a hand as if for a shake, surprising Jimmy, for Gus was not one for handshakes. But instead of meeting flesh, Jimmy's palm came into contact with a hard wad of paper, which turned out to be a roll of twenty-dollar bills.

"What's this?"

"Little walkin'-around money."

"I don't get it, Gus."

"Hey, you're walkin' around Boston, you see something you like, you get it. It's just a thou."

"You don't have to do this, Gus. I saved up. I've been working."

"Yeah, yeah, I know. How many White Castle burgers did you flip this summer, a few million? That's got nothing to do with my gift. You're my brother. You're going to college. You don't take it, all kinds of bad luck'll follow you." Gus laughed. "Listen to me. I sound as superstitious as Pop, rest his soul."

Jimmy put the wad of cash on top of his bureau. It started to open, like a bird ruffling its feathers. The sight of it made Jimmy a little nauseous. How the hell had Gus earned that money, anyway? Jimmy didn't want to think about it. Gus came and went at all hours, and sometimes disappeared for a day or two. Carol never asked questions. *Nobody* asked questions. They were all living better than they ever had while

Thomas Gambuzza was alive, and nosiness could only jeopardize the situation.

"You gonna take it, or what?"

He had to take it. He couldn't let Gus think he disapproved of him in any way. "Thanks, Gus," he said softly.

Gus patted his shoulder. "Buy some fuckin' clothes that look like somethin', for Christ's sake. Where the fuck do you shop, anyway? The math major aisle?"

Jimmy forced a smile. "Gus."

"I'm listening."

Jimmy felt a lump growing in his throat. "You've been really good to me."

Gus shrugged. "You all right?"

"Yeah. Fine. I just wanted to say that I appreciate everything you've done for me. For all of us."

Gus's eyebrows knotted. "You sick?"

"No! What makes you think I'm sick?"

"It's just that this is how people usually talk when they get back the bad biopsy."

"Goddam it, Gus, I'm just trying to tell you that I love you!"

Jimmy was surprised to feel his eyes go wet, and the blur prevented him from seeing that Gus had also gone misty.

"Well, that's good," Gus finally managed to say. "I'm glad." He put his hand on Jimmy's neck, gave it a squeeze. "You know, in the history of this crazy house, that's probably the first time one man ever told another man that he loves him."

"I mean it, Gus. You're a good guy."

Gus sighed, wiped his eyes. "Let's go downstairs. You know how I feel about emotions."

"No, I don't. How *do* you feel about them?"

"They're like the toys my son leaves on the floor.

Lots of fun. Lots of laughs. But you can trip over 'em on your way to the bathroom in the middle of the night."

Downstairs, the Gambuzzas feasted on lasagna, roast chicken, and green salad. Gus sat at the head of the table. Across from him sat Fiorentina, as always in black. Jimmy sat beside Carol on one side of the table. Across from them were eleven-year-old Joey and five-year-old Gus, Jr., delighting as always in each other's company. They were uncle and nephew by biology, but they behaved like brothers.

"You hafta call me 'Uncle Joey,' " Joey teased. "I'm your uncle, you know."

Little Gus looked distressed. "Is that true, Mommy?"

"Yes it is, sweetheart."

Little Gus's face darkened. "I don't wanna call him 'Uncle Joey.' "

"You don't have to," Gus assured him. "Joey's just kiddin.' Keep on callin' him Joey."

"Hey, I'm his uncle!" Joey shouted. "I can tell him when to go to bed. Go to bed, Little Gus!"

The children began to argue, and as Gus smoothed things out, Carol turned to Jimmy.

"I'm so happy for you, Jimmy. We sure are going to miss you around here."

"Me too you, Carol."

She patted his hand. "Thanksgiving'll be here before you know it. You'll come back to visit and be bored with us."

"Aw, come on, Carol."

"Hey. It happens to all college boys."

He could barely stand to look her in the eye for more than a few seconds. If anything, she was more beautiful than she was the night Jimmy met her, six years earlier. With Gus's crazy hours, Jimmy sometimes wound up spending more time with Carol than he did. They'd sit up late waiting for him to return, discussing books and doing crossword puzzles. He carried her groceries in from the car. He read bedtime stories to Little Gus.

Jimmy noticed now that there were a few lines in Carol's forehead, undoubtedly the result of worry about her husband's career. A career he never would have had, if Jimmy hadn't opened that gate.

"Some day," Carol said, "I'll go back to college. Brooklyn College, maybe, after Little Gus is grown. I could do it."

"Of course you could, Carol. So could Gus."

Carol smiled sadly. "No," she gently disagreed. "I'm afraid Gus's education is complete."

A clinking sound; Gus was tapping the side of his wine glass with a spoon. "A toast to my brother, if you please."

The adults hoisted their wine glasses, while the kids held up milk in jelly jars. Everybody clinked glasses, and then Fiorentina entered the room with a cake in the shape of the Chrysler Building, Jimmy's favorite skyscraper.

Everybody cheered. Jimmy felt the tears well up again.

"I did it from a picture," Fiorentina said, in her always quaking voice. "If it don't look like the Chrysler Building, don't get mad."

"It's beautiful, Mom." Jimmy rose to kiss her. The children took turns blowing out the candles on the cake. Gus stood over it with a knife and hesitated.

"Shame to cut this thing," he said.

"Go on, cut it," Fiorentina said. "Nothing lasts forever."

Gus nodded, jerked his head toward Fiorentina. "My mother, the existentialist baker."

Just as Gus sank the knife in to cut the first slice, the doorbell rang. Joey and Little Gus ran to answer it. They returned moments later, with Mr. Albertini himself.

Even Gus was stunned. It was the first time Albertini had ever set foot in the Gambuzza home. He was slim and gray, and wore workman-type clothing, but everything about him radiated power and force.

"Hello, Boss," Gus said softly. "Sit down, please."

"Sorry, I don't have time," he said softly. "Only then did Jimmy notice two burly men in overcoats and gray hats standing at the edge of the dining room.

Jimmy felt his temples pound. He wasn't going to make it. They'd finally figured out who had opened the gate, and were here to take vengeance. Or maybe they'd known all along and just teased it out to the last night, the very last night . . .

Albertini jerked his head toward Jimmy. "You're the college boy." These were the first words he'd ever spoken to Jimmy.

"Yes," Jimmy managed to reply. Albertini turned to one of his bodyguards, and was handed a long package wrapped in plain brown paper. He passed it to Jimmy.

"Going-away present," Albertini said. "Go ahead, open it."

Jimmy obeyed. The package contained a T square.

"You're gonna be an architect, right? So you'll need one of those. That's a T square."

"He awreddy has one," Little Gus chirped. Albertini glared at the boy, then broke into laughter, revealing snowy-white dentures. It was the cue for everybody in the room to laugh.

"All right, then," Albertini said. "So now you have one for here, and one for college."

"Thank you," Jimmy managed to say. Albertini nodded, and walked around the table to shake hands with Jimmy. His grip was like iron. He peered into Jimmy's eyes as if he were trying to read his mind.

"Good luck, son. See you when you come back, right?"

"Yes, sir."

Albertini smiled strangely, as if he'd picked up one of Jimmy's thoughts. Then he turned suddenly and left with his men. They'd been in the house for less than five minutes.

"That was a first," Gus said after they were gone. Jimmy excused himself from the table and went upstairs. He had to change his pants, as he'd wet them. The next morning he rushed to catch an early train to Boston, telling everyone he'd see them at Thanksgiving. By the time Joey and Little Gus woke up, Jimmy was long gone.

"Poor Mom," Jimmy said, more to himself than Gus. "Scared of her own shadow. What a life she's had."

Gus chuckled. "I don't know. She might surprise you."

"Oh yeah? How?"

"Not long after you left, she got official notification that Pop was dead. They do that after someone's been missing long enough. Just a stupid little letter from the government, but it did the trick."

"How do you mean?"

"Guess she finally believed the old prick was really gone for good, that he wasn't gonna suddenly stomp into the house, screamin' for his cigarettes. You'll see, you'll see. Look, baby, we're here."

His heart hammered as they approached the small, dirty red brick house with its low ceilings and mean little heat-hoarding windows—the home that made Jimmy swear to himself as a kid that some day he'd live in tall rooms bursting with light and air. Even his dreams had avoided the memory of this, danced around it as if it were the hole of a volcano. Next door, the same forbidding fence guarded the Albertini property, and the two gas globes burned away.

No; there were *three* of them. Jimmy walked onto the property that the city's boldest newspaperman wouldn't dare to tread upon and went to see who the third flame burned for. It was in a smaller globe, set apart from the flames for the dead boys. BELOVED ENZO, said the Gothic lettering on the small brass plaque beneath it.

He couldn't help laughing, a short, hard chuckle that ended abruptly: a Gus-laugh, and where the hell had his big brother gone? He stood on the family porch, beckoning for Jimmy to join him.

They walked right into the house, as this was still the Sort of Neighborhood Where You Could Leave Your Doors Unlocked.

Smells of home, true home, undeniable home: roast chicken from a hundred dinners ago, furniture polish, the strange, nostril-tickling odor of something between food and cleanser, not one, not the other, but undeniably home. Lights were on. Jimmy glanced at his watch; it was 4:17 A.M. A tall young man and a teenage boy appeared. Both of them had Italian-shaped features, but blond hair and light skin.

"I want you to say hello to somebody," Gus said. The boys didn't budge. Jimmy said to Gus Jr., "Do you remember me?"

"Not really."

"That's all right. I'm your Uncle Jimmy." He turned to the teenager. "You I never met. I'm your Uncle Jimmy."

"I figured if you were his uncle, you were also my uncle."

"Aaay, Lance," Gus said, "don't be a wise guy."

The boys offered their hands for firm shakes. A short woman in a magnolia-pattern nightgown and shocking rusty-blond permed hair entered the vestibule. She suddenly plunged forward to embrace Jimmy around his hips.

"Oh my God, my son, *my son!"*

Jimmy gulped. *"Mom?!"*

"I changed my hair," she said, her face against his shirt front. "Oh, don't say anything. Just don't say anything yet."

Jimmy turned for a look at Gus, who clearly had not told her he was coming. The big man shrugged, unzipped his jacket.

"Hey, so I lied twice. Sue me."

Twenty minutes later Jimmy was up in his old room, in the top bunk of a bed he was sharing with Lance. As he lay on his back, a model airplane dangled within a foot of his nose from the low ceiling that once suffocated him, but now gave comfort. He was home, really home, in a bed above a nephew he might never have known. The kid snored deeply and evenly, paced by the clean dreams of an adolescent. What would his life be like? Or anyone's? Better yet, how the hell did the son of Ghost Gambuzza come to get a name like "Lance"?

It hit him—Carol must have named him after someone in her family, back in Indiana. A wheat farmer, maybe, a man who gaged distances by acres instead of blocks and could tell the time by looking at the sun.

And Gus had allowed him to be so named. My God, Jimmy told himself, how he must have loved her. Yet another way in which his big brother was the far, far better man.

Jimmy fell asleep to the whistling of the same old radiator. It sounded like a lullaby.

CHAPTER 11

Jimmy was the first one awake, rising from blank dreams to bump his head on the model plane. There was no confusion, no sense of where-am-I as he opened his eyes in his old room for the first time in twenty years.

He was careful not to wake Lance as he climbed down past the boy, crept to the bathroom, and peed for the first time in ten hours. Here was the same tiny-tiled floor, a checkerboard of black and white, plus the lion-pawed tub with a tongue-shaped green water stain from a drip that had been falling since his childhood. The taps were the large, chubby-looking porcelain kind, with hairline cracks like the veins in an old lady's palms.

"Why not?"

He plugged the drain with a fat rubber stopper, turned on both taps, took off his clothes, and stepped in. He pulled the bandage off his hand and examined the crescent-shaped scar. Already it had a good, hard scab that could stand a soaking.

When was the last time he'd washed himself with

Ivory soap? He felt like a child, until he stood to lather himself all over with the light white cake. Angry-looking black pubic hairs clung to it, a screaming reminder that he was not a kid but a grown man, one who'd watched a woman die not half a day earlier.

Watched a woman die? Was that how he thought about it, now? What a difference a few hours with your big brother can make! Jimmy no longer thought of himself as a murderer, or a manslaughter-er, or even a woman-shover. His role in the tragedy had been reduced to witness. And at this rate, in a few hours' time, he'd be thinking of himself as . . . *the victim.* Aaay, are you kiddin'? She banged my balls, dropped dead, and left me to dispose of her body! Talk about selfish!

He picked the hairs out of the soap, rinsed himself clean, and dried off with a stiff towel that hung from a rack on the door. His mother had a clothes dryer, but she persisted in hanging laundry on the line—outdoors in fair weather, down in the cellar in bad.

"The dryer eats the clothes," he remembered her saying. "See the lint it makes? That's your clothes getting eaten."

That was the mother he remembered, with her graying hair up in a tight bun. Speaking in semimournful tones, no matter what the subject was. Hardly speaking at all, in fact, except about things like the perils of clothing-eating appliances.

With mild disgust, he slipped into yesterday's clothes, underwear and all. It was the first time in years that he'd worn the same clothing two days in a row, but at least his body was clean. He looked through the medicine cabinet to borrow Gus's razor, but all he could find was a straight razor, the bone-handled job his father had used. Its blade was peppered with stubble and dried soap.

"My God, Gus shaves with Pop's razor."

He'd just stepped outside the bathroom door when he felt a thin hand grip his elbow.

"You're like me," his mother whispered. "Can't sleep late, huh?"

"Not really."

She squeezed his elbow. "We're the only ones, Jimmy. The rest of them, you could blow a bugle, they wouldn't get up before nine. *Madonna,* what I gotta do to get those boys up. Thank God they can sleep late today. Come on, come downstairs, we'll have breakfast."

She held his arm all the way to the kitchen, the bottom of her bathrobe dragging over the floor as she led him.

Coffee was already made. She poured a cup for Jimmy from an aluminum pot with a glass cap, the kind that allowed you to see the coffee bubbling up. Just about everything in the kitchen was as he remembered it, except for a small microwave oven. She saw Jimmy looking at it as she fried bacon.

"Gus gave me that. I don't use it. What am I gonna microwave? What the hell kind of machine cooks food but don't heat up the pan? Aaay, it gives me the creeps."

Jimmy's scalp jumped. This was not the woman he'd known, the frail creature who'd never ventured an opinion or said "hell." She was shorter but bolder, older but stronger, a presence, a force, a person who was not about to fade into the wallpaper. And she was making his breakfast with pleasure, the way a friend would do it, not a servant.

"You want juice? Let me squeeze you some juice."

"No, thanks. Mom, I'm so sorry I stayed away."

"Know what? Let's not talk about it today. We got time. I'm just grateful that I wasn't toes-up when you decided to return. Okay, Jimmy?"

They embraced. "I gotta do the bacon," she said, breaking the embrace. Footsteps sounded above. She looked at the ceiling and grinned. "One of them smelled the bacon. That's the only way I can get them up. Aaay, what am I complaining for, they're good boys. Gus Junior's in law school, you know."

Jimmy contemplated the irony of Ghost Gambuzza bringing a lawyer into the world as his mother laid bacon strips to drain on folded paper towels.

"You married?"

"No."

"Got a steady girl?"

"Just broke up with somebody."

She cracked eggs into a bowl, gave them a quick scramble, and poured them into the pan.

"You're like me," she announced, and Jimmy had to laugh.

"No, I'm serious." She looked left and right. "I never should've gotten married," she whispered. "I'm not the type. I can't have a partner. I get in my own way, you know what I mean?"

"I'm not sure, Mom."

"Listen, I'm not talking about my kids. I love that I had my sons. And my grandsons? Don't even let me get started. But that wife business . . ." She shook her head. "Just wasn't for me."

She set a plate of bacon and eggs before Jimmy and sat across from him.

"What did I know when I married your father? I was so young!" She shrugged. "I liked him all right.

He was good lookin'. Hardly took a drink in the beginning." She winked. "Tell you the truth, he wasn't the type to have a partner, either. We annoyed each other right from the start, but in those days, you stayed married. I shut my mouth, and he got drunk. Crazy. Didn't help that I got pregnant about an hour after the wedding. Aaay, what are you gonna do? Come on, eat, it'll get cold."

Jimmy took a forkful of eggs, and nearly choked on it when his mother said, "I like divorce."

"You do?"

"Oh, yeah. The way I figure it, every divorce is a murder that didn't happen. You hear about a divorce, and everybody says, 'How terrible!' Me, I say, 'Thank God, there's no corpse.' They look at me funny, but what do I care? Eat, eat. You want toast? Just to push the egg on the fork? No? You sure? Milk and sugar for the coffee?"

"I drink it black."

"Me too. See that? We *are* alike. Gus and Joey, they drink coffee milkshakes, is what they drink. Carol took it black." She reached across to touch Jimmy's arm. "Now there was a nice match, Gus and Carol. You saw them together, you knew they were happy."

"I remember."

"Oh, *Madonna,* right to the end they looked at each other like it was prom night. Tell you the truth, it got on my nerves."

She sat back, stretched and yawned. "Who knows, maybe I was jealous. She died hard, the poor thing. Your brother's barely smiled since. He's comin around, though. I can see it."

"Carol was special. I miss her."

"She's on the shelf over the refrigerator."

"What?"

"Take a look."

With both hands behind his back, Jimmy inspected the small metal jar between a ceramic rooster and a plate that read NO MATTER WHERE I SERVE MY GUESTS, THEY ALWAYS LIKE MY KITCHEN BEST. The jar was pewter-colored, with a white tape label reading "C. Gambuzza remains."

"That's it?!"

"Isn't that something? If you saw that can on the street, wouldn't you give it a kick?"

"Jesus Christ . . ."

"She wanted to be cremated. Now what are we supposed to do? Gus tells me, 'Leave it there, don't touch it.' Like I'm gonna touch it. I think he's afraid I'm gonna accidentally season the sauce with his wife."

Footsteps sounded on the stairs. "She was a good girl," Fiorentina continued. "Couldn't cook worth shit, though. *Madonna mi,* Jell-O molds with baby marshmallows. That was her specialty. You'd think she'd just built the pyramids, the way she set it on the table."

Fiorentina quickly put the rest of the cooked bacon on a plate and stuck it in the cold microwave oven just before a yawning Gus entered the kitchen.

"You see this?" Gus said. "For months she told me, 'Don't get me a microwave, don't get me a microwave.' Now she can't live without it. Am I right, Mah?"

"You're right." Gus kissed his mother on the cheek, and as he turned to pour himself a cup of coffee Fiorentina winked at Jimmy, put a finger to her lips.

Jimmy left the house an hour later, while Gus's sons still slept. He did not want a ride back to town. He could catch the train a few blocks from the house, and promised to ride it back that night for dinner.

Gus walked him to the station. They were halfway there when Gus made him go back to the house to put on his dress shoes.

"What's the difference?"

"You walk into Wendy's house wearing those, she'll want a story. Leave the sneakers here, you'll get 'em later."

On the second walk to the train, Gus put his arm across Jimmy's shoulders.

"You all right?"

"I'm fine."

"You don't have to be fine just yet. It's kinda like the roller coaster. You get off, but you feel like you're still riding."

It was strange to see Gus walking more than a few steps at a time. Jimmy saw that despite additional weight and years, there remained a bit of a bounce to his step, as if, in a pinch, he could still be called onto the field to make a tackle. And there was the way he'd caught Jimmy on the bridge the night before. Somehow, it felt like a million years ago.

"Okay, Jim-a-nootz," Gus said. "Now's the time to say whatever you want to say about what happened."

"I don't want to talk about it now."

"No, you don't get it."

Gus caught Jimmy's elbow, bringing them to a stop before the most elaborately Christmas-decorated home in all of Brooklyn. It had a life-sized waving Santa on the porch, its arm controlled by a hidden electric pendulum. Three-quarter size Jesus, Mary, and Joseph figures filled the carpet-sized lawn, surrounded by plaster sheep and camels.

"*This* is the time," Gus continued, squeezing the elbow for emphasis. He nodded toward the rusted elevated subway tracks. "After you get on that train, the subject is closed forever."

"What if the cops come around?"

"They won't. This is clean. This is a capsule." He put his hands together, as if he had a live butterfly inside that he wished to trap but not harm. "No leaks." He wet his lips. "So. You got anything to say now, or what?"

Jimmy hesitated. "You figure the furnace did the job?"

"Don't worry about the furnace."

"You'll think I'm crazy, but I'm worried that she might've been wearing some jewelry . . . something that wouldn't burn."

"No jewelry."

"Gus, you don't know that for sure."

Gus sighed. "She went in naked, Jimmy."

Jimmy could only stare at Gus. "My God."

"What do you think I was doing when we stopped at that New Year's Eve party?"

"My God, Gus."

"I didn't enjoy stripping her, if it helps any." He cleared his throat. "She had a few rings and an ankle bracelet."

"Where are they?"

"Forget about 'em. Her clothes went into the social club furnace. All right? Enough gory details for you, or do you want more?"

"Why?"

"In case we had to dump her somewhere, fast. A naked body's harder to trace. Do you want me to explain why?"

"I think I can figure it out."

"You know enough now? Maybe you should also know there were track marks on her arms. Her legs, too. This was some freakin' package you brought home."

"I told you, Gus, she followed me."

"And it's a lucky thing she did. You want to know why? Because it would have been worse if she'd followed somebody else. Somebody who wasn't as fast as you, who would've taken that knife in the heart, or gotten his face slashed. Let's say he's some poor slob of a family man. One stupid night costs him a slashed face. Now he's got a scar for the rest of his life. He takes it out on his wife, or his kids. And they grow up to take it out on their kids, and so on. See what I'm saying? It's a ripple effect. So maybe it's not such a bad thing that she's gone."

"I love you, Gus."

"I know you do. Last chance to talk about her."

"Did she have a wallet?"

"I was waiting for that. Yes, she did. No money."

"But you know her name."

"Uh-huh."

"You're not going to tell me."

"That's right. Now I want you to tell me why I'm not telling you."

"Because I'd try to find out about her."

"And?"

"And her friends would see me snooping around, and they'd call the police, and they'd question me, and I'd give you up, and Blind Billy would go to jail, and no law firm in the world would ever hire Gus Junior."

Gus whistled in admiration. "That's even better than I would have done it, bro." He pretended to lock his lips and throw away the key. "End of subject. You ever bring it up again, I'll look at you like you've got two heads. I hear the train comin.' You'd better go and do what you've got to do."

"Okay, Gus."

"Think of it as a baseball game. You're the pitcher, and all you need is one more out to win."

"Right."

"Now go strike her the fuck out, and I'll see you at dinner."

"What should I bring tonight?"

"A clear conscience."

Gus gave Jimmy a quick, hard hug before turning abruptly and heading home. Jimmy jogged up the steps to the platform and made it just in time to buy a token and board the Manhattan-bound train. The crooked, stop-and-start, brake-squeaky trip to Forty-second Street took nearly an hour. Grubby, unshaven, and wrinkled, Jimmy took a deep breath before climbing up to the street to begin the short walk to Wendy Orgel's apartment.

CHAPTER 12

Wendy lived in a doorman brownstone building on East Fifty-second Street where she was, though not president of the co-op board, its most vocal member. She saw to it that the garbage cans had chains connecting the lids to the pails, that the doorman's uniform was cleaned regularly, that the brass rails of the canopy (an outrageously expensive improvement she'd lobbied for) were shined once a week with Noxon and soft cloths.

Everyone in the building respected her, though these same people did not always like her. Wendy knew it, and didn't care. She felt it was the price she paid for being a pioneering woman. One day, she believed, females like herself would be appreciated. Her daughter, or perhaps her granddaughter. Only thing was, she had to become a mother first. As she would turn thirty-four on her next birthday, this was fast becoming a Major Issue in her life with Jimmy Gambar, who was not exactly the master of decisions. You could go crazy, watching Jimmy sweat over a menu for twenty minutes before placing his order.

Then he'd call the waiter back and ask if it was too late to change it.

Jimmy had been coming to her place for so long that the doorman, an ancient black man with startling white hair that fluffed out from the sides of his cap, no longer bothered calling up before letting him in. His name was Roscoe, and what he didn't know was that Wendy was working to have his ass fired, having more than once come home late to find this six-dollar-an-hour employee asleep in the lobby armchair. The funny thing about it was that Wendy was the one who'd demanded that they hire a black man for the job. Jimmy, among others, was trying to change her mind about canning Roscoe, who greeted him this morning with a double take.

"Lawd, Mr. Gambar, what happened to you?"

Jimmy rubbed his stubbly cheek. "I'm still trying to figure it out myself, Roscoe. She in?"

"Believe so."

The slow, rumbly elevator happened to be waiting at the ground floor, so Jimmy was on the eighth floor within seconds, smelling the fake fruit scent of hallway carpet cleaner as he strode toward Wendy's door. The pebbled wallpaper was starting to peel near the baseboard. As he pressed Wendy's buzzer he remembered that just the night before, she'd been typing a note to the co-op board about the wallpaper, and when the door swung open the first thing Jimmy noticed was that the same sheet of paper was still in the typewriter carriage. A very bad sign. Wendy Orgel did not leave things unfinished unless she was extremely upset.

Another bad sign was the cigarette in her lips. Wendy only smoked when she was angry, and from the look of the brimming ashtrays, she'd been smoking all night. She blew smoke at Jimmy's face, put her weight on one foot. Her face was all points, her eyes as blank as a shark's.

"Not even a phone call, huh?"

"Hello, Wendy."

"Are you going to stand there, or are you coming in?"

"It's up to you."

"Perfect. Beautiful. Just keep letting me make all the decisions."

He followed her inside. Wendy tightened the belt on her blue terry cloth robe before flopping onto the couch the way a weary prize-fighter slumps onto a stool between rounds. Then she stubbed out her butt, which happened to be a Marlboro. Jimmy had to giggle. His brother's brand. It was the only thing they could possibly have in common.

"Something funny?"

"Not really."

"Of course you won't share it with me."

"No," Jimmy allowed, "I won't."

"And *there* is the metaphor for our relationship. Sit down."

"I don't think so."

Wendy pulled her hair back with both hands, then shut her eyes tightly, as if she were undergoing a minor surgical procedure without anesthetic.

"Are you okay?" she asked in a quaking voice. Jimmy's heart jumped. She cared about him. She really did. For all the things that made her difficult to take sometimes, she had guts. And if there was one thing he'd learned about himself last night, it was that he was no dish of pure delight.

"Think so," he said. "You?"

"I really don't know, Jimmy. I'm still trying to figure

out what happened last night." She noticed the scab on his hand. "What'd you do to yourself?"

Jimmy was tempted to say, "A leopard scratched it." Of course, she would never believe him. He could barely believe it himself. Almost nothing that had happened to him in the past twelve hours seemed in any way real, and on the other hand, they were the realest things that had ever happened to him.

"It's just a scratch," he finally said. He happened to slide his hand down over his pants pocket, and felt the bulge of the robin-egg blue box containing the diamond ring. It was incredible, *beyond* incredible. Just hours earlier, he'd actually intended to ask this woman—no, *beg* this woman—to share the rest of her life with him.

And he would have done it. He would have gone through with every bit of it: the *New York Times* marriage announcement, the wedding under a tent on Wendy's parents' lawn in Mamaroneck, the honeymoon at some Virgin Island of Wendy's choice (sailing–snorkeling–scuba diving–motor bikes), the return to town . . . then what?

Like a movie shown at high speed, the miserable rest of his life sped past Jimmy's eyes—the giving up of his loft, the purchase of a house in Scarsdale, dinner parties, children (but he can't see their faces!), live-in help, separate bedrooms (what did I *do?),* retirement, the move to Florida (condo with pool and gym), and finally the film slowed down so that Jimmy could see his scrawny hunch-shouldered self seated on a wooden bench at an antiseptically clean mall, a too-big white golf cap on his head, waiting for his wife (hope she doesn't forget I'm here) to finish shopping.

Was I nuts? Was I *blind?* Who the fuck was that

jumpy man who'd elbowed his way to the Tiffany diamond counter three days ago?

He looked around the room, at all the paintings, vases, and geegaws in exactly the right places. On the mantel was a photo of the two of them in a raft, plowing over white water, taken by a hustler with a fixed-focus camera on a riverbank. Wendy was in ecstasy; Jimmy looked as if he were undergoing a root canal. The photo beside that was one of Wendy and him with the mayor, snapped at the event his brother Joey had attended; maybe he was watching as the picture was taken.

And beside the photos was a clock the poor cleaning lady had once returned too close to the edge after dusting, an act that earned her a written reprimand.

Notes. Everybody got a freaking note. How many times had Jimmy himself felt his heart sink when, upon opening his mailbox, he'd find a little pink envelope nestled among the bills? How many single-spaced, touch-typewritten notes "FROM THE DESK OF WENDY ORGEL" had brought rain to sunny days? Even when it was a cheerful little "Just thinking of you" sort of thing, Jimmy's day would be ruined. Come to think of it, those were worse than the complaint notes. They gave her something to judge him against, something for him to live up to.

How much had he suffered, and why? And how much had *she* suffered? Like the idea of an afterlife, it was too big a mystery to ponder. All that mattered was to get out of it.

"Huh?" Jimmy said. Wendy rolled her eyes.

"I said, please tell me what you're feeling."

He licked his lips. "I'm feeling that we're all wrong for each other."

She closed her eyes, and her face went gray. This

usually preceded tears, but when Wendy finally opened her eyes, she was not crying. "You know," she whispered, "if I'm honest with myself, I have to admit I'm feeling the same thing."

"It's not anybody's fault, Wen. And listen, I'm very sorry for the way I spoke to you last night. I was way out of line."

Now her eyes glistened with tears. "It was my fault, too. I shouldn't have tried to make you wear the tie. I know how you feel about things like that. Sometimes, I can't help pushing . . ."

"No, no, no," Jimmy disagreed. "What kind of an asshole am I, refusing to even stick the thing in my closet? The way I reacted was ridiculous."

She came into his arms. They held one another tightly.

"Were you with a woman last night?"

"No," Jimmy said. "Just went out wandering."

"Really?"

"Swear to God. How about you? Did you go to the Rainbow Room?"

She shook her head. "Came home and watched *Casablanca.*"

"It was on?"

"I rented it."

"That's one thing we had in common. Good taste in movies." He kissed her cheek. "It's over between us, Wendy," he said gently. "I'm sorry if you feel I wasted your time."

Wendy shrugged. "I had some fun. Didn't you have fun?"

"Sure I did."

"It's just that we've both put off making this decision. Funny, I never thought you'd be the one to break us up." She smiled at him. "Amazing. James Gambar makes a decision."

Jimmy felt himself blush. "I'm a little amazed myself."

"I have to tell you, it's very sexy."

"You're not just after my body, are you?"

Wendy laughed. They were both relieved.

Jimmy hesitated. "You know, I was going to ask you to marry me last night."

"I know."

"What do you mean, you *know?*"

"I saw you take out the Tiffany box when I first came into the restaurant. I was peeking from behind the coatrack."

Jimmy was dumbstruck.

"Let me see the ring," Wendy said. "Come on, big shot."

Jimmy handed over the box. Wendy looked at the ring like a jeweler. "Nice," she said, handing it back. "I must say, you've got good taste."

Jimmy swallowed. "What would you have said, if I'd proposed?"

"What do you think I would have said?"

"Probably 'No.' "

"*Definitely* 'No.' "

"Jesus Christ," Jimmy giggled, "you are a bitch."

Wendy giggled back. "One of the best, when I'm in top form."

They kissed once more for old time's sake, and then Jimmy walked out of her apartment for the last time.

"You're not angry?" Jimmy said at the doorway.

"Not right now," Wendy replied. "I will be. Right now, I just want to sleep."

"Me, too."

"Good-bye, Jimmy."

"Good-bye."

She closed the door, and that was it. It could not possibly have been done any more cleanly.

Down in the lobby, Roscoe opened the door for Jimmy, who took a twenty-dollar bill from his wallet and held it out for the man, genuinely sorry that he wouldn't be seeing him anymore.

"Happy New Year, Roscoe."

Roscoe kept his hands at his sides. "But sir, you gave me money for Christmas!"

"Take it, please."

With genuine reluctance, Roscoe accepted the bill in a crablike hand.

"It's been nice knowing you, Roscoe. I won't be coming by anymore. Miss Orgel and I are through."

Roscoe's momentary look of surprise was replaced by one of comprehension, then approval.

"That is one stone-cold bitch." He looked left and right before adding, "You better off hollowin' out a snowman and puttin' it there, if you don't mind my sayin' so."

"Ah, she's harder on herself than she is on anybody else, Roscoe."

Roscoe nodded. "Why is it we always go for the ones that torment us so?"

"Roscoe, if you ever figure that one out, please let me know."

They shook hands. Jimmy turned to walk crosstown, toward Grand Central Terminal.

"You take care now, Mr. Gambar," Roscoe called.

Jimmy hesitated. "Just for the record, the name's Gambuzza."

"That a fact? You Eye-talian?"

"I sure am. Aaay, but don't tell Miss Orgel."

Jimmy felt twenty pounds lighter as he threaded his

way through the hung-over faces and the yet-to-be-to-bedders on what was turning out to be a beautiful first day of the year. A homeless man in filthy red pants and cracked shoes all but dove in front of him, his sooty hand extended.

"Spare some change?"

Jimmy fished another twenty-dollar bill from his wallet and put it in the man's hand. The guy's mind was so blown that he couldn't even close his hand around it.

"This is too much," he said, thinking out loud. He looked at Jimmy. "You sure about this?"

"Yeah, on one condition."

"Name it, Bud."

"Is your mother alive?" The homeless guy nodded solemnly. "You talked to her lately?" He reluctantly shook his head. "Give her a call today. Will you do that?"

"I surely will," the man replied in a cracked voice.

Inside Grand Central Terminal, Jimmy paused to bathe himself in the glorious light that streamed through the long windows. He stood with tears in his eyes, survivor of an incredible urban safari, and through it all the thought that burned hottest in his mind was of how proud his big brother Gus would be of the way he'd handled everything.

He rode the shuttle to the West Side, then caught a downtown train. On the walk to his apartment he was thinking of how delicious his own bed would feel. But as always, he was interrupted while climbing the stairs by Dennis, whose door swung open at the sound of Jimmy's footsteps on the landing below.

"There he is!" Dennis called in a voice that was wildly shrill, even for him. A man with a terrible complexion, a receding hairline, and a wrinkled

trench coat appeared out of Dennis's apartment, and looked blandly at Jimmy.

"Detective," Dennis said, pointing at Jimmy, "this is the man I was telling you about."

Then a second plainclothes cop came out from inside Dennis's apartment, writing in his notepad. This one was younger than his partner, with a full red mustache that seemed to have sprouted all the way from his nostrils.

Jimmy felt a tickle behind each of his knees. He felt as if he'd just won a fifteen-round decision, only to find that there was one more round to go with a brand-new, fully rested opponent. Jimmy remained on the landing below, gripping the banister and putting most of his weight on it.

The cop with the bad skin flapped open his wallet to show his shield. "Detective Kowinski. Could we have a word with you, please?"

"He's the man!" Dennis screamed, little bubbles of spit dotting his lips. "He's the one!"

The mustache gently but firmly guided Dennis back into his apartment. "We'll talk to him," he said. "Youse just get some rest, and we'll see you later." He closed the door in Dennis's face.

Both cops turned their gazes on Jimmy, who made no motion to move. Kowinski spread his hands.

"You live upstairs, right?"

"I do."

"Well you gonna come home, or what? We got some things we'd like to discuss with you."

Jimmy felt as if he were pulling his feet from patches of tar. His shoes scraped the stairs as he climbed. His muscles ached, his head felt thick, and he thought he could feel his bones creak as he moved, as if his joints needed oil. Something was missing, though, and that was fear. Or if he *did* feel fear, it was a new kind of fear, the sort that was so deep in the marrow that it forced a man to relax, rather than tremble. He was going solo this time, the training wheels named Gus and Joey gone from his bike. And in a bizarre way, it was a fucking thrill. Jimmy walked right past the cops on the way to his door.

"Come on up, fellows," he said almost sleepily as he unlocked the door. He pushed it open to reveal his sun-splashed living room, as neat as it was when the cleaning lady left it.

No; not quite. The lamp that had killed the girl was still on the floor, on its side. Somehow, he and Gus had left it like that.

It was the first thing Kowinski noticed.

"Little disturbance here last night, or what?" He went to the lamp and stood it upright.

Jimmy said nothing. He remembered the advice Gus had given him on the bridge, next time he was in a bad situation: Go easy on the details. He never would have guessed he'd be using the advice so soon.

"Musta knocked it over when you took the rug out," the mustache said. "Hey, Jerry, what do you think?"

"I'd say it's a distinct possibility, Richie."

Now at least I know their first names, Jimmy said to himself. Not that it meant anything. It was just knowledge, and knowledge was always good in a situation like this. *Any* situation.

Jimmy yawned, a real yawn, though he worried that it might have looked like a false attempt to seem casual. "You guys want to tell me what this is about?"

Kowinski took his time answering. "You don't seem surprised to see us."

"I don't?"

"What I'm saying is, you seem pretty cool."

"Detective, please. Get to the point."

Kowinski cleared his throat. "Your, ah, neighbor tells us you moved a rug out of here last night. Is that right?"

"Yes."

Kowinski turned to Richie. "Funny thing to do on New Year's Eve, wouldn't you say?"

"I'd say so," Richie agreed. He had an oddly high-pitched voice, like a muted trombone. "Very odd, indeed."

A lone drop of sweat rolled down Jimmy's back. Otherwise, his skin was dry, his breathing even. He wondered if Richie might have been an English major, then figured no, he couldn't have been. Just another hard-on cop with a high-falutin' way of talking. He was really getting to hate cops, mostly because they were so fucking full of themselves. The one on the horse. The one he tried to bribe. These two clowns.

Kowinski said, "Where was this rug you were in such a rush to move?"

"In my bedroom."

Richie said, "I'm gonna look in the other room."

"Good idea, Rich," Kowinski said.

Richie walked off, his shoes loud on the wood floor.

It occurred to Jimmy that these were two unbelievably sloppy cops, that they should have had a search warrant to do what they were doing. But if Jimmy made a point of demanding that they get a search warrant, they'd believe that something was up. They'd get one, come back with it, and stay in Jimmy's face for hours, just out of spite for having been put through the paperwork.

On the other hand, he couldn't just stand there like a mime while two cops rooted around his home. There's no greater guilt than absolute silence, Jimmy told himself. He wondered if he'd heard that one from Gus, or if he'd come up with it himself. It certainly sounded like a Gus-ism, though at this point he realized that there was more of his big brother in him than he ever could have known.

"Officer," Jimmy said calmly, almost casually, "I'd like to know what this is about."

Kowinski walked over to Jimmy, using the same loud shoes on the wood floor trick that Richie had pulled. For all their swagger, Jimmy realized, cops were not a terribly interesting bunch. Here was one literally in his face, close enough for Jimmy to study the poor bastard's pizza of a complexion. His hangover breath was sour, he'd shaved himself unevenly, and his eyes were the pouting, angry eyes of a child deprived of his dessert. He saw Jimmy as potential prey, certainly, but this is how he saw everybody. What a way to make a buck!

Kowinski rubbed his eyes with the heels of his hands. "You want to know what this is about," the cop deadpanned.

"Yes, sir, I do."

"What do you *think* it's about?"

"I don't know. I walked into my house. My downstairs neighbor shrieked at me. Next thing I know, two cops are in my house."

"Don't you *know* what he's upset about?"

Jimmy's teeth clenched as he remembered that Dennis's windows faced the street. Maybe he'd gone to the window to watch them load the rug into the car? Could the woman's feet have momentarily stuck out from the end of the rug? Had they ridden all the way to the asshole end of Brooklyn and gone through everything they'd gone through, only to have been fucked from the start by that miserable magpie of a downstairs neighbor?

No way. No fucking way. This had been handled by the great Ghost Gambuzza, who did not make mistakes. Even if Dennis had looked out the window, he hadn't seen shit. This Jimmy believed to the point where it was not just faith, it was knowledge.

But just thinking about it had put a glimmer in Jimmy's eye, which the cop caught.

"Hey," Kowinski said, "I see you came up with a theory. You gonna share it with me, or what?"

Jimmy forced himself to shrug, then chuckle. He thought about making a fag crack, but stopped himself. Most cops would appreciate it. These cops looked as if they would appreciate it, but you never knew. One or the other might turn out to be gay, or have a gay brother, or whatever. So instead, he went with a generic put-down of a high-strung single male in lower Manhattan.

"With Dennis, it's hard to know," Jimmy began. "Anything can set him off. Maybe I forgot to rinse out my empties before putting them in the recycling bin. Or maybe I didn't use biodegradable cord to tie up my newspapers."

A bomb. Kowinski didn't even blink. "You're a comedian, huh?"

"No, detective. I'm a dead-tired architect who just dumped his girlfriend, and would like nothing more than to sleep for about a week."

The cop nodded, a tickle of a smile on his lips. "Dumped your girlfriend, huh?"

Oh Christ. What a choice of words. Jimmy had thought that Gus's technique of using a sex story to throw a cop off the trail would help him here. Now he realized he might just have fitted himself with a noose. All he needed now was for Kowinski to say, "Funny you should put it that way. . . ."

Richie returned from the bedroom. "Floor's got this dusty patch on it, like maybe somebody just moved a rug."

Kowinski nodded, not taking his eyes off Jimmy. "Didjoo really move a rug last night?"

"You *know* I did. I *told* you I did. Is there a law against that?" Jimmy sat on his couch, sorry that he'd even mentioned the word "law." He spread his arms across the back of the couch. "Look," he said, "maybe now's as good a time as any for you guys to tell me what this is about."

He was angry, and he'd let them know it. All the cards were on the table, all the money was bet. They either knew something, or they didn't. He stared hard into the eyes of Kowinski, who was the first to break the gaze. He squeezed the bridge of his nose, in a fruitless attempt to relieve hangover pain.

"Your neighbor's very upset," he said, his eyes still shut. "Seems somebody broke into his house after midnight and made off with a lot of his furniture. He thinks it was you."

Jimmy laughed. It was an honest laugh, but again, he worried that it might sound phony. "You think I took his furniture?"

"I don't know, Mr. Gambar. You moved a rug, maybe you moved some other stuff. We're just here to look."

"Let me tell you guys something," Jimmy said. "I did not take any of Dennis's furniture. I wouldn't even want his furniture *playing* with my furniture."

Both cops laughed. Kowinski winced with pain.

"You want some seltzer water?" Jimmy offered. "Coupla aspirins?"

Kowinski nodded. "I'd appreciate it, pal."

Jimmy got the aspirins and a glass of water, careful to be helpful but not servile. Just as the cop was downing them, there was a booming knock on the door. Jimmy opened it, and a sweaty, frantic Dennis plunged inside.

"Officers, I'm *hor*ribly sorry," he began. "It wasn't this man at all. It was my old roommate, Vance."

They all stared at Dennis, who hyperventilated and wiped sweat from his forehead. Kowinski narrowed his eyes.

"You're telling me you know the thief?"

"Yes. Well, he's not exactly a *thief*. He *used* to live with me. He came back to get his stuff. Only, it *isn't* his stuff. He *thinks* it's his stuff." Dennis exhaled, long and hard. "It's a long story. I'd really hate to bore you. But everything's all right."

Kowinski's eyes widened. "All right?" he echoed. "You tie up two cops for an hour over a domestic spat?"

Dennis's lips quivered. "Well. It's not like I *knew*."

"And you accuse your neighbor—your friend—of stealing your stuff?"

Sweat literally dripped from Dennis's ears. "I panicked. I'm sorry. Jimmy, please forgive me."

Jimmy ignored Dennis, who turned to the cops. "Can I go now?" he asked meekly.

"Beat it," Richie said. Dennis fled like a mouse. Both cops apologized to Jimmy. Kowinski even held out his hand, which Jimmy accepted.

"No hard feelings, I hope."

"Could I ask one thing? Do they always send two detectives out to check out alleged burglaries?"

Kowinski sighed. "Things are a little sensitive just now with the gay community. Your friend downstairs happens to be a very vocal member of the precinct's outreach program. So maybe we, ah, overdid it a little with this response."

"No, no, no," Jimmy said. "I just wondered, guys."

"Next time he calls, we'll send an interior decorator." Kowinski winked, then clapped Jimmy's shoulder. "So you dumped your girlfriend last night, huh?"

Sex stories! The Ghost was right—they loved sex stories!

"Yeah," Jimmy said. He pulled the Tiffany box from his pocket. "Had the ring and everything. I was gonna pop the question, you know? Instead, we broke up."

"No shit," Kowinski marveled. "Hey, I'm sorry."

"Nah. It's for the best."

"Better you break up now instead of ten years from now."

Richie said, "They're good about takin' stuff back at Tiffany's. Shouldn't be a problem."

Jimmy realized that these two guys, in their clumsy cop way, were trying to act like human beings. They wished him a Happy New Year and left. Jimmy could hear them laughing about something on their way downstairs.

Jimmy went to the bathroom and rubbed cold water on his face. He looked at himself in the mirror, hard and long, before doing something so unbelievably corny that he could hardly believe it. He winked. Then he dried his face, went down a flight and tapped gently on Dennis's door.

"Vance?"

"It's Jimmy."

Dennis hesitated, then opened it. Jimmy stood and stared at him.

"It was the rug," Dennis chirped. "That rug got me crazy, Jimmy. I mean, I made a crazy connection because of the rug. Why the *hell* were you moving it at *that* hour, anyway?"

Jimmy gripped the front of Dennis's tank top, uprooting several chest hairs in the process.

"You know, I have just one wish for the New Year," Jimmy said evenly. "I'd like to be able to come into my building and walk all the way up to my home without being ambushed by you."

Dennis stood there with his mouth open.

"I don't want to see you," Jimmy said. *"Ever.* If you hear my footsteps, you stay in your apartment until I pass. If you're in the hall and you hear me coming, duck back inside until I'm gone. Got that?" He shoved Dennis away.

Jimmy went to his bed and slept blissfully for five hours, then showered and shaved before going to dinner at his mother's.

CHAPTER 13

One paragraph was all she rated in a Spanish-language newspaper. It identified her as Consuelo Santiago, a twenty-seven-year-old small-time drug dealer who vanished mysteriously shortly after the New Year. Even Gus, who kept his eye out for even the smallest crime-blotter-type stories in the newspapers for weeks after the New Year, never saw this item.

Nobody knew anything. Nobody phoned the newspapers or the police with tips. Her closest family was in Puerto Rico, and she hadn't been in touch with them for years. It was her Bronx landlady who alerted cops to her disappearance, and only because she was three months behind with the rent. And it was a rookie reporter named Arturo Polanco who took the story off the police blotter, because he was a go-getter eager to chase a story a veteran would have ignored as a one hundred percent piece of shit. People disappear a lot in the days after New Year's. Santiago was just the type to vanish, then reappear, to nobody's particular delight.

But Polanco was persistent. The landlady told him about Santiago's favorite hangouts, and on the fourth day of January he traced her to the place she'd been on New Year's Eve. The manager, named Hermano Valdez, happened to have a terrible hangover when Polanco showed up. And hangover or no hangover, he was not the type who was eager to talk with a reporter.

"I hated that bitch," he murmured. "Don't write that down."

Polanco capped his pen, pocketed his notebook. "You want me to get you some aspirin?"

"Already took ten." He squeezed his temples. "Why do you give a fuck about this girl? She was bad news, man."

"Should I take my notebook out again?"

"Fuck, no. I'm just tellin' you what I'm tellin' you." He gestured at the dance floor. "She'd deal right in here. I need that like I need a fuckin' hole in my head."

"What about the people she was with?"

"She was alone. Wait, no." He squinted, swallowed club soda. "That night she was dancing with some suit."

"Remember what he looked like?"

"Hey, are you a fuckin' cop?"

"If I were a cop, would I be this polite?"

Valdez couldn't help grinning. "Guess not. Okay, I don't know what the fuck I can tell you. Ain't seen the guy before or since. Tall and slim. Dark hair. He had this pink tie, is all I remember."

Polanco took out his notebook and wrote it down. "White guy?"

Valdez nodded. "White guy, pink tie. Not around his neck, though. Wavin' it like a whip. Crazy fuck.

Didn't look too bright. Like maybe he hadn't been with a whole lotta women. God knows what she took him for. Probably ripped off his ass good."

Polanco thanked Valdez, and handed him his card. "Will you call me if you think of anything else?"

Valdez shrugged. "He ain't comin' back here, man. You ask me, *he's* the one you should be lookin' for. Probably dead someplace. Believe me when I tell you that whatever he had, she's got it now."

Polanco left. Even with his youthful enthusiasm, he couldn't sustain an interest in the story. He kept a casual eye out for tall dark white men in pink ties in the SoHo area, and didn't spot a single one. Within days he'd sunk his teeth into a story about sweatshop labor in the Bronx, and forgot all about Consuelo Santiago.

The Ghost's instincts about the cop on the horse were in the ballpark, if not exactly on the money. His name was Kevin Mulrooney, and he was indeed the kind of horse lover who'd put a cube of sugar between his lips and let the animal bite it away. He was near the end of his four-to-twelve shift when he saw Gus and Jimmy load the rug into the car, and when he returned to the stable he was eager to mention this odd occurrence to his sergeant, whose first question for any cop checking in was always, "Anything unusual out there?"

However, the regular man had taken sick mid-shift, forcing a sergeant named Frank DeGennaro to fill in at seven o'clock.

DeGennaro's ass was burned, but good. He'd bought two nonrefundable tickets to see Barry Manilow that night, and when the phone rang at his home the last thing he expected was to be called in to work. They didn't give him an option—they just ordered him to report to the job.

Why the fuck had he answered the phone? Why hadn't he let the machine get it? He phoned his girlfriend with the bad news, and told her to take one of her friends.

The girlfriend, Carmela Inguagiata, did not take it well. She'd put in a full day as a beautician on Queens Boulevard, making other women look dazzling for the New Year. She'd told every customer about the big night ahead with Frank, and now this was happening. To make things worse, she goaded him about the way he always let the Police Department bully him.

"I got no choice about it."

"Who'm I supposed to go with now?"

"Take your sister."

"You let them push you around, Frankie."

He slammed his phone down so hard that the receiver split. Happy fuckin' New Year.

DeGennaro's slow simmer had escalated to a steady boil by the time Mulrooney came in to stable his horse. This was always a noisy process for Mulrooney, with a lot of oohing and aahing, patting and nuzzling. DeGennaro watched it and felt his stomach go sour. He could have been listening to Barry singing "Mandy," and instead this was the evening's entertainment. And he knew that this Irish fuck would have spent the night with the horse even if he'd been off duty. For Christ's sakes, another few minutes and the guy would need a condom.

"Speed it up, would you?"

Mulrooney didn't even look at the sergeant. "She's a little skittish."

"Fuck skittish. Finish up and sign out."

DeGennaro took a sip of bitter black coffee from a

Styrofoam cup, regretted it instantly, and set the cup down. With any kind of luck, Carmela would have had a good time at the concert, and they'd salvage the rest of the evening. That was aiming high. Right now, he'd be happy if this Mulrooney fuck would just finish up and check out.

At last he came striding over in his long black boots, like a Canadian fucking Mountie. Irish people. Jesus Christ! They turn the simplest fucking task into the St. Patrick's Day Parade. With an unnecessary flourish, Mulrooney pulled off his helmet and set it on DeGennaro's desk, knocking over the coffee, which rolled in rivulets toward DeGennaro's lap.

"Jesus Christ!"

"Sorry, Sarge." But Mulrooney couldn't muffle a mild chuckle.

"What's that supposed to be, funny?"

A dopey grin split Mulrooney's face. "Hey, it was an accident."

DeGennaro dabbed at his thighs with thin diner napkins that barely absorbed anything. Here he was, wiping stale coffee off his pants, instead of listening to Barry. He looked up at Mulrooney, who was biting his lip to keep from laughing.

"Want me to, ah, getcha a paper towel?"

"Why don't you go over to the stall and give that horse of yours a good bang?"

Mulrooney's face flooded with blood.

"Yeah," DeGennaro said. "That's what you really want. Why put it off any longer, you stupid fucking Mick?"

Mulrooney dove over the desk. His hands squeezed DeGennaro's bull neck, while the sergeant pummeled him in the kidneys. It took four cops from the incoming midnight-to-eight shift to pull them apart. DeGennaro came out of it with a scraped neck and a bloody nose. Mulrooney's ribs were bruised and he lost two teeth, along with the memory of those two guys loading that lumpy rug into the trunk of a car on Greenwich Street.

Those two kids who'd come across the Gambuzza brothers while Jimmy was retching his guts out at curbside got into an argument while the speeding green Oldsmobile was barely a block away.

"*Tole* you it was the fuckin' Ghost," Melendez said. "You didn't fuckin' believe me."

Martinez said, "We still don't know for fuckin' sure."

"Bullshit. We seen him on TV. You blind, boy."

"Fuck you."

"Fuck your mother."

Martinez pretended to turn away, then whirled around and crashed his nearly empty bottle of Ballantine Triple-X against the skull of Melendez, who fell to the street and rolled into Jimmy's vomit. Unfortunately, he did not lose consciousness, so he heard Martinez laughing over the mess on his coat sleeves.

Melendez reached inside his coat, pulled out a 9-millimeter handgun, and pumped three bullets into the chest of Martinez. He died seconds after he hit the pavement, and two hours later Melendez was in a Rikers Island holding pen on second-degree murder charges. His fellow inmates were appalled by the stench of his coat, which Melendez refused to take off. They tried to pull the thing from his wiry body, but Melendez resisted, kicking and punching wildly at anyone who came near him. A prisoner who'd done nothing but lift weights and rip off car radios for ten years took a kick to his nose, and responded by slamming Melendez's head against the wall. It was dawn before the guards noticed the boy's body slumped in a corner, his eyes wide open, the back of his skull caved in. As they carried his body from the cell, two guards held their breath against the stench of Jimmy's dried vomit.

Angelo found out a funny thing about himself at the sweatshop: he was claustrophobic. It hit him while he was huddled with dozens of absolutely silent Asians inside the narrow passage behind the false wall. After five minutes Angelo demanded to be let out, but Chin the supervisor wouldn't let him budge. When Angelo tried to push his way out, the Asians pinned his arms behind his back while Chin held a knife to Angelo's neck with one hand and stuffed a hunk of fabric into his mouth with the other.

"You make noise, you die," Chin whispered.

The Asians and Angelo stayed put for a full half hour before Chin decided that the danger had passed. They all went immediately back to work at their machines while Angelo, sopping with sweat and fighting back tears, cursed them all before plunging outside and running to his car, only to find that the rear tire was flat. His hands shook so badly that it took him more than an hour to change it. As Gus had predicted, birds were singing by the time Angelo got home.

Blind Billy was not much of a drinker, so the few glasses of Cold Duck he'd drunk with the Gambuzza brothers gave him a pounding hangover on New Year's Day. Still, he was as diligent as ever about hauling the ashes from his furnace.

But what a load of ashes! How much coal had he burned, the night before? He carried two pails out to his curbside cans before he started to feel dizzy, then called to twelve-year-old Johnny Perrotta, who happened to be riding his Sting-Ray bike past Billy's house.

"Whaddaya want?"

"Johnny, can you help me carry the ashes?"

Johnny wrinkled his nose, as Billy was a legendary cheapskate. "What'll ya pay me?"

"A dollar."

"What are you, fucked in the head?"

Blind Billy's shoulders slumped, and he sighed like a child. "Is that how you talk to grown-ups?"

"Five dollars."

"You know how long I hadda work to get five dollars when I was your age?"

"They used sea shells for money when you were my age, didn't they?"

"You know, Johnny, that mouth of yours is gonna get you in real trouble some day."

Johnny climbed onto his bike, spun the pedals around to get-away position. "Five bucks, or I'm ridin' away."

"Three."

Johnny hesitated, got off the bike, and held out his hand. "Up front."

Blind Billy counted three bills into the kid's palm, then led the way to the cellar.

"Don't make a mess, now."

"I know how to do it."

"All right, all right. I have to go lie down."

Johnny realized he'd been suckered. There were at least seven more pails to haul! If he'd known that, he'd have demanded seven bucks. But a deal was a deal.

Grumbling, he brought six pails of the stuff outside.

He was going to leave the last load behind, but knew that the old man was the type to call his mother and complain, so he went down to get it.

"Fuckin' cheapskate," he mumbled on the way to the ash cans. He just wanted to be through with the job and ride off on his bike, but as he poured the last load a bright wink caught his eye. Gingerly, he pushed at the filthy ashes and found a little lump of bright yellow metal, melted into the shape of a baby lima bean. He was going to throw it away, but for the hell of it he slipped it in his pocket.

That night at supper, he showed it to his widowed mother, and explained where he'd gotten it. She took it to her cousin, a jeweler, who pronounced it a genuine lump of gold, worth roughly fifty dollars.

Mrs. Perrotta had it made into a locket, which she wore around her neck. Johnny had never seen his mother so happy about anything.

"It's my miracle necklace," she told her friends. "My boy found me gold from a mountain of ashes."

She made them swear never to tell Blind Billy about it, for fear that he'd want it back. A superstitious lot, they agreed to keep quiet, delighted to be a part of the mystery, which was certainly more romantic than the truth—that Mrs. Perrotta was wearing what had once been a double-tooth gold bridge from the mouth of a drug-dealing junkie named Consuelo Santiago.

CHAPTER 14

Jimmy was astonished to learn that his mother had gotten her driver's license at age sixty-three, but it was a mild shock compared to the experience of being her passenger.

When drivers didn't respond to her honking, Fiorentina simply roared around them. Cars, vans, trucks—it didn't matter. A slow driver had one chance to get out of the way before Fiorentina Gambuzza put the pedal to the metal.

It was so unlike the last ride he'd taken in this same green Oldsmobile, three months earlier. Jimmy kept expecting Gus to speak up, to insist upon taking the wheel, but he didn't. With each wild maneuver, Jimmy could hear their luggage sliding around in the trunk.

Gooseflesh. Jimmy imagined what it would have been like if Fiorentina had been at the wheel on New Year's Eve, with the luggage they were carrying that night. They'd all be in jail now, instead of on the way to the airport.

"Mom," Jimmy began, but from the front passenger

seat Gus looked back at Jimmy, put a finger to his lips and shook his head.

Fiorentina pushed in the dashboard lighter, shook a Marlboro into her mouth, then passed the pack to Gus.

"These friggin' people," she murmured. "They're out here sight-seeing."

Mother and son lit up their cigarettes. Fiorentina squinted against her own smoke. "Time's the flight?"

"Relax, Mom," Jimmy said, "we've got plenty of time."

"That's right, Mah."

Fiorentina gripped the cigarette hard between her lips, making it jut upward like Popeye's pipe. "You say that now. One traffic jam and we're screwed."

But they hit no traffic. It was a beautiful April evening in New York, the sky having gone rosy with the setting of the sun through a haze of jet fuel pollutants. Fiorentina pulled up before the Olympic Airways terminal a full two hours before her sons' flight, in accordance with the travel agent's advice.

They each had a suitcase and a carry-on. Tears glistened in Fiorentina's eyes as she said good-bye to her boys. As she hugged Jimmy she whispered in his ear, "You look out for your brother, he panics when he travels." She hugged Gus, got back into the car, and roared away.

"Why the hell'd you let her drive?"

Gus shrugged, lifted his bags. "It relaxes her. Come on, let's check in."

Almost everybody on line was a Greek, bound for home. The man directly in front of them carried a long rectangular package, bound with cord. Jimmy saw that it was a weed-cutting tool. He poked Gus in the ribs.

"Wait'll he gets home and plugs that thing in," Jimmy chuckled. "Europe's on direct current. He'll probably burn down his whole village."

Gus forced a smile. Droplets of sweat appeared along his hairline, which he wiped with the back of his wrist.

"Hey, Gus, you all right? It's going to be fine, you know."

Gus nodded. "Little hot in here," he breathed.

An airline security woman was working the line. She asked Jimmy a series of questions about his luggage: Had he accepted anything from anyone at the airport—a package, for instance? Had anyone handled his bags since he'd arrived at the airport? Did he pack the bag himself?

Jimmy casually answered the questions, and couldn't help smiling about something in his luggage. The night before, Joey had given Gus and him each the same going-away present: one dozen condoms, each packed in a shiny gold wrapper. They were not a brand that Jimmy knew.

"I just got these in," Joey explained. "They don't even sell them in this country yet. From Germany. Best condom in the world."

Gus and Jimmy couldn't help laughing. You had to hand it to Joey. For one thing, he'd taken Jimmy's idea about the return of Blind Billy's eyesight and turned it into an Easter bonanza. Statue sales were soaring in Arizona, thanks to the sculptor's miracle.

And who but Joey could have turned Angelo's bootleg silkworm fiasco into a triumph? He did it by suggesting that the Asians alter their sewing patterns to make athletic warm-up suits instead of dress suits.

"You *want* to sweat in a sweat suit," Joey reasoned. "So what's the difference if it's fake fiber?"

The new scheme worked out so well for Angelo that he was able to quit his supermarket job and devote all his time to the marketing of warm-up suits. He was so grateful to the Gambuzzas that he even gave Joey a bottle of champagne to deliver to Gus and Jimmy, to wish them bon voyage.

But this condom racket was a little hard to swallow, even for the Gambuzza brothers.

"No, I'm not kiddin', here," Joey said. "You can't beat the Germans at something like this. They're a sadistic bunch of bastards, but they kick ass when it comes to technology. They're great at destroying life, and great at saving it. I'm gonna make sure the kids at the parish use them."

"Hand them out at the communion rail," Jimmy suggested.

Joey rolled his eyes. "Laugh now, but you guys'll thank me when you get back. You don't know who you might meet on this trip. You never know what's gonna happen."

That, Jimmy had to admit, was the truth. Was there any way in which his life had *not* changed since the New Year?

It began with Jimmy quitting the firm of Reed & Walter, just like that. His bosses couldn't believe it. They reminded him that a partnership was sure to be his within a matter of months, then demanded to know if he had a better offer somewhere.

"No," Jimmy calmly replied. "Nothing like that. I'm going off on my own. It's something I've always wanted to do."

Jimmy rose to leave, turned at the door and added, "Months, bullshit. I'd be on fucking Social Security before you guys painted my name on the door."

He left his bosses gaping at each other. By early

February the architectural office of James Gambuzza Inc. was open for business in lower Manhattan.

It meant a huge drop in income, but Jimmy made up for it with a lucky break that began with a note that was slid under the door of his co-op. It was from Dennis, writing that he was sorry about the New Year's mix-up. Then the note quickly got to the point: Would Jimmy consider selling his co-op? It seemed that Dennis and Vance were giving it one more try, and knew that if their love was to have a chance this time, they'd need more space. Jimmy acted reluctant at first, to drive the price up, then sold them his place at a fat profit. Dennis and Vance bored a hole through their ceiling and had themselves an instant duplex.

Jimmy decided he'd had enough of Manhattan life. He moved across the river, into a one-bedroom apartment in Brooklyn Heights with a view of the harbor and the Statue of Liberty.

New name, new job, new address . . . it was as if Jimmy had entered the Federal Witness Protection Program. All he needed now was a new girlfriend, but he was in no hurry. Since the breakup with Wendy he'd gone on a few dates, but was nowhere near a commitment. That was okay. He thought of his soul in architectural terms, as a building that had been constructed from ground level up, without a foundation. The building had toppled on New Year's Eve, and he needed time to clear away the wreckage, dig a foundation, and start the slow construction of himself, one row of bricks at a time.

The security woman put stickers on Jimmy's luggage and turned to Gus for the same routine, just in time to miss Jimmy's gasp for breath.

He'd slept over at his mother's house the night before, leaving his packed bag down by the front door.

Could Gus have put anything in his luggage? Would he have done anything that foolish? He told himself he was being paranoid. And anyway, it was too late to wonder. Already the woman was putting stickers on Gus's luggage and wishing him a happy trip.

Five minutes later two men in suits were at Gus's elbow.

"Could we have a moment of your time, Mr. Gambuzza?"

Gus shrugged. Jimmy cleared his throat to speak, but Gus shook him off with the faintest gesture of his head, like a pitcher letting the catcher know a change in signals.

The line inched slowly toward the baggage check-in, and when Jimmy was just about to be served he saw Gus and the suits approaching, resembling three buddies on a golf course. Gus said something that made the other two laugh. They shook hands all around, and then the suits made sure that Gus was restored to his old place in line.

"What happened?"

Gus shrugged. "We had coffee. I'm sorry I couldn't invite you."

"They look through your bags?"

"Look? They unrolled all my fucking socks. Rolled 'em back up nicely, though, I gotta admit. And they got a kick out of those Nazi condoms."

"Bastards."

"What the fuck, they're just doin' their jobs. Exciting work they've got, those feds, checkin' through people's underwear."

"Gus—"

"Do me a favor and don't talk to me until we're on the plane." He lit a cigarette and spoke without looking at Jimmy. "See, I don't think these bozos know you're my brother," he chuckled.

"My old name's still on the passport," Jimmy murmured.

Gus shook his head. "Can you imagine? This is security? No wonder the country's falling apart."

A thin, almost hairless man behind Gus tapped him on the shoulder. "Excuse me," he hissed, "but there's no smoking in this area."

Gus gave him a benign smile. "My mistake," he said, dropping the cigarette to the floor and grinding it out. Jimmy started to giggle, and wondered how that fellow would feel to know that he'd just snapped at Gus "the Ghost" Gambuzza. They'd probably have to bring him around with smelling salts, the miserable bald-headed fuck.

It was not a great takeoff. Choppy winds made the plane feel as if it were slamming through a series of walls as it climbed into the sky. Gus, seated by the window, shut his eyes tightly. Sweat rolled down his face. He licked his lips.

"Do something for me, Jimmy?"

"Anything."

"Would you feel funny about holdin' my hand?"

Even the Ghost's hand was damp with sweat.

"We're going to be all right, Gus."

Gus nodded, eyes still shut. "This is the farthest I ever got in a plane. One time I made them stop and let me out."

"I know."

Gus opened his eyes. "You *know?*"

"Joey told me."

Gus shook his head. "He promised not to tell anybody. Some Vow of Silence he took, huh?"

"Shhhh . . . try to sleep."

"Sleep. Right."

"You'll be surprised at how easy this is. Once we're finished climbing, you'll forget we're flying."

"Until I look out the window."

"So don't look out the window." Jimmy reached across and closed the shutter.

"No," Gus said, pushing it back up. "Leave it open. It's better to know." Gus peered out the window as if to check and see if he was being followed.

"Gus, listen to me. *Look* at me." He squeezed Gus's hand, patted his cheek. "The most dangerous part of the trip was that ride from Mom. This is a breeze. These people are good. They know what they're doing. Let somebody else do the worrying for once, all right?"

Gus sighed, nodded. "You're pretty fuckin' smart, aren't you?"

"Sometimes."

"You swear it's gonna be all right?"

"I won't let anything happen to you."

"I'm gonna close my eyes again. Don't let go of my hand, all right?"

"I won't."

Gus shut his eyes. "Let me know when it's all right to smoke."

"Okay, baby."

A flight attendant came by to ask if everything was okay. Jimmy put a finger to his lips and winked at the woman. A few minutes later the plane reached its top altitude and leveled off at its cruising speed. The NO SMOKING light went off. Jimmy turned to tell Gus the good news, but the Ghost was fast asleep. He snored through a movie and two food services, and Jimmy had to shake him to wake him when the plane rolled to a halt at the Athens airport.

The brothers checked into a hotel and ate their first Greek meal in a small taverna, Jimmy doing the ordering with the help of a pocket dictionary. The waiters listened to Jimmy, but directed their replies to Gus in rudimentary English they'd learned as schoolboys.

It began to annoy Jimmy. "How come *I* talk to *them,* but *they* talk to *you?*"

"Maybe they saw my picture in the *Daily News.*"

Jimmy was exhausted, having barely slept on the plane. They returned to their hotel room, where Jimmy flopped on his bed and fell asleep, fully clothed. Dawn was breaking when he heard the sound of his suitcase being unsnapped. Peeking through slits in his eyes, he watched the Ghost remove a small package swathed in plastic wrap from his luggage and transfer it to his own suitcase before returning to bed.

Okay. So he hadn't been paranoid. This was the way Gus had meant to play it all along. It was a bit of a jolt, but nothing he couldn't get over. Now, at last, they were square. In a funny way, it was a relief. And still he loved the man.

They stayed three days in Athens. Gus loved the food, the wine, the coffee, and especially the Parthenon. He stood in the shadow of the structure with tears in his eyes.

"Look at it," he told Jimmy. "When I'm doing my best thinkin', this is what my thoughts are shaped like. The whole fuckin' thing makes sense. You understand me?"

"I do," said Jimmy, mildly irked. "I'm an architect, you know. This kind of thing is my business."

"Think you could have designed something like this?"

Jimmy shook his head. "Not in the time and place I was born. You've got to have a head free of bullshit to come up with this."

"Well maybe you'll have a head free of bullshit, now that you're your own boss."

"Maybe. I hope so."

"Hey, I've been meanin' to ask you, did it hurt much when they stitched that vowel back on the end of your name?"

"Nah," Jimmy replied. "They gave me a local anesthetic."

Gus put his arm across Jimmy's shoulders and gave him a squeeze. "You're all right. Hey. What do you say we visit the islands?"

So that was it. A drop-off on a remote Greek island. Jimmy sighed, took one last look at the ancient white columns. "Anything you say, Gus."

Early the next evening they boarded a huge tub of a ferry boat that would take them on a fifteen-hour ride to the island Gus had chosen. The boat was barely a mile out of the port of Piraeus when the water turned the incredible blue of the true Aegean. Dolphins followed the ferry, leaping with what appeared to be sheer joy, perhaps over their great good luck at having been born into water so clean and beautiful.

Gus loved it. They'd rented a cabin with bunk beds for the journey but after dropping off their luggage, they went out to sit on the deck. All around them were young Europeans with backpacks and sleeping bags, taking the cheapest of holidays.

The sun had set, and already some of the kids had unrolled their sleeping bags and settled in for the night. Jimmy and Gus drank retsina. A full moon rose, and in its light Jimmy saw that his brother's face could truly have come off a church ceiling. Then he saw that Gus's carry-on bag was between his feet, and realized he was no angel but the infamous Ghost of Brooklyn, who wasn't letting that plastic-wrapped package out of his sight for a millisecond.

They passed small rocky islands, like bits of the lunar surface jutting from the sea. Now and then a goat stared back, with no goatherd in sight. Gus filled their cups with more retsina.

"You ever hear from that Wendy girl?"

The question startled Jimmy. "I thought we weren't supposed to talk about that night."

Gus shrugged. "I'm asking you about your old girlfriend. What's the big deal?"

Jimmy scanned their immediate neighbors. A crew-cut Swedish youth dozed in a sleeping bag at their feet, beside a blond-haired girl who couldn't have been more than sixteen. To their right, an ancient Greek in a striped sailor shirt sat dozing in a deck chair, his stubbly chin resting on the tops of his hands, which gripped the knob of a crooked cane. None of these three were likely to spring to their feet and yell, "Freeze, police!"

Jimmy cleared his throat. "No, I never heard from her again. But I know she got married."

"That right?"

From his wallet, Jimmy removed a two-week-old clipping from *The New York Times* bride page and passed it to Gus. There was a photo of a radiant Wendy beside a dark-haired, grim-faced investment banker named Digby Miller, with whom she was to exchange vows at St. Bartholomew's Church.

"Christ Almighty, she moved fast. You don't know this guy?"

"Nope."

"I'm telling you, she met him that night at the Rainbow Room."

"She never went there, Gus."

"That's what *she* says."

"Gus. Wendy was many things, but she was not a liar."

Gus shook the clipping. "Why are you carrying this around? You miss her?"

"I guess I wanted you to see her. . . . Think she's pretty?"

"She's all right. But that's a fierce face. *Madonna,* Digby's got some life ahead."

"She's okay," Jimmy said. "For the right man, she's just perfect. I wasn't the right man, that's all."

Gus passed the clipping back to Jimmy, who crumpled it up and threw it overboard.

"Looks like you're over her now," Gus said. "Next step for you is to get over Carol."

He beamed a dead-level gaze at Jimmy, who felt his tongue freeze. A small smile tickled Gus's lips.

"Think I didn't know how you felt about her, right from the first night you met her? Think I didn't smell that fresh-bread smell when I went to your room after you screamed?"

"Apparently you did," Jimmy managed to say.

"Think I don't know what you were thinkin', all those nights I got home three, four in the morning? Admit you thought about what might happen for you if I got killed."

"Jesus, Gus."

"Jimmy, come on. Not one fantasy? You didn't have one single fantasy of me gettin' killed, and you steppin' in?"

Jimmy sighed. "Maybe one."

"That's better. How did I go?"

"You got shot."

"Shot. And you were there to comfort the grieving widow, and it took off from there."

"Something like that."

Gus pursed his lips, shook his head from side to side. "All right. You're only human, Jimmy. I'm not bringing this up to torture you. I'm trying to tell you it was all unreal for you. You were a kid. You were nice to each other. It wasn't like a marriage. It was *easier* than a fuckin' marriage, and I think the way you remember Carol is maybe—just *maybe*—standin' in your way of ever gettin' a real wife."

Jimmy looked away from Gus, out at the magical waters of the Aegean.

"I know this isn't easy to hear," Gus said. "Sometimes you gotta fly to the other side of the world just to bring up a subject like this."

Jimmy breathed deeply of the salty breeze. "I'll try to get over her," he finally said.

"That's good. She'd want it that way, too."

"Are you ever going to be over her?"

"I'm workin' on it."

"Gus. Can I ask you something? Something else you can't talk about until you're on the other side of the world?"

The Ghost spread his arms toward the sky. "Anything at all."

Jimmy looked again at their sleeping neighbors. "If you had to that night, could you have killed me?"

Gus rolled a mouthful of retsina around his teeth and swallowed it before plainly replying, "Yes." He leaned close to Jimmy. "Want to hear something even more amazing? It would have been my first time." Gus grinned. "You believe me?"

"Yeah."

"You sure? Because I'm not sure you know what it is I do for a living."

"I know what you do."

"YOU DON'T KNOW!"

Gus was louder than he'd meant to be. The Swedes in the sleeping bags shot angry, slit-eyed looks at the brothers before rolling over and going back to sleep.

"I clean up messes," Gus said softly. "That's all I do. By the time I show up anywhere, everything's already happened. And there'll always be a demand for a guy who can clean up other people's messes. That's one job that'll never get swallowed up by automation." He stood up and stretched. "You hungry? Can we get a meal on this tub, or what?"

In the dining room they ate chicken and a good green salad, served by a waiter whose English was excellent. After serving the brothers he stared at Gus from across the dining room.

"Excuse me," he finally said to Gus, "you are very familiar. You are an actor, no?"

Gus chuckled. "An actor?"

"Yes, yes. I saw you in *The Godfather,* yes?"

"Nah, that wasn't me. Sorry."

"But you look just like him."

"Sorry."

On the way to their cabin Jimmy asked, "Who do you look like in *The Godfather?"*

Gus shrugged. "Fuck should I know? Never saw the movie. Come on, let's get some sleep."

Gus was snoring in no time, and as Jimmy lay on the narrow bed across from him he couldn't help thinking that on the Gambuzza Brothers Murder Tote Board the score stood at Jimmy 1, Gus 0.

* * *

It was not yet dawn when the ship reached the dock at the tiny island Gus had chosen. Actually, the ferry bumped into the dock, knocking a few people on their asses.

Jimmy helped an old woman with a whiskery chin to her feet. She dusted off the seat of her dress and rose on crooked, goatlike legs without a word of complaint.

"Can you imagine?" Gus said. "Something like this happens in the United States, you have a million personal injury lawsuits."

"Greeks are used to things going wrong."

"So am I. Guess that's why all these waiters like me."

The brothers got off with ten other people, all backpackers or islanders coming home. Jimmy tried to figure which one could be Gus's connection, and decided it could be none of them. Whoever it was had to be on the island already, awaiting the arrival of the Ghost.

They took a gear-grinding ride in a small bus up a rocky road to the main village, where the driver pointed them in the direction of the island's only hotel that was open for business. They got a plain whitewashed room with two beds, one bathroom, and three lizards.

Wind moaned and sighed through the open windows, which weren't windows at all but deep holes in the two-foot-thick walls. They slept until late morning, and had coffee and rolls in the village square in the shade of ancient pepper trees. It would have been the most tranquil place Jimmy had ever seen, if not for the four crew-cut German youths at the next table. They told loud stories, roared with laughter at each other's obviously crude jokes, and knocked over beer bottles. Gus shook his head.

"See that?" he asked. "It's like I suspected. No matter where you go in this world, you're in Brooklyn. You're gonna run into assholes."

The Germans began pelting each other with slices of bread. The poor taverna waitress stood by in silent desperation. Gus rose and went to the table.

"Knock it the fuck off."

The laughter stopped abruptly. One of the Germans muttered something and forced a laugh, which died in his throat as the Ghost gazed at him. They hastily paid their tab and went away.

Gus returned to his coffee. "Didn't travel six thousand miles to have my balls busted."

Jimmy asked for the check. The waitress brought it a moment later, along with a complimentary bowl of rice pudding sprinkled with cinnamon for Gus, whose cheek she stroked as she walked away.

Like a pair of meandering mountain goats, the Gambuzza brothers hiked along the island's paths. Flowers of the most brilliant red bloomed everywhere, seemingly straight from rock and dust. An old shepherd passed them, preceded by a flock of belled goats. The shepherd was as toothless as a turtle, with sun-seared skin to match. He said something Jimmy couldn't find in his dictionary. It turned out to be, "Nice shoes!" a reference to the brothers' brand-new bright purple sneakers, going-away presents from Father Joe.

"Christ, it's so fuckin' beautiful," Gus said as they made a turn that opened out onto a beyond-belief vista of the Aegean. A series of terraced farms led down to the shore, where foamy waves broke over flat rocks in shimmering shades of blue that no artist anywhere could ever hope to squeeze from a paint tube.

"Can we walk down a little bit?"

"I'm game if you are, Gus."

For all his hours in the gymnasium, Jimmy could not match the nimble footwork of his big-bellied brother down the slanted terrain. At last they reached the rocks, where they felt the slamming of the waves through the soles of their feet.

Gus turned to stare at Jimmy, his face as grim as it had ever been. "Would you say that this is as beautiful a spot as there is in the world?"

Jimmy nodded. "Couldn't get any better than this."

"All right, then."

Gus squatted to open his ever-present carry-on bag and took out the plastic-wrapped package.

Jimmy scanned the area, but no shady characters were appearing from behind the olive trees. He swallowed to quell the tremble in his throat.

"Been meaning to ask you about that, Gus. How come it was in my luggage?"

Gus grinned. "You knew?"

"I saw you make the switch in the hotel room."

Gus pulled off the plastic to reveal a small metal can with a screw-on lid. "You think I'm gonna let a bunch of feds screw around with my wife's ashes, you got another think comin'."

"Oh my God."

"Hey, I always promised I'd take her to Europe. Things always happened to stop us, you know? This was the best I could do."

Jimmy said, "I thought it was drugs."

Gus laughed. "You got it backwards, Jimmy. The drugs come *from* Turkey and get sent *to* the United States. Not the other way around."

Gus climbed onto a rock and licked a finger to test the wind, which seemed to be blowing in all directions.

"Perfect."

He unscrewed the lid and hurled the ashes straight up. They vanished in a spiral, without the faintest hint of dust falling to earth.

"So long, sweetheart." He threw the can far out into the water, then the lid.

Tears rolled down Jimmy's face, but Gus sighed with dry-eyed relief.

"That's good-bye to my number one nightmare. Aaay, it was only a matter of time before Mah took Carol off the shelf to season a pork roast." Gus rubbed his belly. "Think we could find a place to eat around here?"

HAMILTON TOWNSHIP PUBLIC LIBRARY
3 1923 00316715 8